GOOD DEED, BAD DEEDS

THE DUNN FAMILY SERIES
BOOK 1

RICKY BLACK

CHAPTER ONE

FRIDAY 1 MAY, 2020

FRIDAY NIGHT PLAYED host to another party in Chapeltown, Leeds; known fondly as *the Hood*. People milled around, some drinking, others building and smoking spliffs, talking easily over the thumping drill beats. Most present weren't aware whose house it was, the owner currently visiting her ill sister in Macclesfield. Her granddaughter foolishly decided to have a party, not expecting half the Hood to show. Unable to control the situation, she now stood in the kitchen, getting ever drunker and waiting for it to be over.

Outside, Nathaniel — aka Natty Deeds — grinned, a spliff between his lips, surrounded by his Day-One boys, Cameron and Spence. The trio were in their late twenties and had been close for years. His eyes were on Cameron, bleary-eyed and stumbling around.

'Go on, it's your turn,' he urged, hitting the joint and passing it to another man. Struggling to stay upright, Cameron chugged from the bottle of Hennessy. Finishing, he blinked and shook his head, thrusting the half-drunk bottle at Natty, some of the contents splashing on the ground.

'Your turn. Finish that, or I win.'

Natty snatched the bottle, buoyed by the surrounding eyes. He stood straighter, enhancing his powerful 6-foot frame, knowing he cut an impressive figure; hair neatly shaped up, gold chain bouncing against his designer sweater.

'Go on. Hurry up,' urged Cameron, a bead of sweat dripping down his forehead. Waiting a second longer to annoy him, Natty downed the remaining brandy, ignoring the burning in his throat and chest. After finishing, he held the bottle aloft as people cheered.

'Grab another bottle,' he said, blinking. 'Spence, play too.'

'I'm okay, thanks,' said Spence. He'd calmly watched from the side, nursing the same bottle of Red Stripe he'd had since they arrived. Shorter than Natty, he had hazel eyes, high cheekbones, and soft facial features to go with his slender build.

'He needs his woman's permission,' Cameron sneered. Spence had been in a relationship for a year, but to hear Cameron talk, you'd think they'd started going out yesterday.

'Cam, no woman in their right mind would even go near you.'

People nearby chuckled at Spence's response. Cameron frowned. He had a stocky build, sharp features, and a tapered fade. His dark brown eyes surveyed Spence.

'Laugh all you want, but I get it when I want it. Relationships are for mugs.'

'That's true,' agreed Natty, wiping his eyes as the combination of weed and liquor hit him.

'See? Natty kn—' Cameron stopped mid-sentence and hurried to a nearby bush, where he promptly threw up. Spence shook his head, and Natty laughed.

'I win, lightweight.'

Natty's phone vibrated. Squinting to see the screen clearly, he saw the name *Rudy*. Looking up from his phone, he snorted and stowed it back in his pocket. He had no desire to speak with his boss tonight.

Heading inside, a woman dancing in the corner of the room caught his attention, his eyes locking onto her swaying hips. He made his way toward her, sauntering through the crowd, aware of the hungry stares from other women. In Natty's drunken state, he didn't care.

'Hey sexy,' he said to the woman. 'You look beautiful.'

'Thank you,' she replied, looking away, her dark brown hair

obscuring her temptingly curved mouth for a moment. Natty inched closer, missing the look of alarm on her face.

'How come I've never seen you before?' Natty continued before she could reply. 'People call me Natty Deeds. Let me get you a drink.'

'No thank you.' She shook her head. 'I'm not thirsty, and I have a boyfriend.'

Natty's smirk widened as he swayed on the spot.

'We can just be friends, babe. Doesn't have to affect your relationship.'

Again, she shook her head, her lip curling.

'I'm not interested.'

Even in his drunken state, Natty finally realised she didn't want to be around him. Shrugging, he said, 'your loss.'

Before she could respond, a man draped his arm around her. He had broad shoulders and a muscular build beneath his pocket logo CP Company t-shirt. His eyes surveyed Natty, eyebrows creeping together.

'Do I know you?'

Natty returned the look. 'I don't know. Do you?'

'You're over here bothering my girl.'

Natty could have walked away, but a crowd had gathered. He had a reputation to maintain and couldn't be seen backing down.

'I was talking to her, not *bothering* her. Stop being insecure.'

The woman bit her lip, eyes darting between the pair. Natty stepped toward the man.

'If you really have a problem, we can step outside and deal with it.'

No one spoke. Natty waited for him to move. He glanced at Natty, then lowered his head.

'If you weren't bothering her, then we can leave it.'

Natty smirked, amused at his change of heart. As built as the man was, Natty was bigger. He looked the woman up and down as her man backed up.

'You're too sexy to be with a cowardly man that can't defend you.'

The man's eyes flashed at Natty's insults, but he swallowed and again looked away.

'You need to take a long look at yourself. You're pathetic,' the woman spat, eyes full of loathing.

'Take your pussy boyfriend and fuck off then. Anytime he wants to go, I'll put him on his arse.'

Spence came over after the couple had hurried away.

'Chill out and get some water,' he said, trying to calm him. Natty shrugged him off.

'I'm fine. You know I can handle my drink.'

Spence sighed. Getting through to Natty was impossible at times.

'I'm getting off, anyway,' he said.

Natty rolled his eyes.

'Seriously? We're just starting, and you're running off to your woman?'

'I'm not running.'

'Course you are.'

Spence patted him on the back. 'Be careful, bro. I'll get with you tomorrow.'

Blearily watching him go, Natty stumbled outside. Cameron was still doubled over by the bush he'd thrown up in, moaning. Natty chuckled at his friend's condition.

'You look terrible, bro. Let's get you another drink. That'll sort you right out.'

* * *

THE SOUNDS of someone shuffling around Natty moved him before he was truly ready. Light spilt through multiple slits in the blinds, making him groan, head pounding. Coughing to clear his dry throat, he sat gingerly looking around. The room wasn't his, but he recognised it, along with the woman tidying. His clothing had been carefully laid on a chair instead of the haphazard pile he'd left them in. The woman emptied an ashtray into a white carrier bag.

'Keep the noise down.'

'This is my house, in case you've forgotten,' she replied, hand on her hip as she impaled him with a ferocious glare.

'Calm down, Lorraine.' Natty winced, wiping his eyes. 'Got any painkillers?'

'Downstairs,' Lorraine replied. 'Before you ask, I'm not getting them for you.'

'C'mon, babe. I'm hurting.'

'Stop drinking so much then.'

Natty rubbed his head. 'Wasn't my fault. Cam got me into it.'

'You're always blaming other people, Nat. Take some responsibility.'

Natty waved an arm at her, not listening to her usual spiel. Lorraine glared back, unimpressed. A blue bandana obscured her silky black hair, and she wore an oversized plain black t-shirt and shorts. She was twenty-nine-years old, with light brown eyes, full lips, smooth features, and nutmeg-shaded skin.

'Seriously, Natty. We're not a couple. You can't keep turning up drunk, expecting to sleep in my bed.'

Natty leered, eyes locked onto her silken brown legs.

'I always make up for it in the end.'

Lorraine shook her head.

'I'm not interested in the leftovers from whatever girl you had last night.'

'You've got me all wrong. I was good,' replied Natty, thinking of the girl whose boyfriend he had nearly beaten up. Despite herself, Lorraine's expression softened.

'Get ready. I'll make you some food for when you're done.'

Agreeing with the plan, Natty headed to take a shower. Soaping himself with shower gel leftover from previous visits, he went over the day in his head. He needed to check in with his crew, and then find out what Rudy wanted.

For most of his life, Natty had sold drugs on the streets. He loved the money and the respect he garnered from people for doing it. He worked as a crew chief, one of many who reported to Rudy Campbell. He had seen him a few days ago, and there were no problems at the time, but he knew how quickly things could switch in the Hood.

Once washed and dressed, Natty headed downstairs, still ropey after his night. He saw a small boy playing on the carpet in the living room. Despite the widescreen TV displaying cartoons, he remained in his own world. When he looked up and saw Natty, his face immediately brightened. Natty grinned.

'What's happening, little man? What are you watching?' He bumped fists with the child, listening for a few minutes as he babbled about the show.

'Can we play on the PlayStation?' Jaden eagerly asked.

'Let me get some food in my belly; then we can play for a bit.'

In the kitchen doorway, Lorraine watched Natty and her son, overwhelmed by a surge of affection. For all Natty's faults, he doted on Jaden and spent more quality time with him than his dad. At the same time, she worried about Jaden being so enamoured with a man actively involved in the street life; one that had never truly committed to her and probably never would. She lowered her head, and then headed back to the kitchen.

Natty entered a few minutes later, making a drink and swallowing two paracetamols.

'Have you seen my phone?' He asked, inhaling the fried food scent in the air.

'On the table. I put it on charge for you.'

Thanking her, Natty sat down and tucked into his breakfast, checking his phone. Rudy had called several times, finally sending him a text saying to stop by. Reading several other random messages, Natty put his phone aside and finished his breakfast. Lorraine took away his empty plate, placing a cup of milky coffee in front of him.

'Feeling better?'

Natty nodded, rubbing his stomach. 'That was amazing. Thank you.'

'Whose party were you at? I didn't know anything was on.'

'People based out Rhona's nana's yard. Cam dragged me along last minute. Spence too, before he ran off to see his girl.'

'Leave Spence alone. He's maturing. You should think about doing the same.'

Natty scoffed at Lorraine's usual line of nonsense.

'I'm my own person. I don't need some woman telling me what to do,' he said.

Lorraine folded her arms, leaning against the kitchen sink as she surveyed him.

'That isn't what a relationship is. Relationships are about compromise; supporting one another.'

'Is that what you and *Raider* do?' He snarked, referring to Jaden's dad.

Lorraine's eyes flashed.

'No. You know it isn't. I still know what a relationship is. Do you? Or is this it for you?'

'What are you talking about?'

'I'm talking about life, Natty. What does life mean for you?'

Sliding to his feet, Natty took his coffee, shaking his head.

'I don't want to listen to this shit.'

Without a word, he headed into the living room. A few moments later, she heard him playing with Jaden, just as he'd promised. Lorraine remained by the sink, wishing Natty got it. He meant well, but it was so easy to dislike him. At times, he reminded her of Jaden's dad, but he had a softer side — a contrast to the rougher, darker side the other man routinely showed. It didn't help that Raider knew of her previous involvement with Natty, and suspected there was still something between them.

Raider was easy enough to handle, though. Despite the implosion of their relationship, he typically kept his distance. He tried his luck now and then, but was never successful.

Natty was a different story. Her closeness to him had pushed out Raider for good. Lorraine didn't understand why he had such an issue with relationships, but couldn't see it changing anytime soon.

CHAPTER TWO

NATTY HAMMERED on Cameron's door. After a few moments, he heard several bangs as the door opened.

'You didn't need to knock so loud,' Cameron muttered. Natty followed him to the kitchen, watching him shuffle around.

'You look horrific,' he finally said. Cameron glared back, shirtless, his pyjama bottoms rumpled and livid bags under his eyes. Natty took over and made them drinks. They carried them outside, Natty remaining on his feet, Cameron slumping on the front step.

Cameron lived in a terraced house on Gathorne Avenue. He'd lived with his mum, taking over the house when she remarried and moved in with her partner. An older lady shuffled past, smiling at them both. The house had a patch of dirt masquerading as a garden. Any plants formerly growing had since died with Cameron's disinterest in gardening. It had a black door, mid-sized walls, and an old-fashioned exterior and interior.

As they looked on, the sounds of a crying child punctuated the quiet, his mother dragging him along by the hand, threatening to beat him. It reminded Natty of how his mum had acted when he was younger.

'I'm not drinking with you again,' he finally said, rubbing his eye with his free hand.

Natty grinned. 'It's not my fault you can't handle it.'

'Whatever. You got lucky. Where did you end up, anyway?'

Natty sipped his drink, the coffee scalding his lips, causing him to grit his teeth. Cameron's coffee was horrendous. Natty had complained in the past, even leaving his own coffee at the house, which tasted better.

'Forget that. What happened to the coffee I brought around last time.'

'I used it. So what?'

'So, couldn't you replace it? Your stuff is terrible,' said Natty.

'I'm not paying stupid money for that expensive stuff you buy. Stop avoiding the question: where did you end up?'

'Lorraine's,' replied Natty.

Cameron's eyes gleamed. He rubbed his hands together.

'I'd love to run up in that.'

Natty impaled him with a glare. 'Watch your mouth.'

Cameron grinned.

'If you have a problem with me talking like that, step up and claim her.'

Natty shook his head. It wasn't the first time they'd had the conversation.

'It's not that simple,' he said.

'How come?'

'She's Raider's baby mum.'

Cameron snorted.

'Raider? C'mon, Nat. He's a mug.' He shot Natty a crafty look. 'Plus, it didn't stop you going over there to bang her.'

'We didn't have sex. I just crashed there.'

It was Cameron's turn to shake his head.

'You're turning into Spence, fam.'

Natty chuckled. 'Have you heard from him? He left before me.'

'He rang me an hour ago. He's handling the crew. No hiccups so far.'

Natty nodded. He could always trust Spence to keep things

moving. Spence had always shown a high level of managerial talent, and Natty believed he would make a good boss. Thinking of bosses made him think of Rudy, whom he needed to see. Inwardly, he cursed himself for taking his eye off the ball.

'Cool. Get ready, anyway. Rudy wants a meet.'

Groaning, Cameron clambered to his feet, draining his coffee, making a satisfied sound. Natty looked at him in disgust.

'You need help, Cam.' He poured his own coffee into the dirt.

'Speak for yourself. Hope Rudy's got some work for us. My funds are low.'

'You shouldn't have loaned that silly Rolex off Damanjeet. You got ripped off paying that deposit. I'm sure it's fake.'

Cameron waved that off. 'You're just jealous you didn't get it.'

'Jealous of what? You *need* that fake watch. It's the only way women will go near you.'

'Don't talk shit. I get as many women as you do.'

'You wish.'

While Cameron got ready, Natty messed around on his phone, replying to a few text messages. He thought about what Lorraine had said earlier. Natty felt he was being held to a higher standard based on Spence's willingness to have a relationship, and his reluctance to do so.

Spence had been more reserved than he and Cameron even before getting together with Anika. He often kept them from doing stupid things, always remaining calm, which helped calm Natty — and Cameron — down when needed. Yet, last night, Natty had almost gotten into a fight over a girl, and couldn't even recall what she looked like.

Maybe he needed to cool it with the drinking and partying.

'Seriously, I'm still rough.' Cameron yawned as he stuffed his feet into a pair of trainers. 'Should have done a Spence and left early. How long are we gonna let him keep getting away with that?'

'What are you talking about?'

'Anika. You said in the beginning that she wouldn't change him, and I told you he was pussy whipped. Now look at him . . . leaving parties early when we're having a good time so he can run back to her.'

'They live together now. Spence does what he thinks is right. You don't know that she's having that kind of effect.'

'I know her, remember? We both do.'

Natty shook his head.

'C'mon, let's just go and see the old man.'

Once Cameron was ready, they drove to Rudy's.

'We're out next weekend,' said Cameron, once they'd set off. 'There's an event near Albion Street that's gonna be jumping.'

Natty grinned. 'I thought you weren't coming out with me again after last night?'

'Whatever, man. We're going. I'll take it easy this time,' said Cameron.

'We'll see. What's the event?'

'I mentioned it ages ago. It's been in the works for a while. That DJ from London is performing. The fat one.'

Natty kept his eyes on the road, vaguely remembering Cameron mentioning it. Pushing his earlier epiphany about partying to the side, he nodded and said, 'cool. I'm up for that.'

'Yes! Knew you would be.' Cameron winced. 'We need to stop for paracetamol after this. My head's killing.'

'Sure, sweetheart!' said Natty, as loudly as he could, laughing as Cameron again winced.

* * *

Parking on Francis Street in the Hood, both men strode to Rudy's office, a red-bricked terraced house with a plain white door. It didn't have a garden, with only some messy bushes and a small pathway. Several guys hung around outside, talking in loud voices. They looked up when they saw Natty and Cameron, greeting them with grins and handshakes.

'Rudy in?' Natty asked. They nodded. 'Is he in a good mood? Anyone said anything?' He pressed.

'Same as ever, really,' one of them replied.

Natty left it there. They weren't bodyguards, but Rudy kept them close, using them for different jobs. Walking inside, they went to the kitchen, overwhelmed by the fried food stench. A heavyset woman hunched over the stove, muttering to herself. She glanced at the pair, her eyes lingering on Natty.

'Hey, Delores,' he said, beaming at her. Her stern face softened.

'Nathaniel. How are you? I never see you anymore.'

'I'm out here working,' replied Natty. 'I'll come and see you again soon.'

'Make sure you do. Stay out of trouble.'

'Yes, ma'am.' Natty kissed her on the cheek, turning his attention to Rudy. The older man sat at the kitchen table, sipping a pale concoction. He wore a white shirt and a thin chain, his greying hair trimmed short to disguise his accelerating baldness. Despite his advanced years, he'd maintained his looks. A sharp goatee framed his fame, his piercing coffee-coloured eyes surveying the pair.

He glanced from Natty to Cameron, signalling for the former to sit. Neither spoke at first; Natty used to the older man's theatrics. He looked around the comfortable, worn kitchen, as always unable to understand why Rudy was based there.

'How's it going, Rudy?' He finally asked.

Rudy straightened in his seat, not taking his eyes from Natty.

'Why didn't you answer the phone last night?'

'I was enjoying my night off.'

'We don't have nights off in our business. What if there was trouble, or a raid?'

Natty scratched his chin. 'I'd trust exemplary men like you to have things in order.'

Rudy's nostrils flared.

'Not good enough. You're representing the team, Nathaniel. You're always being watched, so getting drunk and throwing up at parties—'

Natty raised a hand, stopping Rudy mid-flow. Rudy's eyes narrowed.

'What do you think you're doing?'

'It was actually Cam that threw up . . . not me.'

Rudy looked from Natty to Cameron — whose eyes were currently burning into the back of Natty's head — then continued.

'Getting drunk and throwing up at parties, and trying to fight people, is not what's expected.' Rudy's expression remained unyielding. 'You know all this. We've spoken about it in the past.'

Natty resisted the urge to roll his eyes. Humour wouldn't cut it right now. The realisation that someone was reporting his movements suddenly struck him, and he frowned.

'The guy started with me. I wasn't gonna back down.'

'I didn't call you here to listen to your excuses. I need you to arrange a meeting with Elijah.'

Natty's hands clenched before he could even think about it.

'I thought we weren't dealing with him anymore?' He asked, voice thick with anger. Elijah had his own organisation, though there were persistent rumours that he was a front for another gang seeking more power. Natty and Elijah had a strained relationship; one Rudy was familiar with.

'We weren't,' replied Rudy. He glanced to Delores, still muttering to herself, and Cameron, who stifled a yawn. 'It's time we brought things back in line between our organisations. Bad blood isn't good for anyone. We've calmed things down lately, but none of us wants things back to how they were a few years ago, right?'

Natty didn't speak, but knew Rudy was right. The wars that had taken place had changed the landscape throughout Yorkshire, with multiple crews involved and scores of murders and arrests. It had stunted profits in all areas, with only their team remaining strong.

'Nathaniel, can you handle this?'

'I can,' replied Natty, nibbling on his bottom lip. Rudy kept his eye on him a moment longer.

'Elijah is looking to make a move into a new area. Could be something for you to sink your teeth into if you play it right.'

Natty continued weighing up everything in his head. Elijah had caused trouble for their organisation in the past, and the teams had almost gone to war several times. Natty loathed him and the people he kept close. He hoped Rudy had given the idea some thought.

'When do you want me to sort this meeting?'

'I'll let you know. People will be watching. Like I said, it's a great opportunity. Use it to step up.'

Again, Natty almost rolled his eyes. Shaking Rudy's hand, he said goodbye to Delores and went to leave.

'Nathaniel.'

He turned. Rudy surveyed him for several seconds.

'Watch that temper of yours. It'll get you in trouble.' His face softened. 'You're a good man; a good soldier.'

That was the problem, Natty thought to himself as they walked out. He didn't want to be just another soldier.

'No point in me even going,' Cameron grumbled when Natty drove away. 'Rudy didn't even speak to me. Old prick.'

Natty didn't reply, deep in thought about Elijah, considering all the ways the situation could go wrong. He didn't trust him, wondering if Rudy had given him the whole story.

'Natty? What are you thinking about?'

'Elijah,' admitted Natty. Cameron scratched his head.

'What about him?'

'I don't trust him.'

'Him or Raider? You sure the fact your fuckpiece's ex rolls with him isn't clouding your judgement?'

'I'm sure. This is business,' snapped Natty.

'Rudy wouldn't get you involved if there was a chance something could go wrong. You're like a son to him.'

Natty almost reminded Cameron he'd just cursed out Rudy for ignoring him, but didn't bother.

'It's not that simple,' he finally replied. 'Summat's up with Rudy . . . his judgement might be a little off.'

'How?'

'He's got people following me around, reporting back to him. That's a waste of money and time. He's focused on the wrong things, so how do we know he's scoped the situation with Elijah properly?' said Natty.

'Don't overthink it, bro. Have the meeting, get shit organised, and keep it moving. We can get put on in a major way, and trust me, I need that,' Cameron replied, forgetting that he'd recently blown money on renting a snide watch.

* * *

Later, Natty left the gym after a tough weights session, his gym bag slung over his shoulder. It was often his escape; he went to mull things over, to kill time between shifts and sometimes, to forget.

The combined nagging of Lorraine and Rudy had affected his mood. That, combined with the prospect of doing business with Elijah, caused him to seek out a distraction.

After showering and changing clothes, Natty headed to the city centre, finding himself in a bar. He sunk three drinks quickly, not bothering to take stock of his surroundings. Not wanting the profile, he'd deliberately picked a more low-key spot near Briggate. As he sipped Southern Comfort and lemonade, he spotted a woman standing with a group of friends. She kept looking his way. Natty signalled for her to come over, and after a while, she did, allowing him to get a better look. She had chestnut brown hair, deep blue eyes, and a giggly, flighty demeanour. She looked delicious in her little red dress, and he reasoned she would make a good distraction.

'What's your name?'

'Jeanette,' she replied softly, her eyes shining.

'People call me Natty Deeds.'

'Why?'

'Because I'm generous, and I get things done,' he replied, enjoying the smile on her face. 'I'm glad you came over. You're the most beautiful woman in here.'

'Really?' Her eyes widened. Natty maintained eye contact, holding and stroking the top of her hand. He felt her shudder and lean closer.

'Trust me, it's not even a contest. Let me buy you a drink.'

After several expensive drinks and a few highly charged dances, they headed back to Natty's. Jeanette pounced the moment they closed the door, forcing her mouth against his. Responding with equal enthusiasm, Natty easily lifted her from the ground, nibbling on her lips and drawing her further in. Hiking up her dress, he tugged down his trousers and slid her underwear to the side before entering her.

They panted against one another when they were done, catching their breath. Disentangling, Natty straightened his clothes and showed

Jeanette to the bathroom so she could clean up. She tottered down-stairs a few moments later, back to her giggly self, playing with her hair.

'You were so good,' she gushed. 'Shall we get a drink and go again?'

'No thanks. You can go now.'

'What?' Jeanette's mouth fell open.

'I've got things to do. I'll call you an Uber,' said Natty flatly.

Jeanette's eyes flashed.

'You serious? You're kicking me out?'

Natty didn't bother replying. Lip curling, she stalked past him.

'You're scum, Natty Deeds. Don't contact me again.'

'Get home safely,' he mocked. Closing the door on her insults, his smirk faded, shoulders slumping as he sat on the bottom step. Despite his best efforts, he couldn't switch off. Thoughts of Elijah and Lorraine flitted away, replaced by Cameron's words about Rudy being a father figure.

Often, Natty thought about his dad. He'd been in the life too, a big, powerful man with a deadly reputation. He'd been murdered when Natty was 11, and things hadn't been the same since. Even knowing how scared people had been of his dad, all Natty saw was the man who bought him what he wanted, but also taught him how to fight, and never to back down.

Natty had kept that same mindset as he grew older, no matter how much trouble it caused. He'd not truly understood why his dad was murdered, but even at a young age, he vividly recalled wanting revenge.

Sighing, Natty closed his eyes, wondering what the world wanted from him, and how he could get what he needed.

* * *

Two DAYS after speaking to Rudy, Elijah still hadn't contacted Natty. Putting the meeting aside, he went to see Lorraine and Jaden, a new video game in hand.

'I've told you about buying him things before, Natty,' said Lorraine at the door, hands on hips. 'You spoil him.'

'That's my little soldier. I'm just looking out for him,' replied Natty, trying to make his voice as innocent as possible. It was a harmless, throwaway statement. Natty had love for Jaden and wanted to make him happy, but he was aware of Lorraine pausing, and gave her his attention.

He didn't know what had changed, but she was glaring at him, hands on her hips.

'What's wrong with you?' He said.

'My son is not your *little soldier*, Natty.' Lorraine's nostrils flared.

'What are you on about?'

'He's a young boy, and he's going to grow up to do great things. He won't do the stuff you do.'

Natty held up his hands.

'C'mon, you know I didn't mean it like that. I know he is. You know that.'

Lorraine visibly calmed down, nodding.

'Okay. I'm glad you feel that way.'

Natty's face tightened, head lowered, as Lorraine let him in. Jaden greeted him with his usual enthusiasm, which took the sting out of Lorraine's admonishment. After thanking Natty for the new game, they picked their favourite *Fifa* football teams and were off. Natty took the early lead, but Jaden brought it back with a lucky headed goal. With the final whistle imminent, Natty *accidentally* passed the ball back toward his keeper, allowing Jaden to get the ball and score.

'Yes! I won! Natty, I beat you!'

Natty took a moment to watch Jaden celebrate his winning goal like he'd just won the World Cup, an involuntary smile coming to his face at the sight.

After a while, he left Jaden playing and went to see what Lorraine was doing. She was hunched over a laptop at the kitchen table, tapping keys. She pushed the laptop away as he stood there, shaking her head. Natty watched silently for a few seconds until she noticed him, blushing.

'How long have you been there?' She asked.

'Not long. What's all this?' He motioned to the laptop.

'Studying. It's important I keep practising.'

'How long have you been studying? I didn't even know.'

'No one does. I want to have everything finished before I start telling people. My mum knows, because she helps with Jaden, and Rosie does, but that's it.'

'How are you finding it?'

Lorraine ran a hand through her hair, blowing out a breath. 'It's difficult, but I'm not giving up.'

Nodding, Natty went to make drinks for himself, Jaden, and Lorraine, missing the look of disappointment on Lorraine's face at his lack of reaction.

'I'll leave you to it,' he said, placing her tea beside her, then leaving the room.

Natty and Jaden played for a bit longer, then he returned to the kitchen.

'I'm gonna get off now,' he told Lorraine. She didn't react. 'Did you hear me?'

'Yes, you said you were leaving.'

Natty's eyes narrowed. 'What's up with you?'

'Nothing. I thought you were going?'

He stepped into the kitchen and gently lifted her chin to face him.

'What's your problem? Why are you going on dumb?'

'I'm not. I'm trying to work, and you said you were going.'

Natty didn't know why she had switched on him, but he didn't have the time or patience to deal with it.

'That's your problem; you're too moody,' he said, leaving before he ended up starting an argument. He couldn't deal with her weirdness right now.

CHAPTER THREE

LATER, Natty hung with his crew, watching a football match at Cameron's. The remnants of a Chinese takeaway littered the coffee table, along with a bottle of Hennessy and an empty cola bottle.

'Are we ready for tomorrow night then?' Natty asked.

Cameron rubbed his hands together.

'Damn right. Already got my outfit sorted. Spence, you on it?'

'I'll go for a bit. Can we talk about Elijah now?' Spence looked at both men. He'd only joined them because they'd planned to discuss business. Instead, they wanted to watch football and talk about nonsense.

'In a minute,' replied Cameron. 'What do you mean you'll go for a bit? Do you want us to talk to your missus?'

'Why do you always assume Anika's talking for me? I don't want to stay out all night, then be looking after the youngers on the early shift,' said Spence.

'Whatever,' Cameron scoffed. 'You could easily get that squashed. Why else would you not wanna chill with your people?'

'Chill with you . . . like I'm doing right now?' Spence's jaw clenched.

'It's not the same thing.'

'Forget this,' Natty interjected, tired of the back and forth. Silence ensued, both Cameron and Spence shooting the other dirty looks.

'We need to be careful about dealing with Elijah. He's sneaky, and if he approached Rudy, you know there's a reason behind it,' said Spence, his voice level.

'Course there's a reason behind it. It's called money,' said Cameron, rolling his eyes. 'I swear, you lot just like being broke.'

'There's good money and bad money, and bad money has all kinds of strings attached. I like to know what I'm getting into.'

'Look, we can discuss this more after I meet with Elijah. We're here to chill, so let's chill,' Natty interjected. He agreed with both of them. Natty believed he deserved a more significant role, and the money that came with it. He'd seen less worthy people being promoted over him, and knew he had more to offer the organisation.

'What's happened?' Spence asked, sipping his drink.

'With what?' Natty frowned.

'With you. You've been even moodier than normal. We've barely heard from you for the past few days when you're not working.'

Natty rubbed his forehead. He needed to replenish his painkillers; he'd used his stock trying to shift a persistent headache.

'Lorraine's going on dumb again,' he admitted.

Cameron grinned. 'You're mad over her? You're starting to sound like him.' He waved his hand at Spence. Rolling his eyes, Spence surprisingly didn't take the bait, instead focusing on Natty.

'What happened?'

'Don't have a clue. I was chilling with Jaden, and she was in the kitchen. Came to chat to her for a minute when I was making Jaden a drink—'

'Spending quality time with your kid. You're a good dad, Nat,' Cameron teased. Natty shot him a hard look.

'Kill the jokes. I'm not in the mood.'

'What was she doing in the kitchen?' Spence continued.

'Studying. Doing something on the laptop.'

'What was she studying?' Spence straightened, looking more interested. Natty shrugged.

'Was I supposed to ask?'

Spence shook his head. 'Nat, she's your girl.'

'No, she isn't.'

'Even if you're not in a relationship, you spend time with her and Jaden. You trust her.'

'So?'

'So, at the very least, she's a friend, and you could have at least asked about what she was doing.'

'It had nothing to do with me, so I left her to it. If anything, I helped by keeping Jaden out of her hair.'

'Studying ain't easy at any age, Nat. That's why she didn't want to talk to you; you didn't even show interest or ask about what she was doing.'

'Forget it,' said Cameron, clearly bored of the topic. 'Lorraine's not important. The new women at the spot tomorrow *will be*, so let's focus on them. They don't have silly complications and moods. They're just waiting for us to approach.'

Natty smiled at how simple life seemed to be for Cameron. Cameron didn't get it; he didn't understand why Natty was so bothered about Lorraine, and Natty supposed he didn't have to.

'I know we put a pin in the Elijah talk, but make sure the deal makes sense when you meet him,' said Spence, moving the conversation along. Natty cut his eyes to him.

'I thought you didn't trust him?'

'I think he's sneaky, but he's a businessman, and he's successful. He'll have told Rudy . . . or even your uncle, something good to get our team to the table. Focus on that part instead of trying to get laid.'

Natty didn't reply straight away. He didn't show it, but Spence's words had affected him. Spence was a more logical thinker, which always came across in his words. He was always looking at the big picture. Spence's dad had been in the crime game years ago and worked for a kingpin. Like Natty, Spence had been raised to study the streets, and all the major players.

'Back in your pop's day, what do you think he would have done? What was he saying when Delroy wanted to meet with Teflon and make peace?'

Spence rubbed his chin.

'He didn't like the idea of peace, and thought Delroy should be putting Teflon out of business. A few people thought that.'

No one spoke for a moment. Natty weighed up Spence's response, noting that he hadn't said whether he agreed with his dad's opinion.

'Did you tell Lorraine that you could be working with her baby father?' Spence's words jolted Natty from his thoughts.

'It doesn't have anything to do with her,' he snapped.

'She might not see it that way. You should talk to her.'

'Fucking hell, Spence. Are you still trying to pretend Anika hasn't changed you? You never used to talk all this nonsense before.' Cameron stared at him with disdain.

Spence glared at Cameron.

'It's okay to have different opinions, Cam. We don't always have to agree on everything. You think I talk to her about street shit? *Our shit?'*

'Anika got in your head with some nonsense, and now you're trying to do the same with Natty,' said Cameron, sneering.

'You need to grow up,' Spence snapped. 'Anika hasn't changed me, but if women *do* have that effect, you should try harder to get one.'

Cameron's mouth formed a hard line, not liking Spence's words. 'Make sure you ask for permission tomorrow. Wouldn't want her to cry if you go out otherwise.'

'For fucks sake, Cam—'

'Enough!' Natty roared. 'Both of you shut the fuck up, because you're getting on my nerves. I don't know what is going on with you two, but you need to fix it, because this back-and-forth crap is annoying.' Finishing his drink, he shot to his feet and stormed out, leaving his now silent friends behind.

* * *

NATTY LEFT the crew and headed for the spot where the underlings hung out. It was a house just off Spencer Place, with rooms reserved upstairs for the team to chill. Entering, Natty greeted a few faces, glancing at the screen, where people were gathered around watching two runners play *Fortnite*. The person Natty was looking for sat in the corner drinking a Lucozade, a battered Nokia on his lap. Carlton was one of the more reliable youngsters. Natty had schooled him, slowly giving him more responsibility.

'How's it going?' He asked. Carlton nodded.

'All good, boss. Almost sold out.'

'Bolki aware?' Bolki was in charge of delivering product, ensuring each team had what they needed.

'We're on his list. He's stopping by later with the reload.'

Natty patted him on the shoulder. 'Let me know if anything pops off. I'll be nearby.'

'Got you.'

Leaving the spot after hanging around for a few more minutes, Natty drove to his mum's house. She lived in the middle of Hares Avenue. Natty always felt weird being in the area; as if he was under surveillance. He'd heard rumours of a former distributor having an office in the area, protected from police presence by the nearby mosque, and all the political ramifications that came with it.

His mum lived in a red-bricked spot with a brown door, blended nicely with the other terraced houses around it. He'd never understood why she stayed there. She had the money to live in a better home, but she refused anytime Natty brought it up.

His mum sat on the sofa, smoking a cigarette and watching television. She gave him a sharp look when he entered. People often told Natty he had his dad's build, but his mum's facial features, which was never more evident than when he was with her. He had her nose and cheekbones, and she was currently giving him the same hard look he often gave others. The room stank of cigarettes, with various family photos dotted around, namely of Natty's dad in his younger days. Two cups rested on the coffee table.

Natty kissed his mum on the cheek.

'Do you want a drink, mum?'

'No.'

Natty took both cups from the coffee table and placed them in the kitchen sink. After making a coffee, Natty sat next to his mum.

'Got a cig for me?'

'This is my last one.' She handed it to him, and he took two long drags, passing it back.

'How are you?'

'Life doesn't change.' She shrugged, eyes back on the screen.

'It changes if you want it to. Do you?'

She scowled.

'Do I what?'

'Do you want things to change?'

'I don't have time for this,' she snapped. 'How many times have I told you not to bring that smart mouth around me?'

Natty didn't respond, already regretting visiting. He loved his mum, but she was challenging to be around.

'Spoken to Unc lately?'

Finishing the cigarette, his mum flicked the remains into a nearby ashtray.

'He had dinner with Rudy and me the other night.'

'You should have invited me. I'd have liked to see him.' Natty wondered why Rudy hadn't said anything.

Rudy and his mum had started seeing one another after Natty's dad had died, shortly before Natty began working with Rudy. He'd grown used to their relationship, but that didn't stop it from aggravating him from time to time.

Rudy was in a perfect position to put in a good word to Natty's uncle, but hadn't. It was galling.

'Suck up to your uncle in your own time. I won't be used so you can do it,' his mum said.

Natty glared at her. '*Used*? I come and see you all the time. You're the one who never has anything to say.'

'Maybe if you were genuine, I would.'

Natty swallowed down his anger.

'I'll stay for dinner, and we can watch a film or something. What are you having?'

'You're only offering to try to prove me wrong,' his mum replied.

'You're fucking impossible.' Natty rubbed his forehead.

'Don't swear at me. I won't have you in my home if you're going to disrespect me.' His mum's eyes narrowed.

'I'll leave then.' Natty drained his coffee and shot to his feet.

'See? You're selfish. You don't care about me. Just like your dad. That's why you're walking out now.'

Without a word, Natty slammed the door behind him.

CHAPTER FOUR

BY THE TIME the event rolled around, Natty's lousy mood hadn't abated. He hated that Lorraine and his mum were taking out their issues on him. Spence was right when he'd said Natty should have paid more attention, but Natty was sick of the games. He wanted women to be straight up, the way he was. He entered Cameron's, psyching himself up.

'Was starting to think you weren't gonna show,' said Cameron. He sat on the sofa, building a spliff, a bottle of E&J by his side. 'You wanna hit this? I've got some coke too, if you want some.'

Despite being tempted to say no, Natty nodded, snorting a line, before pouring a drink.

'That a new outfit?' He said, wiping his nose and sniffing. Cameron wore a tight navy blue t-shirt with a pocket logo, jeans and cream Balenciaga's. He topped it off with his thickest chain, and the snide Rolex.

'Yeah. Cost me two bags, but worth it.'

'You spent two grand on the clothes?' Natty's eyebrow rose.

Cameron shrugged. 'So what? That outfit you're wearing doesn't look cheap, either.'

Natty had foregone wearing a chain. He had a black shirt he'd recently bought, ripped jeans, and shoes.

'Whatever. Where's Spence?'

'Probably on his knees begging to go out,' snarked Cameron. Natty gave a short laugh, which appeared to please Cameron.

As Cameron called Spence, Natty wondered why he had such an issue with Spence and Anika. Unbeknown to Spence, Anika and Cameron had been a thing once upon a time, before Cameron ended it. Neither Natty nor Cameron ever mentioned it, and despite not entering into relationships, Cameron remained partial to casual affairs.

As far as Natty was concerned, if Spence was happy and kept working hard, it didn't matter. Seemingly, Cameron disagreed.

Spence arrived a while later, outfitted in a crewneck sweater and jeans.

'Looking sharp, gents,' he said, grabbing a glass and pouring his drink.

'Didn't think you were gonna turn up,' said Cameron, eyeballing him.

'I almost didn't.'

Cameron's eyes narrowed. He shot Natty a look, and then glared at Spence.

'I definitely need to have a word with your missus. You're fucking whipped, and it's sickening.'

Spence sighed.

'Once again, I'm capable of thinking for myself. Not everything revolves around my girl.'

'Seems like it does,' Cameron retorted.

'Are you jealous? You talk about Anika more than I do.'

Cameron laughed darkly. 'Jealous of you? She's been around the block. Only you would want *that*.'

Tossing his glass to the floor, Spence lunged for Cameron.

'Stop!' Natty broke them up before they could start swinging. He shoved Cameron away as the pair shot daggers, breathing hard. 'You two need to calm the hell down, fighting over this nonsense. Cam, go outside and cool off.'

'What about him? He's the one who can't handle the truth.' Cameron's nostrils flared.

'What?' Spence struggled against Natty, but Natty easily kept him in place.

'Just go, Cam. Don't make things worse.'

Cameron stomped from the room. Natty let Spence go a few moments later.

'I'm not gonna stand for the repeated disrespect,' Spence warned, eyes hard.

'Spence, ignore him. You know what he's like.'

'That's not the point.' Spence jerked away, continuing to take deep breaths, trying to calm down. Natty couldn't argue, but didn't know what to say. They had been cool for the longest, but things seemed strained with Spence and Cameron, and he didn't know how to get around it.

If they fought, would he have to take a side? If he did, which side would he pick?

* * *

LATER, Natty was at an apartment in the city centre. Despite all the hype, the event had been a bust. When a woman he'd clicked with suggested an after-party, he'd seized the potential distraction. He'd lost the woman in the shuffle of people, but wasn't bothered.

The two-bedroomed apartment had a spacious living room with a connecting kitchen. It had light cream walls, immaculate flooring, and a black and white rug taking up most of the space. A large sofa and several smaller chairs and tables were dotted around the room. The party was full of people dressed in tight, flashy clothing. Drugs freely flowed, a bevy of people lining up to partake.

Cameron and Spence had made up after multiple shots. They were talking to some women in the corner, Spence nodding along and backing up Cameron. Natty felt entirely out of place. He didn't like the crowd, and his bad mood hadn't shifted. He kept thinking about his issues with Lorraine, plus the Spence and Cameron drama. This was a night he'd have preferred being by himself.

Spotting an attractive brown-skinned woman conversing with some people, he wandered over, enjoying how her eyes widened when she saw him.

'Natty,' he said, introducing himself by taking her free hand and kissing it. Her face flushed, and he knew he'd had an effect.

'Alana,' she replied in a soft voice. The other women shared glances, then excused themselves with polite nods.

'How did you do that?' She asked. Natty grinned, maintaining eye contact.

'Guess they realised we were destined to talk.'

Alana rolled her eyes, but couldn't stop her lips twitching. She still held his hand and, upon noticing, flushed further and let him go.

'You're sweet.'

'That's one word to describe me.'

Alana arched a perfectly shaped eyebrow. 'Give me another.'

'*Determined.*' He kept up the eye contact, knowing it was crucial. A moment later, she looked away, blowing out a breath.

'I . . . need to speak with someone. Nice meeting you, Natty.'

'You too.' He could have stopped her from leaving, but didn't. Based on her body language, he assumed she had a boyfriend and didn't want to get carried away. Getting another drink, he made his way to Cameron and Spence.

'Having fun?'

'It's live in here,' Cameron slurred, his arm around Spence. 'Could have banged those little cokeheads if I'd tried harder.' He squinted at Natty. 'See you're finally smiling. You got over your shit?'

'I guess so,' said Natty. Even a few seconds of flirting had been enough for him, his worries abating for the moment. Scanning the room, his gaze rested again on Alana. She was sipping wine and speaking to a group of women. His eyes widened when he recognised one of them. Without a word, he moved in their direction, ignoring Cameron calling after him.

Alana's mouth opened as he neared, but ignoring her, he focused on another woman. She wore a fitted blue dress accentuating every delicious curve, and her hair was styled in neat box braids. Natty blinked, unused to seeing Lorraine looking so dressed up. He wondered for a foolish moment if he had manifested her presence.

'What are you doing here?' He asked before he could stop himself.

Lorraine blinked, surprised to see Natty. There was a moment where they continued staring at one another, each taking in the other's appearance. Behind them, the other women exchanged looks, Alana included. Lorraine's mouth opened and closed before she finally composed herself.

'I could ask you the same question.'

Natty frowned, caught off guard by the response. He wasn't pleased with just how sexy Lorraine looked. He thought about their last conversation and how cold she had been. The earlier feelings of annoyance returned.

'Where's Jaden?' He looked into her eyes, not wanting to get caught checking her out.

Lorraine folded her arms, drawing Natty's attention to her impressive chest for a moment. 'He's with my mum for the night. You know she loves to see him.'

Natty couldn't argue. He'd met Lorraine's mum dozens of times, and she was besotted with her grandson and enjoyed looking after him.

'You have a free yard then?' He wasn't sure why he said it, or where he was going with the question. Lorraine's eyes narrowed.

'Please don't think you'll be drunkenly crashing at my place, Natty. If you show up, I won't let you in.'

'What's your problem?' He snapped, tired of the attitude.

'Even if I told you, you wouldn't care. Have a nice night.' Lorraine stalked off, Natty glaring after her, his mood worsening when he saw several guys eyeing her up. Alana shot him an incredulous look, rolling her eyes. Cameron and Spence were talking to some more girls, so Natty went back over and joined in the conversation.

The women were younger and currently attending university. He quickly grew bored and couldn't help looking over to where Lorraine was. She was laughing with the same group of girls, and the guys from earlier surrounded them. Alana looked back at him, but Natty turned away.

As the party continued, people left, with more faces showing up. Some faces Natty recognised appeared; men he knew were connected to Elijah. He wondered if it was a coincidence. One of them noticed Natty and wandered over. He was a slim, light-skinned man with a neatly trimmed fade and a diamond stud in his ear. He slapped hands with Natty, a large chain around his neck jingling.

'What's happening, Nat? Didn't think I'd find you here.'

'I was at some event in town, and someone mentioned this spot.'

Wonder nodded. 'They have these parties every once in a while. Ellie's cool, and it's a good little breeding ground for making connections.'

'I'll have to come again in future,' said Natty.

Wonder sized up Natty, looking around before he spoke again.

'I heard we're gonna be doing some business together.'

'I heard the same,' replied Natty, wondering what Elijah had told his team. He glanced past Wonder, his eyes again resting on Lorraine. Wonder noticed, his eyes flitting between them before he spoke.

'Is that Raider's baby mum?' He asked, already knowing the answer.

'Yeah.'

Wonder raised an eyebrow. 'I heard you two were close. Raider's mentioned it before.'

Natty shrugged.

'We're friends.' For some reason, the words felt bitter as they left his lips. He wasn't sure what they were, but relegating it to friendship felt wrong. It was made worse because he couldn't seem to get anything right where she was concerned. Even the way she had walked off earlier riled him. His paranoid brain was working overtime. Elijah was up to something; he was sure of it. It was too coincidental that his people happened to show up when Natty and Lorraine were talking.

'That's cool, bro. Just be careful, because you know Raider sees her as his.'

At another time, Natty might have shrugged off Wonder's words as general advice. He couldn't stop him from hanging around Lorraine, and whether Raider had an issue, he'd continued to see her and Jaden.

In the mood he was in, he saw the words as a challenge.

'Why doesn't he see his son as *his* too?' Wonder opened his mouth to respond, but Natty talked over him. 'Raider needs to recognise when something, or someone, isn't *his* anymore.'

Wonder's eyes narrowed.

'Don't forget, Raider is on my team, Natty. We're cool, but play nice, and don't talk reckless.'

Natty took a step toward Wonder, closing any space between them. Wonder stood his ground. They both knew Natty would wipe the floor with him in a fight, but he didn't back up.

'Save all that tough talk for someone else.' Natty noticed the men Wonder had come with, inching closer, and defiantly met the eyes of each. Several of the partygoers picked up something was wrong, backing up and whispering amongst themselves.

Ignoring it, Natty focused on Wonder and his crew, piecing together a plan of action. There was little space in the cramped room, but he would have to deal with that if they rushed him.

'I don't want to start any shit, Nat. I just need you to be respectful.'

'You already started something when you approached me trying to give warnings,' replied Natty.

'You're always on one.' Wonder shook his head. 'I'm just giving you some friendly advice about *Raider's* baby mum. Chill.'

Natty continued to size up the crew, ready to throw the first hit.

'Nah, it's not happening like this,' said a voice from behind Natty. Cameron and Spence appeared on either side of him. The stench of liquor was overpowering, but they seemed to have quickly sobered, ready for whatever happened next. With the odds a little fairer, Wonder and his people lost their spirit.

'We were just talking,' said Wonder. 'No drama.'

Natty didn't say a word as Wonder and his men backed away. Cameron turned to him, still scowling.

'What was all that about?'

'They were talking about Lorraine and Raider. Wonder thought he could warn me off.'

'She's here, isn't she?' Cameron had a lewd look on his face.

'Thought I saw her earlier, looking super sexy. You're a fool for not claiming her.'

'I don't have time for this shit. I'm off to get another drink.' Natty walked away, still struggling to calm down after what had transpired. As he poured himself some brandy, his hands shook. It wasn't from fear. He wasn't scared of Wonder or anyone he had with him. He'd wanted the fight so badly, and it was something he could control. He could handle violence. Violence didn't play games and try to mess with his head. It was easy and had a resolution he could handle.

Natty took several deep breaths. He'd just downed the brandy and poured another when Spence made his way over, Cameron again trailing.

'Nat, I'm gonna bounce,' said Spence.

'Because of Elijah's people? Don't worry about them,' said Natty, waving his free hand.

Spence shook his head. 'I'm not scared of them. If you want me to stay and back it, I will.'

'You need to stay, anyway,' interjected Cameron. 'If they see we're a man down, they might try to rush us.'

Spence looked to Natty, waiting for his response.

'You're cool, Spence. Those pussies aren't gonna do anything whether you're here or not.'

'Are you sure?'

Natty sipped his drink, struggling to get a handle on his feelings. His frustrations bubbled to the surface, and he struggled to keep them tethered. Wonder was talking on the phone, his eyes on Natty. People furtively watched both groups, having seen the earlier exchange.

Out of the corner of his eye, Natty saw Alana and the other women leaving, the men that had crowded them, helping with their jackets, shooting nervous glances back at Natty.

Wonder kept his eyes on Natty. Natty's eyes narrowed; Wonder staring had his blood boiling. The anger had returned. He needed the drama; Wonder was the physical representation of his problems, one he wanted to smash through.

'These lot are getting too big,' growled Cameron. 'They really think they're running things out here. Spence, if it kicks off, go for Wonder. Natty and me can handle the others.'

'You need to get some water and chill, Cam. We don't need things getting any worse at a public party,' said Spence. Despite his earlier words, he'd stayed, too loyal to leave his friends, a resigned expression on his face.

Natty's fists clenched. He knew there would be consequences for the fight and that Rudy would undoubtedly find out, but right now, he didn't care. Wonder had tried talking down to him. He grabbed the brandy bottle, ready to smash it over Wonder's head.

Before he could take another step, Lorraine stepped in his path. Eyes remaining on Natty's, she took the bottle from his hand, then led him from the apartment. In the elevator, he snatched away his hand.

'What the hell are you doing?' He snapped, when they reached the ground floor and headed outside.

'What are *you* doing, you mean?' Lorraine replied with a question of her own. 'Are you *really* trying to fight Wonder and his boys? Were you *really* going to smash a bottle over his head? In public?'

'You shouldn't have taken me out,' Natty said, ignoring her questions. 'I won't have those little twats thinking I'm soft.'

'Natty, who cares what they think? What is going on with you? Why are you so determined to cause carnage?'

'What I'm doing has nothing to do with you. I'll tell you one thing: Wonder was ringing someone up there, and my guess is it's Raider. So, when your wastrel baby father shows up, I'm gonna deal with him, and you don't wanna be around to see that happen.'

'Don't be silly, Natty. You're going to end up getting arrested if you carry on. It's Ellie's party, and she's already threatening to call the police on all of you.'

'I can handle prison.'

Lorraine's eyes flashed, her nostrils flaring as she shook her head.

'Nat . . . I care about you and know how you are, but this isn't the way to go about things. I want to help you, so please tell me what is going on?'

'I'll tell you what's going on, seeing as you wanna know so badly. I'm tired of the women in my life taking out their moods on me. I'm tired of the bullshit games, and I'm tired of people not fucking respecting me!'

'Respect? What are you talking about? Who doesn't respect you? Wonder and his crew, who you don't even like?' Lorraine sighed, resting her hand on Natty's shoulder. He wanted to move it, but found he was powerless to do so. 'You're a great guy, and I have a lot of time for you. Everyone does. You walk around with a chip on your shoulder, though, and you think the world owes you something.'

'What the hell do you know about it?' He roared, stung by her words. 'What does any of this have to do with you?'

'Fine!' Lorraine snapped, fiercely meeting his eyes. 'Do what you want. I don't even care anymore. You and Raider are as bad as each other.'

Lorraine stormed off down the road. Natty closed his eyes, sighing deeply. He wanted to go after her, but knew he would only worsen things. He let the cold air sober him up, trying to get his bearings.

A few minutes later, a midnight blue BMW pulled up. Elijah slid from the car in a yellow and green Brazil football training kit. Natty straightened, knowing that despite his negative feelings toward Elijah and his team, he was a man who he needed to give his due to. Noticing him, Elijah nodded. Natty's hands clenched as he approached, unwilling to let his guard down.

'Where's Raider?' He asked, glancing at Elijah's ride, unable to see inside.

'At this time, probably drunk in a strip club somewhere,' Elijah replied. 'Wonder called. Mentioned there might be a potential issue.'

'He was talking reckless, acting like he wanted to go.' Natty was unnerved by Elijah's calm demeanour. There was barely an inch in height between them, and Elijah's powerful build was on a par with Natty's.

'I will handle Wonder. I want good relationships between our firms. I've spoken with Rudy. There's plenty of money we can make together.'

'What's your angle here?' Natty asked. 'Rudy trusts you, but you've done some slick shit in the past, and I don't know if I can just forget that.'

Elijah glanced around and signalled for Natty to sit in the car. He took in the fancy leather interior for a moment, then focused on Elijah.

'There was dirt on both sides,' Elijah finally replied. 'When all that stuff happened years ago, we were both there. Afterwards, our teams wanted to benefit from the power vacuum, and we bumped heads. It went away, though. It didn't linger. I've made money on my own, and you lot are absolutely killing it.'

'So, why bother working together if we're doing well separately?'

Elijah maintained eye contact. It was unsettling for Natty to see his strategies being used against him, but he persevered.

'Because the streets are ready for a change. Other little gangs are banding together, wanting more power and prestige. It's only a matter of time before people start looking at our teams and wanting to get some of what we're getting. If we work together, they won't try us. It won't be worth the risk.'

The idea had a lot of merits, and it was easy for Natty to see how Elijah might have been able to sell the concept to Rudy. He'd also noticed subtle changes in how the crew was perceived. There were a lot of compliments masking envy; passive aggressive remarks about the team taking a more significant piece of the pie than other smaller firms. Natty hadn't paid too much attention, but Elijah clearly had.

'I don't fully trust you, and I don't fuck with Raider. He's a piece of shit.'

Elijah held the stare a moment longer.

'I understand it's personal with you two, and I won't get in the middle of that. At the same time, Raider is my brother, and I can't have you disrespecting him in front of me.'

Natty could have made an issue out of it and forced a fight. Part of him wanted to. In the grand scheme of things, it would be pointless. It wouldn't get him what he wanted, and despite not trusting Elijah, he knew he was right with some of the things he had said.

The streets were ready for a change, and they had to make sure they changed with them. The old days were done with. The way things were set up, it was hard for one person to rule anymore. Maybe that would change in the future, but for now, this was how things were, and Natty had to deal with that like everyone else.

'Fine,' he finally said. Elijah nodded.

'Let's go inside and get a drink.'

Neither man spoke as they took the lift back up to the party. Several more people had left since Natty had gone outside. When he entered with Elijah, he saw Cameron's eyes widen. Spence had gone by now. Elijah and Natty headed for the table. They poured drinks of brandy, and Elijah held out his glass. Natty clinked it, and they both nodded. Elijah turned and headed over to Wonder.

Placing his glass back on the table, Natty walked away to find Cameron.

'What the hell was that about? Who invited him?' Cameron frowned at Natty.

'Wonder called him,' replied Natty. 'He thought things might get bad between us.'

'Where's Lorraine? I figured you two went back to hers, the way she dragged you out of here. Wouldn't have blamed you either.' Cameron smirked.

'We had another fight, and she stormed off.'

'A fight over what?'

Natty shrugged. 'Nothing. She just didn't want me to fight, that's all.'

Cameron sniggered. 'Gotta say, I was shocked when you picked up the bottle. You were gonna smash it over Wonder's head, weren't you?'

'If I had to.' Now that he'd calmed down, Natty felt foolish at the idea of bottling someone in the middle of a busy party.

As annoyed as he was with Lorraine, Natty was glad she'd stopped him from making a huge mistake.

'What did Elijah say to you?'

'He wants our teams to align, because other little teams are starting to band together. He doesn't think they'll come for us if we're united.'

'He's making sense. I know bare little teams that are working together, and not many of them like us.'

Natty agreed. Their team was in a strange predicament. They were successful and made big money, but they didn't have much say in how things were governed in the streets.

After the fall of the last big crews, the police and the streets, in general, seemed to have a vested interest in preventing any team from getting too big. The only reason their crew had prospered was that they were well-positioned before the change. It gave them a head start that others didn't benefit from. Their supply was mainly unaffected by the storms, and by the time the other teams got their acts together, they sat pretty.

'What else did he say? I know where one or two of those little crews hang. We can tool up and go sort them out.'

'Later, bro. Let's chill on the business now.'

Cameron sneered at Natty.

'Okay . . . let's focus on you moving to Lorraine's friend in front of her and kissing her hand like you're Prince Charming!'

Laughing, Natty took his ribbing for a while, then the pair headed to speak to some of the remaining women. The mood slowly started to pick back up after the tension, and Wonder even came over to apologise after a while. It was clear he had been prompted to do so by Elijah, but it was a nice gesture.

As the party continued, Natty noted how people were positioning themselves around Elijah and sucking up to him. Regardless of Natty's feelings, the man had presence and knew how to use it. He felt a little less unnerved about having to work with him, but resolved to keep an eye on him and his team, just in case. He continued drinking, even having a few shots with Wonder, and the night became a blur.

* * *

THE FOLLOWING DAY, Natty woke in an unfamiliar bed, with a strange woman draped over him. His head pounding, he extricated himself from her grip, gathered his clothes, and walked out without waking her. The place was an absolute mess, and he had no intention of helping her tidy up.

CHAPTER FIVE

ELIJAH'S WORDS stayed with Natty over the next day. He grudgingly found himself agreeing with what he'd said, and was warming toward the idea of working with him.

It remained to be seen just how much money they would make together.

Natty wondered which teams Elijah was concerned about that would make him seek out Rudy for support.

Ripples in the underworld were always met warily. Everyone recalled the dangerous, bullet-riddled years. Afterwards, the streets were wide open, and people took advantage, making quick alliances to survive the complex world.

Things had calmed since, but people remained cautious.

From complicated street politics, Natty's thoughts strayed to another complication . . . Lorraine; the argument they'd had outside the hotel. Whenever complications arose, he always fell into battle mode with Lorraine. He didn't like that she'd snapped at him, or that she had accused him of having a problem. Natty knew he was confident, but he didn't believe he had a chip on his shoulder, and didn't know why she was so mad with him. He decided to let her cool down before he spoke with her again.

The other thing Natty didn't want to admit was how good she looked. Natty knew Lorraine was attractive. There had been a vibe between them from day one, and he was no stranger to her body, but he was used to seeing her in sweatpants and hooded tops, or worn out from looking after Jaden.

The reminder of how she could look when she was trying was a gut punch, and he wasn't sure what to do next. He cared for Jaden and wasn't intimidated by Raider the way others were, but thinking about a commitment was another story altogether. He wasn't sure how to handle that.

There was also the issue of Cameron and Spence.

The pair had got along at the end of the night, but they had almost come to blows, and it wasn't something he could afford to let happen again. The issue of Anika seemed to be driving a wedge between them, and Natty couldn't understand why. He decided it was a bridge he would have to cross and that speaking to Cameron might help him understand what was happening.

* * *

'I WAS WONDERING when you were gonna show up,' said Cameron a short while later. They were in his kitchen while he made breakfast. Natty stood at the back door, smoking a spliff. Cameron didn't have a problem with him smoking inside, but Natty wanted fresh air at the same time.

'What do you mean?'

'You were absolutely gone last night. I thought you and Ellie were gonna start banging in front of us,' said Cameron.

'I might have gotten a bit carried away with the liquor,' Natty admitted, smiling.

Cameron sniggered.

'A bit? You were out of it. One minute Ellie's yelling at you about bringing drama to the spot; the next, she's grinding and kissing you in front of the whole room. I dunno what you have, but they like it.'

Natty sighed. He remembered flashes of having sex with Ellie, but a lot of the build-up was foggy.

'What are you doing here, anyway? You've got the day off.'

'I wanted to talk to you.'

Cameron nodded. 'The Elijah thing? I've been thinking about that myself since I woke up.'

'It's not about that, but go on.'

Cameron frowned, but finished making his breakfast and took a seat.

'I think it's a good move to be working with him,' he started, tucking into his food. 'As snakey as Elijah is, he's got connections, and he's right about one thing; teams are circling. I give it a few months before one of them gets their shit together and tries to take us out.'

Natty's eyebrow rose at Cameron's words, but he saw their merit.

'After last night, I'm guessing we'll set up a meet. There's no use waiting around,' he said.

Cameron nodded. 'What did you wanna talk about, anyway?'

Natty sipped a coffee he'd made before Cameron started cooking, again silently reminding himself to bring his own next time he came.

'This thing with you and Spence.'

'What about it?' Cameron's brow furrowed.

'I want to know why his relationship is such a big deal.'

'It isn't.' Cameron's voice rose.

'It clearly is. You bring it up at every opportunity, and you sound bitter. I need to know what's happening, and I want the truth.'

Cameron shrugged. 'I dunno what you want me to say.'

'Tell me what the problem is. Am I gonna have to worry about you two falling out?'

'That's up to him,' replied Cameron. 'I'm not the one selling out my boys for pussy. I'm right here with you.'

'So is Spence. You may not like what he's doing, but he still chills with us, and he works as hard as anyone, so kill it and dead the silly remarks.'

Cameron's nostrils flared. 'You're telling me that you're happy about them? She's basically living off him since they moved in together.'

Natty made a face. 'I don't care. If he was pillow talking and putting us at risk or her ahead of business, I'd have a problem. My main problem with her is that she was with you, but never told Spence. I think that's foul.'

'Why don't you say something to Spence then?' Cameron demanded.

'It's too late. We have to live with it, but you need to get over your shit.'

Cameron scowled. Natty let the words sink in before he spoke again.

'Leave Spence be. Focus on helping me make our team even stronger. If he ever becomes a problem, we'll deal with it.'

'What about Lorraine?'

'What about her? Didn't we already speak about Lorraine?' Natty's left eye twitched.

'I saw your face last night. You're into her, and it's not just about banging her.'

'No, I'm not.'

'Yeah, you are, and the fact you're lying about it only makes it worse.'

'The only one lying is you,' said Natty, annoyed at Cameron's repeated comments.

'You and Spence are changing and growing pussy whipped over women, but you both wanna act like I'm the problem.'

'You *are* the problem. Who the fuck is pussy whipped, you silly prick?' Natty's muscles tensed. He glowered at Cameron, who stood his ground.

'You are. Don't be getting all hostile with me. I'm out there repping the crew, making sure people fear us, while you're almost scrapping and getting in fights all over the place. Did you forget you were ready to take on Elijah's whole crew over that girl you claim you don't like?'

'Are you silly? I was ready to fight because they thought they could disrespect me. The same way you're trying to disrespect me now.' A vein in Natty's neck pulsed, his eyes flashing.

'You wanna fight me now? Is that it?' Cameron glared at Natty, who returned it. The look between the men grew more intense until, finally, Cameron took a deep breath.

'I'm sorry, okay? You're my brother, and I'm not gonna fight with you over some nonsense. You want me to leave Spence alone, then I will. When he fucks up because he's too busy thinking about Anika, I'm gonna be the first one saying *I told you so*.'

Natty grinned, knowing Cameron would do just that.

'Fine. Now, let's drop it and talk about something else.'

* * *

LATER, Natty drove to Lorraine's and parked across the road, not wanting to go home. He'd hoped to hear from her by now, but evidently, she was still angry.

Staring at the house, he thought about what she could be doing with Jaden, wondering if he should make the first move and knock on the door. He sat there for several minutes, then his phone buzzed. He looked down, seeing a text message from Ellie, speaking about their night. Glancing from his phone to the house, he took a deep breath, then replied to Ellie's message as he drove away.

Rudy had also sent several messages, wanting to speak to him, but Natty kept putting it off. He had no desire to listen to another lecture and was still annoyed at him for meeting with Natty's uncle without including him.

Natty had a contentious relationship with his father's brother. Mitch Dunn was a menace from day one, and one of few people to be in the same league as other respected Hood legends that had passed on. After Natty's father's death, Mitch continued to go from strength to strength, slowly removing himself from the public eye. Like Delroy Williams, he worked through his network and right now, Rudy was the man he spoke with.

Thinking of Rudy made Natty recall the argument with his mum. He hadn't spoken to her since and felt guilty, but she didn't make things easy. Rudy didn't either.

They had access to his Uncle Mitch. Natty hadn't spoken to him since he'd come to Natty's mum's for Christmas dinner, and even then, they hadn't talked business.

Maybe he needed to arrange a meeting?

He didn't know what he would say, however. He wanted to make money and more responsibility, but he also didn't want to be an idiot on the string, seduced by promises of a better life that would ultimately lead to nothing. Natty knew people like that, both in and out of the crew; the down-for-whatever types, who would kill, maim, or anything they could to get clout. To get put on; to get that reputation that would lead to the money and power they always wanted.

The cemetery was littered with the type.

One way or another, Natty needed to work out what he wanted. Until he did that, he was stuck in a rut.

It was well after eleven when he finally entered his house. Heading upstairs, he turned on the bath and stripped out of his clothes, doing press-ups while the water ran. His gym schedule was shot, and that reflected in his general mood. He'd not pushed, grunted, and sweated his problems out for a few days, and it showed. When Natty finished, his arms ached, but he felt slightly better. He glanced at his phone, seeing a text notification, which he ignored. He climbed into the bath when it was ready, playing a hip-hop album on his music dock. Closing his eyes, he let the heat take over, trying to bury his problems for good.

The talk with Cameron had been interesting. They'd been close to blows, but had been friends a long time. Neither held back, and that sometimes boiled over, but rarely lingered. Cameron had agreed to cease his comments about Spence and Anika, which Natty saw as a win.

He planned on having a similar conversation with Spence, and then from there, he would deal with Rudy.

* * *

'WHAT DID he say when you spoke to him then?'

Spence and Natty were in Natty's front garden the next day. Natty had a spliff in his hand, a beer bottle resting between his legs. Spence remained stood, holding a bottle of his own.

'He said he would leave things alone with you. Dunno how much stock I'd put in that if I was you, though.'

Spence nodded, sipping his beer.

'Have you thought about why he acts like he does?'

Natty shook his head. He was distracted for a moment by the flashing light and vibrating of his phone, but ignored it when he saw who it was.

'Cam is always gonna be Cam. He doesn't know any better, and I don't think he even wants to.'

'Do you think I'm doing something wrong with Anika?'

Natty weighed up his words carefully. As he'd said to Cameron, Spence's relationship hadn't affected his business, and they still hung out — as they were now. The pros outweighed the cons.

'No. Your girl is your girl. I don't think you'd be telling her things you weren't supposed to, so she can't hurt the team. Personally, I don't get why anyone would be in a relationship, but it doesn't threaten me that you are.'

Spence grinned.

'I appreciate that, fam. It's been a while now, though. We kept things low at first, but we're living together, and it hasn't changed me. I still take my job seriously. Now, I have more to focus on.'

'I can't promise things will be any easier, so just stay calm. That's all I'm asking,' said Natty.

'I will. Other than that, how are you?'

'I'm fine. Why wouldn't I be?'

'You nearly got into a fight with Elijah's people, for one. Then I heard you came back in with him a while later and seemed cool. That's on top of the whole Ellie and Lorraine situation.'

Natty scowled.

'There is no *Ellie and Lorraine situation*. It's handled.'

Spence stared ahead, his fingers gently tapping his bottle.

'I'm not trying to interfere, but I'm here if you need to talk. Are you gonna keep things going with Ellie?'

Natty grimaced. 'Definitely not.'

'Didn't you enjoy it?' Spence cut his eyes to him. Natty shrugged.

'Honestly, I don't remember much of it. I woke up, and I was just in bed with her. Cam said we were all over each other.'

'She's friends with Lorraine.'

'So?'

'So, you and Lorraine are cool, despite whatever nonsense comes out of your mouth. I saw how angry you were that night, but you still went outside with her.'

'So what? What does that mean?' Natty's eyes narrowed.

'I'm not saying it means anything. Your life is your life. I just think you need to accept the possibility that there might be something more between you.'

Natty didn't respond, even if he knew his friend was right. Things with Lorraine were at an all-time low, and when she found out he'd slept with Ellie, he guessed they would get worse. He would need to bite the bullet and deal with it. Mentally, he added the issue to his to-do list. He would eventually need to speak with Rudy and deal with his lecture, and then he was onto other business.

CHAPTER SIX

LORRAINE WAS HOME, watching Jaden play his game. Her mum had looked after Jaden earlier so she could study, but she'd spent most of her time stewing over Ellie's party and her argument with Natty.

'Are you hungry?'

Jaden shook his head, not taking his eyes from the flashing screen.

'Did you have a good time at Nana's?'

He nodded. 'She let me watch football.'

'That's nice. We can do something fun next week if you like.'

'Okay, Mummy. Can we bring Natty too?'

Lorraine blew out a breath. She didn't know what the thing was between them, but it was never easy. She had known Natty a long time; they had been on and off more times than she could count. Natty was a great guy; he was funny, smarter than he acted, and cared more than he wanted to admit. He had charisma and a way of pulling people toward him. He was loyal to his friends and often generous — hence the *Deeds* nickname. At the same time, he had a temper that he seemed unable and unwilling to control. He had never put his hands on her, but they'd had several screaming arguments where she thought he was going to.

During an off period with Natty, she and Raider had become closer. He was a few years older and seemed to represent everything Natty didn't. He was polite to her, considerate, and she was young and dumb enough to fall for his slick talk. She didn't see the flaws until it was too late. By contrast, Natty had never hidden his flaws.

Before long, she was pregnant, and Raider faded into the woodwork, claiming she had intended to trap him. She'd seen the real side of Raider at this point; a nasty, abusive side. All the false niceties and politeness immediately vanished once she'd refused to get an abortion. Lorraine buckled down, ready to be a single mother.

To her surprise, Natty stepped up during this period, often driving her to appointments and looking after her. She never asked him why, and he never explained himself. She'd often wondered if he'd felt guilty for letting her fall into Raider's clutches, but she was scared of the answer.

After Jaden was born, Natty remained around. He helped with feeds from time to time, and even took Jaden out with him. They would watch television, and go to the park. As Jaden grew older, he became used to seeing Natty. He knew Natty wasn't his father, and seemed to look at him as an older brother, which Lorraine was conflicted about. She didn't think Natty would willingly corrupt her son, but she had misgivings about his lifestyle. There were enough temptations around to lure young boys toward the street life, and she didn't want her son to be another statistic.

Lorraine's phone rang. Reading the screen, she saw it was Rosie, her best friend. Walking to the kitchen and taking a seat, she answered.'

'Hey, girl.'

'Hey, Lo. You okay?'

'Yeah, just having a lazy day. You?'

'I'm good. Have you spoken with Ellie?'

Lorraine frowned. 'Not since I left her place after the party. Me and Natty got into it, and I ended up leaving early. I don't even think I said bye.'

'She called me a bit ago. I've just got off the phone with her.'

'Why do you sound so weird?' Lorraine asked, not liking her friend's tone. She sounded like she had grave news.

'She and Natty got close after the party.'

Lorraine's stomach lurched before she could adequately comprehend those words.

'I heard that they were flirting,' she admitted, resisting the urge to be sick.

'They slept together, Lo. What happened with you and Natty? You said you got into it?'

Lorraine explained about Natty's standoff with Raider's friends, and how she had led him from the party before he could get into trouble.

'Are you okay?' Rosie asked.

Lorraine sighed.

'I can't *not* be okay, babe. Me and Natty aren't like that. I don't quite know what we are, but I don't think it gives me the right to get upset.'

'Course you do. Natty was drunk as hell, but he should have known better, and Ellie definitely should have. She said she's sorry, by the way.'

'Nothing to be sorry about. Natty is single. He doesn't belong to me.'

'Girl, this is me you're talking to,' said Rosie.

Lorraine's eyes narrowed. 'What does that mean?'

'It means I know you, and you and Natty are not *just* friends. He's basically a dad to Jaden, and you two are closer than you want people to think. He went off and got drunk after his argument with you because he needed a distraction. After arguing with him, you stormed off home and left a party early.'

'So what? We're not together. He's not Jaden's dad. He can do what he wants.'

'So, you two have some weird holding pattern that I don't understand, but everyone knows there's something there.'

They spoke for a while longer before ending the call.

Lorraine made herself a drink, thinking about Natty and Ellie. She was in two minds about what to think. She knew Natty was furious that night, and based on what Rosie had said, he was completely out of it. There were feelings that she didn't quite understand between her and Natty, but she didn't know if it was worth the long-term potential heartbreak. She had a perennial worry about him abandoning Jaden, as Raider had.

Tired of thinking about it, Lorraine resolved to focus on her son, rather than putting her energy into Natty.

* * *

THE NEXT DAY, Natty sat on the wall outside his house. Spence stood nearby, whilst Cameron leant on his car. The sun was out, yet grey clouds loomed above, and there was a chill in the air. Not that this bothered Cameron, who wore a grey vest.

'I'm telling you, I've found a tough new workout,' he said, flexing his bicep. 'Gimme a couple months, and I'm putting everybody to shame!' He exclaimed.

'Are you forgetting what happened last time you went gym with me?' Said Natty. 'You tried lifting 80 kg, showing off for those girls, and you nearly killed yourself.'

Spence sniggered, having heard the story before. Cameron pursed his lips.

'Bullshit. You dragged me to the gym, even though you knew I was feeling under the weather, and you tried to make me lift heavy. Fact of the matter is, I'm on it now. Bought some creatine earlier too.'

'What's with the sudden urge to get back into shape?' Spence asked, chuckling. Cameron's eyes narrowed.

'Get back into shape? I'm already in shape. Look at me.' Again, he flexed. Natty shook his head.

'You're gonna end up getting pneumonia before you make any gains. It's not warm enough for that little vest,' he said.

'Nat, you need to stop hating. I'm fine, this weather is nothing.' Cameron beat his chest with his free hand, still holding the joint. 'You've got bigger worries, anyway; let's not forget about your *Prince Charming* shit; kissing hands and searching for glass slippers.'

'What are you talking about?' Spence barely held back his laughter.

Natty took the joint from Cameron and inhaled, savouring the potent weed.

'Didn't you see it?' Cameron started. 'He moved to a woman at that party, kissing her hand like he was in a play! Funniest thing I've seen in ages.'

Spence burst into laughter.

'That's such a Natty thing to do. I've seen it before. He transforms when there's women around.'

Laughing, Cameron approached to take the spliff from Natty just as a blacked-out car pulled up next to them. Rudy stepped onto the pavement. Cameron froze with his hand out. Spence gawped at Rudy as the laughter vanished. The eyes of the trio lingered on Rudy, but he only had eyes for Natty.

'Seventeen phone calls. Eight text messages. No response,' said Rudy in a low, calm voice that fooled no one. Natty locked eyes with him, getting the measure of the man. He knew he was in for it. As the moment stretched with neither man speaking, he finally rubbed his forehead.

'I've been busy. I was gonna get back to you today.'

'Not too busy to be sitting outside, getting high and joking around, when you could be working, though?' Rudy shook his head. 'Get in the car.'

Natty's eyes narrowed.

'You don't need to come at me like that, Rudy,' he snarled, irritated at the way he was being spoken to. Rudy didn't respond, simply keeping his eyes on him.

With a huff, Natty took a hit of the joint, then slapped hands with Cameron and Spence. As he climbed into the car, he heard Cameron laughing. He shot his friend a hard look, and Cameron's laughter evaporated.

Natty closed the door, and the car pulled away. One of Rudy's men was driving, and he kept his eyes on the road. Rudy looked out the window in the passenger seat next to him, paying Natty no attention.

'Where are we going?' He quickly grew tired of the silence.

'Figured we'd go to the pub, seeing as you're so fond of drinking recently,' said Rudy.

Natty tried to swallow down his mounting anger.

'I barely drink,' he responded, but Rudy ignored him, and the driver pretended not to hear. Eventually, they pulled outside a pub in Middleton. As Natty climbed from the car, he noticed the clouds had thickened and turned darker.

Natty followed Rudy into the pub, wondering why they weren't going to Delores's place. It had an old-fashioned layout, with an old wooden partition and several tables, chairs and stools that had seen better days. The burgundy decor wasn't much better, but it was cleaner than Natty expected. The stench of beer hung heavily in the air. Someone jostled against Natty as they moved through the busy crowd. He shot the person a hard look and nearly pushed them back, but restrained himself. Rudy nodded to a fleshy, grey-haired landlady, and after a minute, they had a table. A football match played in the background, capturing the bar's attention.

The landlady took their orders. Rudy ordered a coke, and Natty had a lemonade he didn't want. He glanced around the pub, looking for women he could focus on. There were none.

'Talk me through it,' said Rudy, sipping his coke.

Natty resisted the urge to roll his eyes. The atmosphere in the pub heightened every time Leeds United touched the ball. As a player came close to scoring, the yells of encouragement gave Natty an extra few seconds.

'What do we need to talk through?' He finally replied.

Rudy's nostrils flared. Putting his glass down, he rubbed his temples. Noticing his mounting frustration, Natty spoke again.

'Wonder ran his mouth.'

'So?'

Natty shrugged. Rudy shook his head.

'What am I supposed to do with you . . .?'

'You tell me. I don't get any real sense of direction nowadays,' Natty flippantly replied. Rudy's eyes widened, shocked at Natty's audacity.

'If you're ever going to make anything of yourself, you need to start working out when it's the time to close your mouth and do what's best for the people above you.'

'Wonder ran his mouth. Not me.' Natty didn't respond to Rudy's words, though they'd cut him deeply.

'Nathaniel, we're trying to do business here. Make money. Is this the time for your little gangster shit?'

'There's no gangster shit here.'

'You're just fighting over a girl you're not even involved with. Where's the sense in that?'

Natty's jaw tightened.

'I wasn't fighting over her. It's not about her. It's about them.'

'Elijah's people are harmless, so I need you to ignore them and stop making the wrong moves.'

Natty sipped his drink, eyes blazing. Rudy sighed.

'Nathaniel, the streets are always watching. I don't need to tell you that. Your Unc is watching too, and this dumb shit always gets back to him. I know you're unhappy with how things are, but you need to see this as an opportunity to prove yourself.'

Natty levelled Rudy with a look.

'What more can I do?'

'What is it you think you *have* done? You have a problem with authority, Nathaniel, and you're too quick to flip out at the wrong times.'

Natty's eyes narrowed, but he didn't have an answer. He liked being part of the organisation, yet knew he deserved more. Putting that into words was difficult.

Realising an answer wasn't coming, Rudy continued.

'You have everything you need to get to the top. To lead. Lose that chip off your shoulder and go after what you want, but do it for you, not for what you think people want you to do.'

Natty shook his head. 'I don't care what people think of me.'

'Yes, you do. People know it, and if you let them, they will use it.'

Swallowing his frustration, Natty kept his voice level, scowling as the crowd noise increased again.

'You could have spoken to my uncle at any time and told him to elevate me, but you haven't. Save the preaching.'

Rudy's eyes bore into Natty's younger pair.

'First, watch your mouth. Second, I don't tell your Unc anything.

Outside of your mum, nobody does.' Rudy's nostrils flared. 'You've been in the game long enough to understand that one wrong move can have disastrous effects. It can even cost you your life.'

Natty wanted to keep arguing but decided against it.

'If Raider even looks at me wrong, I'll finish him.'

Rudy again shook his head, eyes tinged with sadness and disappointment.

'Is that all you are?' He asked, voice almost a whisper. 'You wanna be like your old man, is that it?'

'Don't talk about my dad.' Natty's fists clenched.

'I knew him, remember? Roughest of the rough, putting bodies in the ground. Where did it get him? It got him de—'

'I said, don't talk about my fucking dad.' Natty leapt to his feet, their drinks clattering to the floor. 'He was more of a man than you could ever be. Keep his damn name out of your mouth.'

Before Rudy could reply, Natty stomped from the pub, leaving a shocked, silent crowd in his wake.

Outside, Natty trembled with rage, glaring at Rudy's driver. He needed to get away before he did something he regretted. Whilst in the pub, it had finally started raining. Nostrils flaring, Natty put his hands in his pockets and began walking, cursing his lack of a jacket as he stomped on.

* * *

RUDY WATCHED NATTY LEAVE. Bringing up his father had been foolish, but he needed him to slow down and look at the situation. All eyes would be on him, and Rudy wanted him to succeed.

Sliding to his feet, he approached the bar. Dropping several notes on the bar top, he nodded and left.

CHAPTER SEVEN

ON THE NIGHT of the meeting, Natty prepared for Elijah. Spence and Cameron offered to go with him, but Natty decided to go alone.

He thought about Rudy and what he was expecting from this meeting. Natty hadn't spoken to him since their altercation at the pub. He regretted what was said, but he admired his dad and the toughness he brought to the streets. The thought of his memory being used to make a point evoked a wave of enduring anger.

Still, Rudy had done a lot for him and his mum, and as Natty picked up a pack of cigarettes from the coffee table, he knew he owed him an apology.

Unravelling the plastic from the packet, Natty pulled out a cigarette and lit it. Taking a long drag, he zoned out, thinking about his dad and his life. He wondered how he could have killed people. What it felt like. Who they were. There were rumours, but he didn't indulge them. It was one of the many unwritten rules of the streets.

Natty was terrified at the idea of dying. He knew people who had died — even his dad died violently, but the idea of life ending worried him, especially now. He hadn't done enough for people to remember him. He recalled the tepid response to his dad's murder. It was quickly

forgotten, no one speaking about it other than contemporaries of his dad, waxing poetic about what a *real* guy he was.

Natty shook off the thoughts. He didn't want them clouding his mind right now.

Natty and Elijah met at Jukie's. Though it was his name on the building, Jukie was semi-retired and rarely moved around in the public eye anymore. There were rumours about him receiving a large amount of money in 2015. A few trusted family members now ran the business.

Natty had been in the gambling spot before, but it wasn't his scene. The crowd was a bit older, and he wasn't into cards or dominoes.

He greeted a few people when he entered, and ordered a beer. Scanning the room, he saw Elijah sitting in the far corner. The place was packed, so Natty was surprised he'd procured such a spot. It spoke to the clout the man had around Chapeltown these days. They shook hands, and Natty plopped into the seat opposite Elijah, glancing over his shoulder. He felt exposed, facing away from the rest of the room.

'I'm not going to off you in public,' said Elijah. 'I'm serious about wanting to work together.'

'Rudy mentioned that but was a bit vague,' admitted Natty.

'Vague in what way?' Elijah leaned in.

'I don't know why it had to be me in the chair.'

Elijah smirked. 'Plenty will step into your shoes if you don't want to do it.'

'Raider one of those guys?'

Elijah's smirk widened. 'Raider has a different type of skillset, but one that's equally useful.'

Natty didn't reply, thinking about Lorraine. They had yet to clear the air, but he missed her and Jaden. Natty didn't understand why he couldn't just walk away from them, and that confusion frustrated him.

'Raider will toe the line, if that's a worry of yours,' Elijah continued, wrongly believing Natty was mulling his words.

'I don't study Raider.'

'You study him far more than you should. That's part of the problem.'

Natty frowned, rubbing his forehead. He considered this the main reason why he and Elijah didn't vibe. Elijah thought he knew everything about everyone. Taking a moment to compose himself, he thought about Rudy's pep talk. There was a lot of subtext he was missing, but he didn't want to miss an opportunity to elevate his game to a new level. He breathed deeply before he replied.

'I'm here and want to make this work, Elijah. I can put shit aside if I need to.'

Elijah blinked, clearly surprised.

'Well, that's good to hear. Is the only issue you have with me because of Raider?'

'Is that important?'

'If we're going to work together, then we should clear the air and get it all out in the open. I'll go first: I always thought you were a waste of space.'

Natty immediately went to jump to his feet, but Elijah held up a hand.

'That right there, is exactly what I mean. You dive in head-first, then you think afterwards. You're much sharper than everyone gives you credit for, but your temper gets in the way.'

'I don't let anyone treat me like a little man, and I never will. You might let people disrespect you, but I don't go for that shit.'

'Neither do I, but there's a time and place for anger, and the time isn't every time someone does or says something you don't like.' His eyes bored into Natty's. 'Pick your battles.'

Natty rubbed his nose, not enjoying Elijah talking to him like this. They were around the same age, both growing up in Chapeltown, knowing many of the same people. At the same time, Elijah seemed sharper than Natty, which was unsettling. His words seemed to hold more weight. He carried himself like a boss; unruffled, always meeting Natty's eyes, dressing the part in shirts, trousers, and shoes — other than when he'd shown up to Ellie's party in a tracksuit. Natty didn't like how insightful Elijah seemed, wondering where he'd learned to dissect people as he had.

Ultimately, Natty acknowledged that Elijah was being respectful with what he was saying, and realised it matched what Rudy had said last time — before he brought up Natty's father. He sighed, knowing more than ever that there was another deep conversation with Rudy in his future.

'It's your turn,' Elijah finally continued. 'Don't hold back.'

Natty didn't.

'I think you're sneaky. I also don't like the company you keep around you — Wonder runs his mouth too much, and Raider's a piece of shit.'

Elijah's eyebrows rose, but apart from that, he remained unruffled by Natty's words.

'Is the Raider problem to do with the woman you both like? His baby mother?'

Natty's nostrils flared. 'It's not about liking her.' He stewed, wondering why people kept saying it to him. Everyone seemed to think they knew him better than he did, which was galling.

Raider was a fool, and Natty didn't like his neglect of Jaden. That was it.

'What's it about then?' Elijah steepled his fingers, looking genuinely interested.

'We have history and I look out for her.'

'Raider also has a history with her.'

Natty gritted his teeth. 'I know he does, but he also ducked out on his responsibilities when he abandoned his child.'

Elijah bowed his head for a moment, then sighed.

'I'm not saying I agree with every decision he makes, but he's loyal, and I respect loyalty.'

'How can he be loyal to you if he's not even loyal to his son?'

Elijah rubbed his eyes, not hastening to reply. It was clear to Natty that he had stumped Elijah, and he allowed himself a small moment of triumph.

'I try not to involve myself in the personal lives of my team, but I can admit you've made some good points.' He grinned. 'Now there's a bit more understanding on both sides, we can get down to business.'

Natty straightened, ready to listen. Elijah glanced around again.

'I've scoped out some fresh territory in Little London.'

Natty's eyebrow rose, and he was immediately intrigued. To his knowledge, there were several little crews based in Little London, operating in a scattered but successful fashion. Alongside this, the council had renovated a lot of the area, building new apartments and catering to a younger, student demographic.

'There are several streets near Oatland Close that the gangs appear to have overlooked.'

'They might be overlooking it now, but when we bustle in and set up shop, we'll be on their radar, and we both know what that means.'

Again, Elijah nodded.

'That's where the resources of your team come in. We take over the blocks as a joint effort and see what sorts of moves the locals make. If anything goes down, we handle it.'

'Do you think anything will go down? Things have been relatively calm in Leeds since the big shootings.'

Elijah acknowledged this with a small smile.

'Of the players down there, only Warren will be a problem. He's one of those . . . hotheads too stupid to listen to reason.'

Natty acknowledged the pause, considering if it was a snipe from Elijah. He chose not to react, filing away Warren's name for future reference.

'The area is fertile. Plenty of students and sales around, and they love to get high. All they want is to do so safely, and if we can provide that, they'll do our marketing for us and spread the word on our product and discretion.'

Natty agreed with that. He had a few students and young workers that bought from him, and it was all they thought about, other than getting laid.

'What split are you thinking?'

Elijah didn't hesitate. '60-40 sounds fair.'

Natty agreed, but decided to push.

'60-40 our way works better.'

Elijah frowned. 'Our team did the due diligence. We saw the potential in the area.'

'True, but you came to us, and you need the muscle of our team. You've already admitted it might come down to war; even if it doesn't, the reputation of my crew trumps yours.'

Elijah rubbed his chin, mulling this over. Natty watched, his heart racing at his effective negotiating. He hadn't gotten aggressive. He'd stayed in control, using what he had just learned, to make his point calmly. He sipped his drink and waited.

'Fine. 60-40 your way. We'll see what the money is like when we get down there. I think there's more than enough to go around once we start.'

They shared another drink, talking about football and a bit of Hood news, before Natty shook his hand and left. He felt he had a greater understanding of Elijah. He didn't deny much of what Natty had said to him, and placed great emphasis on believing in loyalty. Natty wondered how much of his dislike toward Elijah had been perpetuated by what other people had said to him.

Hours later, Natty was home when he received a call from Rudy.

'We need to talk.'

* * *

THEY MET AT DELORES'S. She had already gone to bed, but Rudy had a key. He led Natty to the kitchen and poured him a glass of white rum. Under the flickering kitchen light, his face appeared more lined than usual, and there were bags under his eyes.

'You look tired,' said Natty. He sipped his white rum, the liquor burning his chest.

'I've been in and out of town all week. Haven't had more than a few hours sleep at a time. Not important, though. Spoke with Elijah earlier, and he said you got the deal done. I want to hear your side.'

Natty gave a quick overview of the conversation.

Rudy beamed.

'That is great work, Nat. I purposefully didn't give any instructions about the split, because I wanted to see how you handled it. Sixty percent is well beyond what I expected.' He gave Natty an approving look. 'I'll be telling your uncle about this, and he'll see it the same way I did. This is exactly what I was talking about last time, when I spoke of your potential. You're one of the best guys we have when you're locked on and focused.'

Natty's shoulders straightened, and he couldn't keep the smile off his face, happy Rudy was showering him with so much praise. The joy he'd felt earlier when doing the deal, came back tenfold. In the past, only fighting and successfully seducing women had given him the same rush. Now, he realised it was possible to get the same feeling when doing business the right way.

Rudy gave him a small smile in return before continuing.

'I want you working directly with Elijah, getting everything in order. Keep relatively hands off, but I don't need to micro-manage you on it. Get one of your people to cover your current day-to-day duties. I'm sure you have people in mind. Who are you going with?'

Natty took a few moments to consider. Cameron was more forceful and would likely crack the whip to ensure things got done. Despite that, Spence was the right person for the job, and the fact he was more confident overall, shone through.

'Spence is the right choice.'

Rudy nodded.

'Good. Cameron has skills, but he's not the most subtle person. Spence comes from good stock. His dad was a handful for Delroy back in the day. Anyway, I've spoken with Elijah about some of the particulars. Raider is to be kept away from the project. Wonder might be marginally involved. Keep doing what you're doing, and good things will happen.'

'Thank you, Rudy. About what happened last time. I'm sorry for how I acted. It's tough talking about my dad.'

Rudy laid a hand on his shoulder.

'I know, Nathaniel. I shouldn't have baited you, but I'm glad we're cool now. Spoken with your mum lately?'

Natty shook his head. They hadn't spoken since their argument the last time he'd seen her. Rudy sighed.

'She loves you, but she just worries sometimes. Doesn't always know how to say what she's thinking.'

'I don't think she's ever held back in her life.'

Rudy chuckled.

'I know it's not my place to get involved, but I care about you both. Talk to her.'

'I will,' said Natty. After finishing his drink, he left, Rudy following shortly afterwards.

* * *

NATTY MULLED over the conversations he'd had with Rudy and Elijah. He remained pleased with how he'd handled the situation even a day later. He called Spence and Cameron, arranging to meet in the afternoon at Cameron's.

Unable to muster the energy to go to the gym, Natty settled for continuous press-ups until his arms ached. Afterwards, he went to check on the main spot, speaking with the youngster, Carlton.

'Any issues?'

'Nah, Natty. Everything's calm. Police have been asking questions and driving around, but everyone is being careful.'

'How come the police are around?' Natty was suspicious.

'Someone got stabbed a few streets away. Teenager.'

'Fuck's sake.' Natty scowled. He didn't like kids stabbing one another in general, but he hated it when it happened near his spots. It made everything hot, making it harder for people to make money.

'Do we know who was behind it?'

Carlton shook his head. 'Some beef that started on the internet. You know what some kids are like.'

'If you find anything out, let me know. If it's over some nonsense, then the people involved need dealing with. Can't be having people think that sort of shit is cool.'

'Okay, boss. I'll keep my ear to the ground and see what I learn.'

After slapping hands, Natty left and went to see Cameron and Spence. They were there when he arrived. He'd stopped to get food beforehand, and they tucked into some chicken and rice. When they finished, Natty spoke.

'The meeting went well. We're in business.'

Both men grinned, thinking of the financial implications.

'How was Elijah?'

'He was cool. We had a decent chat.'

'Do you trust him?' Spence had his eyes on Natty.

'I do.' Natty wasn't exaggerating. He didn't think Elijah had an ulterior motive in wanting to work with the team, and his reasons made a lot of sense. Cameron snorted.

'Couple' meetings and you're sold on the guy,' he said.

'I'm willing to give him the benefit of the doubt,' replied Natty.

'It's in his best interests to play it safe. If not, it's war. I don't think any of us want that,' said Spence.

'I don't give a fuck about a war. I stay ready,' replied Cameron. 'Every now and then, it has to happen. Look at the last one. It changed the game.'

Natty frowned. 'The last *war* was between Roc and D-Mo.' They were two youngsters who'd run around shooting one another, recording it online for clout. The police had swiftly arrested both crews, hitting them with huge sentences and crippling both gangs.

Cameron shook his head. 'I'm talking about Teflon's wars. Those guys are legends.'

'The game is bigger than that, Cam. I want a career and the money that goes with it. I don't want pointless clout.'

'Behave, Nat. As long as I've known you, you've wanted a name on the streets. Look at the shit you used to get into, trying to build a rep,' Cameron finished with a sneer.

'It's okay to change. I still think Elijah is sneaky, but the plan is a good one and makes a lot of sense. We can do our legwork and drive around the area, check things out.'

Cameron's nose wrinkled. 'It's a shithole. There's no point.'

Natty glanced at Spence, who didn't say anything.

'With all the extra work I'm gonna be doing to get this off the ground, someone needs to step up and run the crew day-to-day.' Natty saw Cameron's eyes gleam, but pressed on. 'Spence, you're up.'

Spence nodded, giving Natty a small smile. Cameron's eyes bulged. His nostrils flared as he looked at both men, incredulous.

'Are you serious? Did you forget I've been down since day one and always had your back?'

'Course not. You've never shown any interest in running things. I don't see what the big deal is.'

'Spence hasn't either,' Cameron pointed out, but Natty shook his head.

'Not true. We've had conversations in the time about how things run, and what to look out for. He's contributed strong ideas.'

'Why haven't you had the same conversations with me?'

'Because you never asked, and Spence sought me out to learn. That's the difference.'

Cameron frowned, scowling at Natty.

'Well, I want the information too.'

'Good. You can learn it from Spence.' Natty stared into his friend's eyes. 'This is a big move for all of us. We can use it to really put ourselves on the map.'

Cameron's scowl didn't shift.

'It's a big move for you lot more than me. I've been repping this crew since day one, putting myself on the line when we needed it, and I'm being left behind.'

'Cam, it's not like that,' added Spence, but Cameron shook his head.

'Yeah, it is like that. You didn't speak to me about any of this. You just expected me to fall in line. That's fucked up.' Cameron jerked his hand at Spence. 'How can you depend on this guy to lead? He can't even drag himself away from his girl.'

'Are we going on about that again?' retorted Spence. Cameron shot him a scornful look, shaking his head.

'You need some time to chill and get your head around things,' said Natty. Cameron responded by lighting a spliff and flicking on the television. Natty held up his hand, the same way Elijah had with him during their meeting.

'This is exactly why you're not ready to lead, bro,' he said. 'You lose your temper, and then nothing else matters. You just switch off.'

Cameron took a long drag of the spliff, shrugged, then continued watching the television.

* * *

Spence and Natty didn't stay long. Cameron's mood had soured the night. They sat outside Spence's, Natty on the wall, and Spence sitting on his step. Anika had come out to check on Spence, then left the pair to it.

'Maybe you should have him run it instead of me,' said Spence.

Natty shook his head.

'You're the best man for the job. I can't change that for the sake of his ego. We'll give him time to cool off and get used to the idea. If the money is good, that's all Cameron will care about. We both know that.'

Spence nodded, a look of approval adorning his features.

'You seem to be in a better place,' he said softly.

'What are you talking about?'

'You seem calmer; like you're thinking more clearly.'

Natty thought about that. He hadn't noticed, but now that Spence had mentioned it, his mindset had undoubtedly changed. His talk with Elijah had helped establish some common ground, and there was even some merit in the things Rudy had said about his father, and how that had affected Natty.

'Maybe I am,' he finally said. 'It's like, sometimes I just feel angry at the world, and I don't even know why.'

'I think we all get like that sometimes.'

'When I do, it's like all I have to offer is violence, and that's when I want to start fighting people, and get rid of some of the emotion.'

Spence mulled that over before he spoke again.

'Have you spent any more time with Lorraine?'

Natty shrugged. 'Not yet. We didn't leave things in a good place after Ellie's party.'

Spence grinned. 'Talk to her. See where her head is at now.'

'For what?'

'For anything,' replied Spence. 'Fun, love, comfort . . . whatever. You don't need a specific reason.'

Natty let Spence's words resonate, blowing out a breath as he placed his hands in his pockets.

CHAPTER EIGHT

THAT NIGHT, Spence relaxed on his sofa, Anika snuggled against him as they watched the end of a Netflix documentary. The meeting with Cameron and Natty was on his mind. Spence liked the idea of stepping up, pleased Natty had chosen him. He had ideas to help grow the business and make them all more money. Natty had made an intelligent decision and seemed to be carrying himself differently. Because of this, they had an opportunity to step up, meaning everyone had to play their role.

Including Cameron . . . He thought.

'Are you okay?' Anika murmured as the show came to an end. She was mixed race, short and curvy, with curly black hair and brown eyes so dark they were almost black.

'Yeah,' Spence replied. 'Just work stuff. I'm gonna be busier going forward.'

Anika reached for the remote and paused the television.

'How come?'

Spence stifled a yawn. 'Natty's gonna be busy, so I'm stepping up. Money goes up too, which is good.'

Anika didn't say anything. Spence glanced at her.

'Are you okay? I probably should have discussed this with you earlier, but it all happened so quickly,' he said.

'Your business is your business, Spence. You know that.' Anika's tone was strangely cold.

Spence shook his head.

'We're partners, babe. Do you remember what we recently spoke about?'

Anika's stomach plummeted.

'Refresh my memory,' she replied.

'The future. We have this place, but it would be nice to start pooling money and aiming for something bigger. We could even rent this place out.'

'I'm still thinking about it,' Anika said. 'You have to admit, it's a big commitment.'

'No bigger than this commitment.' Spence pointed around the room. 'You wanted us to move in together.'

'Are you saying you didn't?' Anika narrowed her eyes. Spence chuckled.

'Course I did. Don't flip out on me. I'm just saying, saving our money to get another place isn't a bigger commitment.'

'It's a much bigger financial commitment. What if we didn't stay together?' she said, interested in how Spence would respond.

'I see no reason that we wouldn't,' he replied. 'We're compatible, and I like to think we compromise and talk about things when they're on our mind, like we're doing now. Still, I don't want to pressure you. Tell me about work.'

Anika frowned. 'What do you want to know?'

'How is it going? Do you still enjoy it?'

'Better than going into an office every day,' Anika replied. She was a self-employed beautician and enjoyed it, for the most part. She could pick her hours and had loyal clients. She didn't contribute as much monthly as Spence did, but made a decent living. Anika was content where she was at and had no great desire to push things. At the same time, she liked being challenged, so she kept an open mind.

It was hard explaining that to Spence sometimes.

'Yeah, I wouldn't want to work in an office either. I wouldn't mind owning one or two, though,' he said. Moving away from Anika, he picked up his laptop, booting it up and going online.

Anika glanced over his shoulder, seeing he was on his investment portfolio portal, looking over the numbers. He did this often, having taken to investing with a level of zeal that Anika hadn't expected. He would read books on investments and financial strategy, and his internet search history was littered with bookmarks from articles and financial tips.

For the most part, she was proud of Spence and the fact he used everything to make himself stronger. He was constantly pushing ahead, with a desire and thirst to learn and do more. It was inspiring, but it was also cloying and caused her insecurity to flare.

She often felt that she couldn't keep up with him, and that eventually, he would realise, and things would become harder for her.

Trying to push the negative thoughts to one side, she snuggled back up to Spence, resting her head on his shoulder and closing her eyes.

* * *

THE NEXT DAY, Natty decided to see Lorraine and clear the air between them.

Before going, Natty cleaned himself up, going for a haircut and trimming his beard. He didn't know why he was making an effort, but instinct told him it was the smart thing to do.

Lorraine answered the door, her face blank. Natty wondered what she thought about him and Ellie. He wouldn't bring it up unless she did, though.

'Hey,' he finally said.

'Hello,' Lorraine replied, her tone as neutral as her face. He hoped it was just down to their argument, but it was telling that she hadn't yet invited him inside. He couldn't remember the last time they had stood at the door to talk, which wasn't a good sign.

'How are you?' Natty inwardly cringed when Lorraine scowled, hand on her hip, blocking any attempted entry. She was casually dressed in an oversized t-shirt and jogging bottoms, but Natty recalled how she had looked on the night of the party. No matter how much he tried, he couldn't get the image out of his head. He wondered how things might have gone, had things not got so heated between them. Whether he would have ended up in her bed instead of Ellie's. His stomach clenched, but he fought to remain neutral.

'What do you want, Natty?'

Natty almost flared up, ready to snap back at her, but inwardly calmed himself.

'I'm sorry for flipping out on you the other night,' he said. Lorraine remained silent, her expression unchanged. Realising it wouldn't be that easy, Natty blew out a breath. 'I was going through some stuff, but that's no excuse for my behaviour. You were right about some of the things you said, and I know I need to fix up. I guess I just needed you to know that, and that I really am sorry. You've always been real with me, and taking out my issues on you isn't the way to go.'

Before he could know if his words had any effect, they were interrupted by Jaden bounding to the door, beaming when he saw Natty.

'Natty! Have you come to play *Call Of Duty*? Where have you been?'

'I've been working, little man.' Natty couldn't hide his smile. He was genuinely happy to see Jaden, but he also knew that now that he'd seen Natty, Lorraine would let him in.

Grinning, Jaden tugged on his mum's sleeve.

'Mummy, can Natty stay and play *COD* with me?'

'Natty's busy, baby, so he can't come in.'

Smile widening, Natty replied.

'Actually, my plans have changed. I can stay.'

Jaden's eyes lit up.

'Please, Mummy. I'll be good. Promise.'

Lorraine cut her eyes to Natty, who maintained his grin. She sighed and stepped aside to let him in as Jaden cheered.

Jaden led Natty into the living room, talking a mile a minute about school.

'How's Anton doing?' Natty knew Anton was Jaden's best friend at school.

'He's good. We're not talking to Robert, though. He said he's a better footballer, and he told Ms Rainer that we were talking in class.'

Distracted, Natty observed Lorraine leaving the room.

'You been playing football?' He asked, not hearing the reply about Robert. Jaden nodded.

'I've been using some of the things you taught me. I scored two goals in the last game,' he said proudly. Natty ruffled his hair.

'That's my boy. Keep it up, and you'll only get better. I was a sick footballer when I was younger.'

'How come you never played in the Premiership?' asked Jaden.

'I went in another direction,' replied Natty. He'd been nowhere near the standard, and didn't want to disappoint Jaden by admitting it, nor did he add that he'd started selling drugs instead.

After a while, he left Jaden playing and headed into the kitchen. Lorraine was at the counter, her phone playing *Jorja Smith*. Natty knew she was a fan of the singer, but she was too soft for his liking. He was a rap fan, preferring *Skrapz* and *Nines*.

An awkward silence ensued, Lorraine continuing to add seasoning to some lamb chops near the kitchen sink, working around Natty. He jammed his hands in his pockets, wondering when things had become so complicated.

'How's the studying going?' He finally asked, unable to cope with the tense silence.

'Just stop, Natty,' she replied.

'Stop what?' He frowned.

'You're not interested, and you don't have to pretend to be,' she said icily. Once again, Natty almost lost his temper and stormed out, but somehow maintained his composure.

'Look at me,' he said. Sighing, Lorraine paused her music and faced him, eyes flashing.

'If you're interested, then I am too,' he said. 'I'll make us some drinks, and you can tell me all about it.'

Lorraine's mouth hung half open as Natty made her some green tea, and himself a black coffee. He sat at the kitchen table, giving her an expectant look. She shook her head.

'You're the most annoying man I've ever met,' she said softly.

'I always aim for the top.'

Lorraine giggled.

'Idiot.'

Natty waved her words aside.

'Right then; studying. How long have you wanted to do it?'

'I thought about it a few years ago, but I didn't think I could do it.'

Remembering what Spence had said about taking an interest, Natty had his next question primed.

'Why did you think that?'

Lorraine shrugged.

'It seemed hard, and I didn't think I was good enough to do it.' She lowered her head a moment. 'Eventually, mum and Rosie talked me into it.'

'For what it's worth, I think you can do it too. You're the smartest person I know.'

Lorraine rolled her eyes, but it was evident by the slight smile on her face that his words had touched her.

'What is it that you're studying, anyway?'

'I want to get into software engineering.'

Natty's eyebrows rose. It was the last thing he had expected her to say.

'What? With cars?'

Lorraine giggled.

'Not with cars. At the moment, I'm learning how to code,' she replied.

'What made you want to do that?'

'It's hard to describe, but it's like magic . . . close as you can get in reality, anyway. The opportunities are endless. I mean, if you can imagine it, you can pretty much do it. The limit is your imagination. Where we are . . . how we grew up . . . I felt trapped; like I'd been dealt my hand and that this was it for the rest of my life. Learning to do this; it lets me express myself, and kinda break away from that.'

Natty sat in stunned silence, in awe of Lorraine's passion. He'd never heard her speak like this before, and he felt terrible that he hadn't had a clue, when she was clearly so invested in it. Still, this wasn't about him right now. It was about Lorraine. As she reached for the drink he'd made her, he intercepted and squeezed her hand.

'You'll be great, Lorraine. Don't ever think any different. I'll help you in any way that I can.'

They held hands, the moment lingering for several seconds. Lorraine pulled her hand away, and straightened herself.

* * *

CAMERON LAY IN BED, staring at the ceiling with a small smile on his face. A woman was pressed against him. He'd met her at a party, and it hadn't taken long for his charm to work. They'd left the party to go back to his place. The sex had been good, and they'd finished, rested, and gone at it again.

'You need to go,' he said.

'What do you mean?' She said sleepily.

'I've got some things I need to do. I'll get you an Uber.'

'You're really kicking me out like that?' She sat up.

'Don't start,' said Cameron. 'I just told you I had things to do.'

'How can you just use me and kick me out?'

'We both had fun, and now it's done. If I wasn't busy, I wouldn't be making you go.'

She scowled. 'Whatever, Cameron. Fuck you. I'll get my own Uber.'

'Suits me.'

Cameron lit a spliff when she'd gone, having already forgotten about the woman. He found his thoughts drifting to Spence, and the argument they'd had. He liked Spence, and thought he was sharp. He differed from Cameron and Natty, which meant they balanced one another. Cameron didn't like the effect Anika had on him; the way Spence had changed since getting with her. He believed she'd softened him, which wasn't suitable for any of them.

He wanted Spence to return to what he considered *normal*, which was how he and Natty acted.

Deep down, he didn't want Spence anywhere near Anika, and he knew it.

Cameron had his dreams, the same as anyone. His plan had been consistent since he was young. He wanted to be a major player, and constantly recalled the older days; the things he had seen, and the stories he'd heard.

The level of power that former Leeds kingpins' had was intoxicating. Cameron wanted that. He wanted the juice, and the money that went with it. He wanted a mansion, a fleet of cars, and for people to show respect whenever he entered the room. Natty understood that dream to a degree, but his family were practically royalty.

Cameron didn't understand why they hadn't taken a firmer hold of the streets. They had everything in place, but had focused more on maintaining.

If Cameron had the opportunity, he would be ruling Leeds with an iron fist, making all the little teams pay a street tax, and bribing the police to keep them in line. Instead, he was down at the bottom with Natty and Spence.

Cameron was fully aware that the trio complemented one another. Natty was charismatic, and people gravitated toward him. Spence was structured and subtle, often providing a diplomatic voice of reason.

As for Cameron, he was the forceful one, always willing to go out and make something happen. With their combined efforts, Cameron felt they could truly run the streets. Unlike the others, he recognised they needed to keep Rudy sweet to do that.

Shaking the thoughts, he read a text message on his phone, pulled on a hoody, and left the house, hitting the streets.

CHAPTER NINE

OVER THE NEXT FEW DAYS, Natty and Elijah got to work in Little London. They procured numerous spots in the area, making deals with the people renting the houses to ensure they stayed out of the way. Natty had surmised that the locals wouldn't be a problem, as long as they played ball and kept things low-key.

Elijah put the crew together, everyone handpicked by him and Rudy, a mix of the two teams. On the first night, they gathered in the neatest of the spots. Elijah and Natty stood before them as they crammed into the living room. Natty briefly glanced around, hoping he'd made the right decision by choosing to trust his rival. Brushing aside these worries, he stood straight, meeting the eyes of those assembled.

'We wanted to link up and run you through what we have going on here,' said Elijah, his eyes sweeping the room. 'This is opportunity in its purest form, and we need you guys to remember that and represent yourself accordingly.'

Natty was impressed by Elijah's speech. His cadence was smooth, and his words were carefully chosen. It was evident by the straightening of backs and the emphatic nods, that they'd also had an effect on the team.

'We're not here to cause trouble. There's more than enough money around here for everyone, and we're definitely going to take our piece of it. This is a chance to take things to the next level. We're gonna move the usual stuff; white, dark, spice, weed, and pills. All the shifts and teams have been organised, so don't mess around, and you'll be treated well.'

There were more nods now, and even a few smiles. Natty, too, bought into the speech. If Elijah wasn't selling drugs, he'd be cleaning up making money as a salesman. He had it down to a T. His consistent narrative left no doubt as to what his intentions were.

'That said, I want to hand the floor to Natty, who has something to say.'

Natty hid his surprise as all eyes were suddenly on him. He hadn't thought of anything to say, and it hadn't been discussed that he would speak. Elijah had thrown him under the bus, though; it was sink or swim time. Swallowing down his moment of nervousness, he immediately composed himself and spoke.

'. . . Elijah said most of what I think needs to be said, but remember, it's possible to beat the game we're all playing. One of the most important commodities is teamwork; having one another's back. Two crews that haven't always gotten along, are now working together. Toward a common goal. A goal that will improve all of our lives. The only way we can do this is by leaving old grievances in the past, and moving forward.'

When he finished speaking, there were even wider smiles and some firm nods, and Natty felt good, even as his heart raced.

Later, Elijah caught up with him.

'You did well.'

'Is that what you wanted to happen?' Natty hadn't forgotten Elijah throwing him the ball without warning.

'I was curious,' Elijah admitted. 'Everyone knows how good you can be. You're not gonna get a better chance than this to show everyone. Remember, *you* gave a speech about unity. We can do a lot of good here, and we can get super rich at the same time.'

Natty touched his fist, committing to giving it a try.

GOOD DEED, BAD DEEDS

* * *

AFTER THE MEETING ENDED, Elijah stayed with the team, who planned to order some food and have a small party. Natty walked the area, wanting to get a feel for things. He was walking down a street when he saw a woman openly watching him from the window. She jumped when she saw him, but he gave her a small smile, an idea forming. He knocked at her door, and she answered after a few moments, suspicion etched onto her face.

'Yeah?' She said. Natty's smile widened. She was on the heavier side, with lank brown hair and tired blue eyes. Behind her, Natty heard kids running around, making noise.

'Good evening. My name is Natty,' he said smoothly. The woman looked around him, clearly still startled.

'Julie,' she finally replied.

'Nice to meet you, Julie. Listen, I'm new to the area, and I figured you were someone I could speak with about what goes on around here.'

'Why me?'

'You were watching out of the window, for one. I'm guessing you have a good idea of who's who. That could be useful.'

Julie licked her dry lips, eyes dancing. Natty saw he was losing her and took out a twenty-pound note, which her eyes locked onto. He held it up.

'This is yours; there's more where that came from.'

Julie visibly relaxed and invited him inside. Before closing the door, she peered out onto the street, looking each way before closing the door behind her.

'Sorry about the mess,' she said.

'Don't worry about it,' replied Natty, the thundering of footsteps and commotion amplified now he was through the door.

'Oi, shut up! I'm sick of all the bloody racket!' Julie screeched. 'Take the noise upstairs!'

The kids — three unruly young boys — promptly ignored her, until she grabbed and smacked one of them. After two more hits, he ran upstairs crying, and his brothers followed.

81

'I'll crack you all if you break anything,' she called after them. Natty wasn't phased by her threats to her kids; he'd grown up around similar threats, and had seen it all of his life. He followed her into the living room, stepping over various toys. Despite not being particularly dirty, the room was undoubtedly untidy. Natty plopped on the sofa, which creaked beneath his weight. A large television was mounted on the wall, and Natty imagined that was the main reason it was unscathed.

Julie sat next to him, biting her lip, eyes darting all around the room. She gnawed at her nails, waiting for him to speak. Natty winced. He'd always hated the sound people made when biting their nails.

'Why don't you go and make yourself a drink?' He said, wanting to relax her. Julie leapt to her feet like she worked for him, hurrying to the kitchen.

Natty glanced at the television, distracted by the yells coming from upstairs. There was a loud bang, then the sound of someone crying. He thought of Jaden then, and the fact he had no brothers or sisters to roughhouse with. It made him wonder if Lorraine had ever wanted more kids.

Julie returned with a cup of tea and sat back down.

'I guess I won't have a tea then,' Natty joked. Julie laughed, and it cut through the tension.

'I can make you one if you like?'

Natty shook his head, still smiling. 'It's fine. Seriously.'

'Sorry about the kids,' she said. 'They're an absolute nightmare when they're cooped up like this. Run around doing what they want.'

'Don't worry about it,' replied Natty, taking control of the conversation. He took out a wad of money, watching her eyes lock onto it, then laid another twenty-pound note on the chipped coffee table. 'What can you tell me about the local area?'

'Are you police?' She asked, eyes narrowing. Natty shook his head. 'You know what I am.'

Julie sipped her tea, visibly more relaxed.

'It's bedlam. I don't want any trouble, and I don't know much. There's a lot of gangs in the area. Warren's crew are the worst, but I'm guessing you already knew that.'

Natty didn't immediately respond. Warren was the main threat in Little London, and his name was linked to numerous murders. He was definitely going to be a problem, and he had everyone in the area terrified of him. They would need to devise a way to handle him if they were to establish themselves.

'Why's Warren so bad?'

'He's horrible. Likes to hurt people. A lot of the kids around here are just following his lead. I can't even let my lot play out. They'll be running for him by the end of the week.'

Natty didn't dispute that. Julie was right. The lure of the money always got to most youths, making patterning them a breeze.

'Other than Warren, who else should I be looking out for?' This time, Natty laid a ten-pound note on the table. Julie nearly spilt her drink to gather up the money.

'Harry and Rodney,' she finally said. 'They're young, keep themselves to themselves. Got a few kids working for them, and they study. I don't know what, though. They seem to stay out of people's way. Guess they're only bothered about the money.'

'Personality-wise, what are they like?'

Julie shrugged. 'They're nice to me, if that's what you mean. They've never given me money before, though.'

A plan was unfolding in Natty's head as Julie spoke. One of the main ways to take over in any area, was to understand the terrain. Julie was going to be a major cog in that information bracket. He slapped five more twenties on the table, thinking how lucky it was he'd happened to carry more money than usual. This time, Julie didn't go for them immediately.

'What do I need to do for it?' she asked.

'Nothing that will get you in any trouble. I just want you to keep an eye on things for me. I want to know who is doing what and where. There's more money in it for others who want to earn.'

Julie tensed back up. Natty smiled, again looking to disarm her with his charm.

'Listen, I just want the area to thrive. I want to make money, but I want you to be able to let your kids play footy outside like they should be. We can do a lot around here, and with my people in charge, I promise you nothing but positive vibes.'

Julie nodded, successfully mollified. Natty stood and walked to the door.

'Right, I'm gonna head off. Let's see if I make it where I need to go without dehydration taking me down.' He grinned, and Julie again laughed. 'I'll check on you soon.'

The smile vanished when the door closed behind Natty, and his face tightened, back in business mode. Leaving Julie's garden, he spotted a young fiend — a *sale* — limping down the street. His clothes were worn, and his face drawn, but he didn't have the battered look of a fully developed addict, and quickly stopped to talk when Natty called him.

A deal was quickly struck. Natty offered to buy him a cheap camera phone, in exchange for the sale discreetly taking photos of the various dealers around Little London, offering to pay for each name and face. He wanted to know precisely who everyone was, and who they worked for.

'You can earn a few hundred for helping,' he told the sale, 'and get a little discount for yourself.'

Needless to say, the man was tripping over himself to sign up, and Natty inwardly beamed, knowing he'd made significant steps.

* * *

THE NEXT DAY, Cameron headed out. He had a job to do. Christian Price was one of Rudy's clients. He lived in a dreary house at the top of Beck Hill Grove, and had taken the piss paying for drugs. Cameron had been contacted by one of Rudy's men and offered the job, with instructions on handling it.

Cameron had previously dealt with the client, so he hadn't questioned the task. He took a taxi down the street from Christian's address, then headed up the road, keeping his head down just in case anyone was watching.

He knocked at Christian's door, watching the man pale when he saw him. Christian was slightly taller than Cameron, with a ponytail and designer stubble, his t-shirt stretched tight around a gut accrued from excessive takeaways.

Cameron smiled.

'Hi mate. Are you going to invite me in?'

Christian glanced around the room, looking like he would rather be anywhere but there. Cameron chuckled.

'C'mon, bro. We're good, and I know you don't want to talk business on the doorstep where everyone can hear us.'

Christian's shoulders slumped, and he allowed Cameron to enter. They went to the living room. Cameron slumped into a seat on the sofa, then put his feet up on the coffee table. Christian's jaw tensed.

'Look, Cam. I'm sorry I've fallen behind. Some of the lads I work with have given me the runaround.'

'And that made you think you could give *us* the runaround too? You know that's not how the game works.'

'I know, but there was nothing I could do, and I didn't think you would be understanding if I approached you about it.'

'We'll never know, I guess.' Cameron shrugged. 'Do you have it now?'

Christian nodded. He left the room and returned with a plastic bag. Cameron looked inside at the contents, seeing the notes hastily banded together. He took them from the bag and began counting. His eyes narrowed as he neared the end of the count. Christian cleared his throat.

'Erm, look, I have most of it, but—'

'Why did you tell me you had it?'

'Because I didn't want you to think I was playing games.'

'You *are* playing games,' Cameron snapped. 'Rudy isn't a patient guy, and neither am I. First, you don't get in touch and keep ducking when we're trying to speak to you. Then, you say you've got the full eight grand, when you only have six. What the fuck is going on?'

'I'm sorry . . .'

'I don't wanna hear how sorry you are. Doesn't mean fuck all to me. Tell me what the hell is going on?' Cameron's feet slid from the table.

'I told you. I've got people slipping me, messing with my drugs, trying to put me out of business. Why do you think I'm so far behind?'

'I think you're a greedy little prick. You should have gotten in touch and didn't, so now we're gonna get deep.'

Christian stepped back as Cameron rose to his feet.

'C'mon, Cam, other than this I've been loyal. You don't need to go on like that.'

Cameron sprang forward, covering the doorway so Christian couldn't escape. Christian put his hands up in surrender, but Cameron slammed his fist into his flabby stomach, then kicked him backwards, laughing when Christian toppled to the ground. He kicked him in the ribs when he tried to stand, then did the same thing again.

'You've been warned before about playing with us, you little prick.' Cameron kicked him after every word. 'You'll think twice about doing it again in future.'

Before he could hit Christian again, he heard a scream of rage and turned. At the last second, he was able to get his hand up, instinctively deflecting the knife that hurtled towards his face. It cut deeply into his wrist, the snarling woman raising her hand to strike again.

'Bitch!' Cameron snarled, backhanding the woman and sending her flying across the room, the knife clattering to the ground. Groaning, she crawled towards it, slowly stretching out, feeling for the blade. As the tips of her fingers touched it, Cameron's boot came crashing down on her hand. Screaming in pain, she cradled her hand as Cameron moved closer, breathing hard.

'Shouldn't have involved yourself,' he said, drawing his foot back and kicking her in the ribs. She let out a groan of pain, holding her hand, rolling into the foetal position. He kicked her again.

'Stop it!' Christian yelled. 'I'm sorry, that shouldn't have happened. Please, just leave her alone.'

Cameron whirled toward Christian, his eyes blazing.

'I'm coming back tonight. You need to have the rest of the money, plus an extra five bills, or else.'

* * *

CAMERON PULLED up outside Delores's, locking up the car and heading inside. He'd wrapped his wrist, the cut not as deep as he'd first thought. He and one of Rudy's men had stopped by Christian's as planned after he'd sorted his wrist. Cameron didn't know what Christian had done to get the money, but he'd taken the threat seriously, and had the rest of Rudy's money, along with the penalty fee.

Cameron hadn't seen Christian's girlfriend, and he assumed she was upstairs resting after the beating he had given her. He didn't feel bad. For the most part, he didn't believe in hitting women. The girl had tried to kill him, though. If he hadn't turned, the knife would have caught his head.

Pushing the thoughts away, he knocked on the door, smiling when Delores answered. She glared at him, even as his grin widened.

'Hello, Delores. You're looking well tonight.'

'He's through there,' she replied, kissing her teeth at him and turning away. He closed the door, his smile vanishing. He had no idea why the old bitch always looked down her nose at him. Anytime Natty was around, she was smiling and grinning, offering to make him food and drinks, treating him like her son, whereas Cameron was routinely treated like something on the bottom of her shoe.

Rudy sat in the kitchen as always, a folded newspaper on the table in front of him, next to a beer. He looked up when Cameron entered, putting the paperback he'd been reading to one side. Cameron handed him the money without a word, his heart hammering against his chest. He rarely saw Rudy without Natty there, and he didn't have the same dynamic Natty had.

'You take a piece?' Rudy enquired, counting the money. Cameron shook his head.

'Nah, I'd never do that. He gave me extra too, because of the runaround.'

Rudy smiled tightly. His eyes flicked to Cameron's injured hand.

'I figured you'd have kept the extra.'

'It's not my money,' replied Cameron. Rudy continued to survey him.

'You're not that bad, are you . . . we definitely picked the right person for the job. You're loyal.' Rudy peeled off some notes. He held them out to Cameron, then pulled back and added more to the pile.

Cameron thumbed through the money. His eyebrows rose.

'You didn't need to give so much. You said five.'

'Don't you want the extra?'

Cameron grinned. 'I didn't say that.'

'Good. Don't worry about it then. How did it go? Did Christian learn not to fuck around going forward?'

Cameron nodded. 'I gave him a beating he won't forget. His girl got involved, so I had to smack her around too.'

Rudy shrugged. 'I'm sure she deserved it. How is Nathaniel doing?'

'Natty's the same as ever.' Cameron almost rolled his eyes. He swore Rudy thought he was Natty's protector sometimes.

'I know about the party in town you all went to a while back,' said Rudy.

'What did you hear?' It wasn't a shock to Cameron that Rudy had heard. There were a lot of people at the apartment that night, and any of them could have passed word on.

'I heard he squared up to several of Elijah's men. You were there with him, right?'

'I was, so was Spence. That was Natty's thing, though. I backed my boy.'

'Like I said, you're loyal.' Rudy wasn't smiling anymore. His eyes were hard. Cameron instinctively straightened, noticing Rudy hadn't asked him to sit.

'Look, Natty is mad about a lot of things, but mostly that you've taken so long to give him more to do. He's here grinding, we all are, and we all want more.'

'Is that Nathaniel talking, or you?'

'Natty's the leader. I watch his back, same as always.'

'We have a lot riding on this, as you know. Nathaniel and I have cleared the air and he's getting on board, but we both know how he can get. I need you to keep him safe.'

'Natty can look after himself,' said Cameron.

'He doesn't always think. The day we left you and Spence, he threatened me in the middle of a pub.'

'What?' Cameron's eyes widened.

'I pushed him too far. Mentioned his dad.'

Cameron nodded his understanding now. Natty could be rough at the best of times, but he drew a line where his father was concerned, and speaking ill of him was a dangerous move.

Cameron recalled seeing Natty stomp people out for disrespecting his dad on more than one occasion. He wondered if Natty would have hit Rudy if he had continued.

'That'll do it. Natty doesn't take that shit laying down.'

'Regardless, keep an eye on him. You know how we do it. This will benefit everyone, and in the long run, everyone will make more. You're a good kid. That Spence is too. He's a student of the game. I spent time with dudes like *Teflon* and learned how they think. The game is the game. The money . . . the money can be absolutely everything. If we do it right. Are you with me?'

Cameron nodded, swallowing down a response to the comment about Spence. 'I'll keep you posted on Natty. Cheers for the bonus.'

* * *

AT HOME THAT NIGHT, Cameron sipped a brandy, ignoring a few calls and text messages. When he couldn't get hold of Natty or Spence, he had a few others he liked to hit the clubs in town and spend money with.

Lately, he wanted to be alone. He had a lot to think about.

Rudy's words about Spence being a *student of the game* had irked Cameron. Cameron had been in the crime life most of his life. He'd known Natty longer, and had proved himself numerous times. Spence had skills but was too passive; he didn't go and take what he wanted. His dad had been a menace in his day, but Spence wasn't like that.

Then there was Anika. Spence had fallen in love with her, and he didn't even know her.

Not like Cameron did.

Soon, Cameron found himself on Anika's social media profile page.

Checking her Instagram, he scrolled through her photos. He lingered on a few images, but when he saw a picture of Anika and Spence, his fists automatically clenched, and his nostrils flared.

A wave of anger cascaded through his body, and he struggled to get it under control. He read the comments praising their looks and close-ness with gritted teeth. The longer he stared at the photo, the more his eyes started to water from the intensity.

Seeing she had recently updated her Instagram story, he noticed that she'd posted about going to a club in town for her friend's party — there was a countdown, which ended on a night Cameron knew Spence would be working. That meant he wouldn't be with her or be scheduled to turn up.

Cameron decided right then that he would go, even if he didn't have a plan, or know what he would say.

CHAPTER TEN

ANIKA BEAMED. She'd been planning her friend Carmen's birthday for some time, and was pleased it was all going off without a hitch.

They had met at Anika's for pre-drinks, then headed to several clubs. They had the full treatment in their current club. It was near Call Lane, and had a warm, inviting interior, with comfortable seating areas, a fancy bar, and a spacious dance floor. They'd done their dancing earlier, and now sat in a VIP section, drinking champagne, having taken photographs when the gold buckets and sparklers came earlier.

Carmen's face was flushed as she spoke with their friends, giggling and animated. Anika found herself studying her. Carmen was so different to her that she found it intriguing. She was engaged to her boyfriend; they lived together and wanted to be married.

Anika didn't understand why. Anika's parents had separated when she was younger, and her dad hadn't given her the time of day. He had a whole new family now — one she had never met.

She was happy for her friend, but couldn't relate. Anika had her dreams, and often fantasised about travelling, going off the grid and not having people relying on her. It was the opposite of what she had going on with Spence.

Deep down, Anika worried that Spence was a rebound guy. Somebody she had become fond of, but didn't properly love. Like a lot of people, she was scared of being hurt. It had happened before and she was determined it wouldn't happen again.

She closed her eyes. She didn't want these thoughts, but couldn't help it. At times she felt trapped in her own life, too scared to make the decisions she knew would drastically change her surroundings.

'Nika?'

Anika's eyes flew open, unaware she had zoned out. The group of girls were all watching her with various levels of curiosity.

'Sorry, I got a bit distracted. Are you okay?'

'Yes, babe. We were just wondering when you and Spence will get married?'

'Yeah, you guys have been together forever. You must be getting those thoughts now, right?'

Anika wanted to tell them that it had only been a year, but didn't.

'We need to sit and properly talk about it, I guess.' She dipped her head as she laughed for a moment. 'I'm just going to walk around for a bit, see if I can see anyone else.'

'We can see everyone from here,' said Carmen, awkwardly pointing around the club.

'I just want to stretch my legs. I'll be back soon.'

Anika hurried away from her friends without looking like she was doing it. She wished she had stayed home now, feeling she was ruining the vibe. Her friends deserved to be able to enjoy themselves without her overreacting and making things about herself.

Making her way through the crowds of people, she queued for the bathroom, checking her face in the mirror, and taking deep breaths that had the women at the next sink giving her strange looks. She forced the thoughts out of her mind and exited the bathroom.

Deciding she would go back to her friends and be in a better mood, her thoughts were scuppered when someone appeared in front of her. She glanced at them, then froze when she realised who it was.

'Hey, Nika.'

'Cam?'

Anika's stomach lurched, her chest tightening. It couldn't be a coincidence that Cameron happened to be here tonight. He was as good-looking as ever. He dressed nicely and liked fancy jewellery, but she had never cared about that. She always dug Cameron's passion for her, and the fact he did his own thing and took no shit. It was intoxicating.

The old flames stared one another down for a long moment, and then Anika sighed and tried to step past him. Cameron gripped her wrist, stopping her in place.

'What's your hurry?'

'I don't want to get into it. Least of all with you.'

'You don't have to hide. Spence is working, so you don't have to worry,' said Cameron.

'I know where my boyfriend is, thanks. Just like he knows I'm out with my friends.' She glanced around Cameron, realising he appeared to be alone. 'Why are you here?'

'Why aren't you with your friends?' Cameron avoided the question.

'I wanted a moment away from them,' Anika admitted. Cameron nodded.

'You look good.'

Anika shook her head.

'I'm not doing this with you.' She pushed past him and was ready to leave when he said a single word.

'*Fiji.*'

Again, she froze. Turning to face him, her eyes met his.

'You always wanted to live in Fiji for a year. You told me about it, way back when. Does Spence know?'

Anika gritted her teeth. 'Stop it.'

Cameron's expression remained the same.

'No matter what happened with us, I still remember what you said.'

Anger flared in her.

'You mean the bits you want to remember. You tend to ignore the rest.' She sighed, feeling tears prickle in her eyes. 'I don't want to do this with you.'

She expected Cameron to argue or counter, but instead, he tilted his head, shooting her an almost sad look.

'I hope you get what you want; what *you* want . . . not you trying to live up to *their* expectations at the expense of your own.'

Anika's mouth opened and closed, her heart hammering. She wasn't going to do this. She wouldn't get caught up in this again. Without a word, she walked away, and he didn't stop her this time.

She sat with her friends and tried to involve herself in the night again, but she was distracted. Her mind wandered, thinking of distant beaches and tranquillity. She wondered if Cameron being in the club was a sign, and was shocked that he'd remembered about Fiji. It wasn't like him, and he'd shown no reaction when she'd mentioned it all those years ago.

Anika had a few more drinks, wanting a distraction from her swirling thoughts. Her friends sensed something was wrong, but she lied and said she was okay.

Eventually, her phone buzzed when she was finishing her latest drink. It was from Cameron, and though her instincts told her to delete it without reading, she quickly opened it.

> Do you ever wish things had turned out differently?

A few seconds later, another message came:

> You don't need to reply. I really do hope you have a good night.

Anika put her phone down, holding her empty glass, feeling overly emotional, hoping she didn't break down and start crying in front of her friends.

Her phone vibrated again, and she steadied herself. This time it was Spence:

> Hey beautiful. I hope you're enjoying your
> night. Let me know if you want me to bring
> anything in for you. Speak to you later.
> Love you.

Anika stowed her phone away, unable to respond to the message. She had a few more drinks and a few dances before she replied with some generic mess. She couldn't shake her introspective thoughts despite her attempts to distract herself. Finally, she took out her phone and sent a message:

> I think about how things could have been,
> every single day.

* * *

CAMERON LOOKED DOWN at Anika's message and smirked. He'd gotten his point across. It didn't matter how much Spence wined and dined her. Her heart still belonged to him; he'd proved it. He'd discretely watched Anika try to pretend to herself that she hadn't spoken to him, trying to distract herself with drinks and dancing and her friends, but nothing had worked.

They had unfinished business, and now she realised that point too. He was living in her head, completely rent-free.

Taking stock of his surroundings, he finished the drink he'd ordered, making small talk with a bartender for a while. After a few more drinks, he decided to leave.

Going to the club to confront Anika had been a brainwave and as he strolled up Call Lane to book a taxi, he was pleased he'd planted a seed.

CHAPTER ELEVEN

TWO WEEKS PASSED. Natty met with Julie several times, getting the lay of the land. He learned more about Warren and his reputation. He didn't seem particularly smart, but had heart and aggression in spades. Natty wondered if he would be a problem to work alongside, concluding he would be.

The young drug addict Natty hired had taken to his task well, identifying numerous smaller players, enabling Natty to learn more about them. Most were on the younger side, just playing at the life. Several were supporting growing habits by dealing. Natty had spoken with Elijah and believed they could relieve the burden on these types by supplying them, getting them to take care of the distribution on their behalf.

Elijah was on board with the plan, and today, they were meeting Harry and Rodney, the dealers Julie had mentioned.

They met in the middle of a nearby park. Natty glanced around, feeling exposed out in the open. The youths, barely old enough to have facial hair, looked twitchy, dressed in similar black and grey tracksuits. One of them, a lanky, big-nosed kid with wavy brown hair, stepped forward to do the talking, his eyes warily straying from Natty to Elijah.

'What are you lot saying then?' He asked.

'Which one are you?' replied Natty.

'Harry.'

'You know why we're here,' said Natty. 'We're moving in, and we want to work with the natives rather than the alternative. We know you guys are decent little hustlers, and we want you to get down with us.'

'Get down how?' Harry glanced at Rodney, who didn't respond.

'Take our supply. You'll get our protection on top of that.'

Again, Harry looked to Rodney, then back at the pair.

'What if we don't want to work with you?'

Natty had expected a little resistance, and was ready to objection handle.

'Why wouldn't you?'

The question threw Harry, his eyes widening. He opened and closed his mouth. Natty continued.

'We have the infrastructure to make big things happen for you. There's even a little signing fee for working with us.' Natty was laying it on thick, but it would be worth it in the end.

'Oh yeah, what sort of fee?'

'Couple grand, at least. Enough to have a nice treat and then get on board with a winning team. If you're interested, we'll give you the full details.'

Harry rubbed his face, giving no sign of the direction he would pick, despite his jittery movements.

'We're interested, but there's one big problem, mate.'

'What's the problem?' Natty kept his eyes on him.

'Warren.'

Rodney nodded, showing more emotion than he had thus far.

'What about him?' Natty pressed.

'He's a fucking madman. He won't even like us meeting with you. He leaves us alone, but that'll change if we start taking sides,' said Harry.

'We'll talk with Warren; make him see sense.'

Harry scoffed.

'Good luck with that. Warren'll kill you. He's done it before.' His eyes furtively swept around the park. 'Nice to meet you lot, but we can't work with you. Warren's the man.'

'Looks like we have some work to do,' Elijah remarked when the youths had scurried away.

Natty rubbed his forehead, trying to hide his annoyance. The way the dealers sounded, they weren't going to make much headway in the area until they'd spoken with the local psycho.

'Yep,' said Natty with a sigh.

* * *

Spence took Anika out for dinner. She liked Italian food, and he had been meaning to try out a place on Park Row.

As they ate, he spoke to her about Natty and Lorraine.

'I don't get what's happening with them,' he admitted between mouthfuls of his food. 'Lorraine has always had a thing for him, and Natty can't admit he feels the same for her.'

'Do you really think he does?' Anika asked. She was interested in the back and forth between the pair. She had seen Lorraine around and knew Natty through her involvement with Spence and Cameron.

A wave of nausea hit her. Natty had been around back in the day when she and Cameron had their fling. If he remembered or told Spence, it would get awkward, and she couldn't face that.

She hadn't told any of her friends. She and Cameron happened so fast, and they got in too deep, too quickly. It hadn't lasted long, and she had tried to mask the pain, not wanting to face up to the depths of her feelings.

Even now, Anika was playing a dangerous game. Cameron could tell Natty what she had done. He could even tell Spence. She was risking it all, but couldn't help it. The day after she sent Cameron the message, she'd spent the whole day in a panic, thinking Spence would find out.

Cameron hadn't replied, which didn't surprise her. Deep down, she was hurt that he hadn't texted her, and wondered again what his game was, and if he just wanted the attention.

'Babe?'

She blinked, glancing at Spence, who looked at her in concern.

'Are you okay?'

She nodded.

'I'm just a bit tired. It's been a long day.' She toyed with the rim of her wine glass, worrying her bottom lip. 'What does Cameron think of Natty and Lorraine?'

Spence snorted.

'He thinks she's fit. Typical Cam way of looking at mature situations. He wants Natty to fuck her and to beat up her baby father. That's Cam all over. I think sometimes he comes across as bitter.'

'Really?' Anika had never heard Spence talk like that about Cameron before. Then again, he'd not said much about him in general besides grumblings about Cameron calling him whipped. It seemed a lot more visceral right now.

'I think he has some real issues where women are concerned.'

Anika sipped her wine, listening to the words, her stomach in knots hearing about Cameron. She tried to cobble together what she remembered about the old days, but they were mainly superficial thoughts. Cameron had turned so cold on her when she'd thought they had something, and trying to sift through those memories was painful.

'You know, it doesn't seem like you even like Cam sometimes.'

Spence pursed his lips, a sour expression on his face. He sighed.

'Cam's a cool guy most of the time, but he has a lot of dickhead traits, and he's constantly on my back.'

'Why?' Anika asked, her heart hammering.

'I've told you about it before,' huffed Spence. 'He's constantly bringing up our relationship, like it's some kind of bad thing.'

'Relationships aren't for everyone,' Anika replied, wondering if this applied to her. Spence made a lot of sense on paper, but she didn't feel the way she thought she should, and had no one she could speak to about it.

No one but Cameron, who was currently ignoring her text.

'I agree they're not for everyone. That's why it's important to find the right person, and to build together.' Spence squeezed her hand. 'Cam doesn't have that, and I don't think he ever will.'

When they finished eating, they headed home. Spence went to

shower, leaving his phone on the sofa. Anika looked at it for a minute, and then picked it up. He'd previously shared his pin with her, and she scanned his social media messages, her stomach turning when she saw conversations with other women.

She read the messages, unsure what she was searching for, but wanting a reason to be angry. She was in for a shock; the conversations were brief. Either short, friendly dialogues with no sexual undertones, or Spence shutting down other exchanges when they got flirtatious, openly saying he wasn't interested and had a girlfriend.

She put the phone away, and fixed herself a drink, mulling her dilemma, sure now that she was the problem, not Spence.

What kind of woman hoped her boyfriend had done wrong, so she had the excuse to be angry with him?

By all measurements, Spence was a good guy. He adored her, and he showed it every day. It made her wonder why, because she couldn't see what he saw in her. Her self-esteem was in the dirt and had been for some time. Anika didn't know how to take the necessary steps to heal, and doubted she even had the strength to do so.

Her phone vibrated as she sipped her drink, and she opened the message, her heart soaring when she read it:

I haven't forgotten about you. We have a lot to talk about.

Anika hated how hot and alive the simple message made her feel. She immediately replied, saying she was looking forward to getting some closure.

By the time Spence returned, wearing a pair of shorts and a plain t-shirt, she had a smile on her face.

'You seem in a better mood. What cheered you up?'

'I just got a text message that made me happy, that's all.'

'From who? Your mum?' Spence plopped onto the sofa next to her.

'No, it was from Carmen. She's always got something to say,' Anika lied.

Spence hugged her tightly, smiling, kissing the top of her head as he turned the television on. She was a horrible person, she mused, as she sat and thought about Cameron whilst his best friend hugged and kissed her, but she couldn't help it. She felt something she had been searching for when she thought about Cameron.

She remembered Spence's words about relationships, and she believed that she could be the reason why he was how he was.

Why had he stopped to talk to her? What had he hoped to gain by doing it? She couldn't tell.

* * *

THE NIGHT after their meeting with Harry and Rodney, Natty met Elijah in a club in the city centre. He'd been there a few times before, and always liked the vibe. It was on Briggate, near the top end of the city centre, and it catered to a more hood crowd. Consequently, Natty saw many faces that he recognised, and some he knew would be surprised he was meeting Elijah.

As always, Elijah was already there, and had procured seats that allowed him to see all the comings and goings. He wore a simple black shirt and jeans, not trying to stand out. Despite this, he still had a few ladies making eyes at him.

Natty stopped to hug a female he hadn't seen in a while, then kept it moving, sliding into the seat opposite Elijah. They shook hands.

'Ordered you a brandy. Figured you'd want something strong,' said Elijah by way of greeting. Natty thanked him and sipped the liquor. It was Courvoisier, which was second to Hennessy on his favourite brandies list. Nonetheless, he enjoyed the taste, taking in the overall vibe of the spot. He was surprised Elijah had come alone. Almost every time he saw Elijah, he was by himself.

Natty wondered why.

'So, let me just say I'm impressed,' said Elijah. 'I wasn't sure how you would do when Rudy put you forward, but you're solid. It's surprising you haven't been moved up already. You have the right instincts, and you're a moneymaking machine. Have you ever considered that maybe you're on the wrong side?'

Natty had, on more than one occasion. He'd wondered in the past if he was being held back because of who he was related to, but there was nothing to prove it. It was surprising that Elijah had picked up on it.

'Are you trying to recruit me?'

'You'd never work for me. Maybe working for yourself is something to consider.'

'My people don't like competition.' Natty knew enough about how his uncle operated to know that.

'They've allowed me and others to ply our trade. I'm not stupid, Nat. Everyone knows that your people were the strongest after Teflon and his people were done with Leeds. The police came down hard, but you lot could have pushed to control the Hood, but you didn't, which suggests that the people you're working for, want to do things quietly. That means allowing others to do their thing, as long as they play the game right.'

Natty said nothing, listening to Elijah talk. He liked what he was saying, though.

'The police pretty much leave us alone when we're not shooting and stabbing one another in the Hood. They're cool as long as we keep the dealing quiet in the catchment areas. They'll bust a few of us to hit their quotas, but they like order and hate boredom. A couple of us in the Hood, quietly going about our business, it drives them crazy.'

'Where are you going with this?' Natty frowned, surprised when Elijah smiled.

'All I'm saying is that you have serious talent, Natty. You could do your own thing, just like me. You don't have to be reliant on anyone, family or not. You've proved that to me, so give it some thought.'

'I will,' replied Natty, secretly buoyed by the compliments. He wondered if Elijah was trying to butter him up for something, but dismissed it. Elijah had nothing to gain from encouraging Natty to go out alone. Natty found himself considering how it could work. He could take Spence, Carlton and Cameron, and get a few youngsters. He wouldn't be making millions, but he would be his own boss, and could dictate more of what he did.

'You do that. For now, back to Little London. What's the next step?'

'The locals are ready for change, and the whole area is open. The money is good, but there is much more to be made if we can completely sew it up.'

Elijah grinned. 'I must say, I expected it to be a cash cow, but the money we're already making is what I'd projected after six to eight months of solid grinding. Getting some of the locals on board has been excellent for us. I thought it might just be a drain when you first tried it.'

'Speaking of drains, Warren's the damn *Deebo* of the area, and as positive as we are for people, he's still the one that the masses defer to. Everyone is scared of him, and he's got people shaking in their trainers. Look how Harry and his mate reacted.'

Elijah scratched his chin, savouring his red wine.

'Sounds like we should put him to work.'

'If we want things to continue, we need to do something. The early takings are creeping up, as you said. What we're putting out there is solid, and we're building a stable line that people want to get behind.'

'The money will be divided in two days. I'm planning on using mine to pay out some bonuses.'

Despite what he knew about Elijah's generosity, Natty frowned, surprised at the action.

'Why?'

'We're paying for the illusion of honesty, Nat. Do you understand what I mean by that?'

Natty shook his head.

'It means that loyalty is rarely earned anymore. It comes from perception, and money. We pay out bigger bonuses, people work harder, and they feel like they are part of something far bigger than what we actually have.'

'I'm not sure about that,' Natty admitted. 'We might build a workforce of entitled soldiers if we move like that. That's your thing, though. I'm interested to see how it turns out, but for now, Warren's the problem.'

'Warren won't be a problem.' Elijah pushed out his chest. 'We'll make him an offer.'

They spoke some more about the streets. Mindful that Elijah had ordered his last drink, Natty hit the bar to get the next round. He was almost there when he bumped into a more petite woman, steadying her to ensure she didn't fall. He grinned when he recognised her.

'Rosie. Fancy seeing you here.'

Rosie's eyes sparkled as she recognised Natty.

'Nat! What are you doing in here?' Rosie continued to take in Natty's appearance, and he grinned. 'You look good.'

'So do you. You look stunning.' Natty returned the compliment. Rosie wore a shimmery grey top and some jeans, her toned arms on display. Natty had never noticed how good her posture was before, but it was arrow straight. 'I'm meeting someone. What about you?'

'I'm chilling with some friends. It's my girl's birthday,' she replied. 'Who are you meeting? Spence?' Her eyes glittered. Natty chuckled.

'When did you start taking an interest in Spence?'

Rosie smirked. 'Spence has always been fit.'

Natty chuckled again. He remembered Spence having a thing for Rosie back in the day. At the time, she was in a long-term relationship, so nothing transpired.

'You're trouble, Rosie. Leave my boy alone. He has a girl,' he teased. Privately, Natty believed Spence and Rosie had better chemistry. He preferred Rosie in general between Rosie and Anika, but things hadn't turned out that way.

'I just asked if you were meeting him. It's been a while, but I remember how sharp he is. He knows his stuff.'

Natty nodded. 'He does. His head is definitely in the right place.'

'What about your head?' Rosie looked Natty in the eyes. He shrugged.

'I'm getting where I need to be,' he replied. 'How's Lorraine doing with her studying? Have you spoken to her lately?'

'Earlier today. She's stressed. You know how she gets with it. She told me you've seen her working in the kitchen when you're over. You should go back and make her feel better.'

'Feel better how?' Natty's eyebrow rose.

'In any way you feel would help her. I think she would definitely appreciate it.'

'Has she said something to you to make you think that?' said Natty.

'No, this is just someone who knows her friend and understands her needs well,' replied Rosie.

'Why?'

'You know why.' Rosie moved aside to allow someone to pass. 'Lorraine talks about you a lot, and I think you're a good influence on her.'

Natty was thoughtful as Rosie spoke, and he wondered how true that was. He didn't think he had ever been a good influence on anyone, especially a woman. He was usually the guy trying to tempt them to do silly things with him, at the expense of whatever else was going on.

Lorraine wasn't like that. He wanted her to succeed.

'Whatever, Rosie. Maybe I will. I'm gonna get these drinks and head back, anyway. Don't be getting my boy in any trouble.'

After hugging Rosie, Natty ordered and paid for his drinks, then headed back to Elijah, who stowed away his phone just as Natty returned.

'I'll arrange a meeting with Warren. I know a few of his people,' he said.

'Do you think he'll go for the meeting?' Natty asked.

'People will be looking at him sideways if he turns it down cold. In terms of a resolution, I'm not sure he would benefit from working with us, but he's not the sharpest guy. Some people are too stubborn to work with others. I used to think you were like that.'

'Fuck you,' replied Natty, his eyes narrowing. Elijah laughed, picking up his drink.

'I said *used to*. I'm happy to say I was wrong.'

Natty chuckled, not really angry with Elijah.

'In terms of a deal for Warren, what are you thinking?'

Elijah sipped his drink, then scratched his chin.

'I'm not sure. It's gotta be something that lets him see the benefits of working with us.'

'What about a discount?'

'What sort of discount?' Elijah frowned.

'Well, we want him to buy from us, so what if we give him a break on buying boxes?'

'What sort of break?'

'Two grand discount per kilo.'

Elijah's eyes widened. 'You're serious?'

'We want him to play ball, right? Like you said, it's gotta be something that benefits him.'

'I know, but that could get costly in the long run. It's not something I would want to do long-term.'

'So, we'll sort something out temporarily. He'll see the benefits by then, and we can move things along. Once Little London is fully set up, we'll be laughing. We can step it up to other areas.'

'That won't be easy. People are squirrelly nowadays about working together.'

'If they see us doing it, and getting big money, that might shift a lot of that reluctance,' said Natty. Elijah nodded.

'All right, I'm on board. You've clearly given this all a lot of thought.'

'I want us to succeed,' replied Natty, smiling.

The pair raised their glasses and clinked them together.

CHAPTER TWELVE

THE FOLLOWING DAY, Anika was home, lazing on the sofa. She had no early bookings, deciding to pass the time by reading. So engrossed was she in the book, a bang at the door jolted her out of the zone. Her heart hammered against her chest, more in hope than fear. She didn't know who was on the other side of the door, but she knew who she wanted it to be.

Surely, he wouldn't risk coming to Spence's house unannounced?

'Natty?' She said after finally opening the door. Natty smiled, towering over her, his build prominent under his simple white t-shirt. A few of Anika's friends had gone after Natty in the past, and she couldn't blame them. She wasn't interested but could certainly see what they saw. He had a nice smile, broad shoulders, and an appealing ruggedness. His smile widened.

'Easy, Nika. Spence around? I was meant to meet him, but he's not picking up. Figured he might still be asleep.'

Anika chuckled. 'Spence gets up early every day, no matter when he gets in. Refuses to *waste a day*.' Although harmless on the surface, her tone betrayed her feelings. In truth, a lot about Spence's character irked her. 'You missed him, though. He left a while back.'

Natty snorted. 'I've been dragged on a few early runs with him, before I put a stop to it. I didn't even notice the car wasn't there. Thanks, I'll catch him at one of the spots. Take care of yourself, love.' He turned to walk away, but Anika spoke again.

'Natty?'

Natty span around, a confused look on his face.

'Yeah?'

Anika's muscles twitched. She cleared her throat, trying to decide what she wanted to say. Natty's brow furrowed as he waited. The moment lingered for several more awkward seconds, before she finally spoke to cut the tension.

'. . . How are you and Lorraine getting on?'

Natty's expression was unchanged.

'Getting on how?'

'I just mean . . . you two are close, right?' Anika didn't know where she was going with this.

'We're friends. I'm sure she's fine.'

'Are you happy?'

Still puzzled, Natty watched her for a long moment. Anika's heart hammered against her chest, wondering if he could sense her inner conflict.

'What . . . Why would you ask me that? Everything okay with you and Spence?'

Hurriedly, Anika nodded. Natty tilted his head to the right, then rubbed his chin.

'Yeah, I'm happy. A big part of me wants more, though, and I'm trying to work out how to make that happen.'

It wasn't the answer she expected, and she was surprised he'd even given her one.

'If you had a way to get closer to those answers, would you take it?'

Natty didn't hesitate to nod. 'Of course. Why punish yourself by wondering when you can find out for sure? Are you sure you're okay?'

'I'm fine. I just wondered what you would say. Thanks for being honest.'

'Anytime, love. Look after yourself.' Natty bounded away. Anika remained by the door, unmoving. Although Natty didn't realise it, his words were a green light to Anika. A sign to press forward and get the answers she needed.

* * *

IT TOOK Anika a day to gather herself. Knowing Spence was working, she left their house the next night and took an Uber to Cameron's, taking the time beforehand to do her makeup and style her hair.

When Cameron opened the door, he had a hungry expression on his face, eyes gleaming as he took her in. When she'd sat down, he fixed her a drink, then sipped his own.

'Do you want anything else? I've got pills, coke, or some weed.'

They shared a spliff. After a while, Anika relaxed. She was half finished with her second drink when she finally spoke.

'A big part of me knows I shouldn't be here.'

'Is that why it took you like two weeks to reach out to me?'

Anika cleared her throat.

'I wasn't sure. Like I said . . . I shouldn't be here.'

'You think too much.' Cameron laughed, glancing at her legs. 'You're here for a reason.'

Anika's eyes narrowed.

'Does everything boil down to sex?'

Cameron swirled his drink around his glass before taking a long sip. Smacking his lips, his eyes fixed on the glass. Eventually, his eyes met hers.

'Why did you finally come to see me?'

'I want closure.'

Cameron shook his head. 'You want freedom, not closure.'

'That probably means getting bent over in your world.'

Smirking, Cameron didn't reply.

'I spoke with Natty,' Anika said.

Cameron jerked, spilling his drink.

'Shit.' He dabbed at his clothes, scowling. 'Does he know we're talking again?'

'Course not.' Anika shook her head.

Cameron took a deep breath, visibly relieved. He wiped at the stain on his top one last time, then left it.

'Good. Natty wouldn't understand.'

'How do you know that? He's a gyalist. He'd probably support you.' Anika knew Natty had been through his fair share of women, and hadn't displayed feelings for any of them, save for Lorraine. She recalled his reaction to her cringing questioning yesterday, inwardly shuddering.

Cameron shook his head. 'He and Spence are tight. He'd see anything I did as a violation.'

This reminded Anika of something she'd wondered for a while.

'Does Natty know how deep things were with us?'

Cameron studied her for so long that Anika started to think he wouldn't answer. Eventually, he shook his head.

'That's in the past. He knew we had a little thing, but it doesn't matter anymore.'

Anika's stomach plummeted when Cameron described what they had that way. Despite her best efforts, it was apparent they had vastly different ideas about what they'd shared back then. She drained her drink and poured another.

'Why did you never love me?'

Cameron rubbed his forehead, eyes narrowing.

'How do you know I didn't?'

'If you had, we would have been together.'

'If that's how you felt, you wouldn't have got with my friend.' Cameron's tone was like ice, and Anika blanched, before taking a deep breath.

'Spence cares about me.'

Cameron snorted.

'He's soft.'

'You two don't seem to like one another. Why do you still think you're friends?'

Cameron shrugged.

'We're just different.' He again looked Anika in her eyes. 'Doesn't mean you should have gone for him, though.'

Anika rubbed her eyes, growing steadily more frustrated with

Cameron's responses. 'I never had to guess how Spence feels about me. He tells me and shows me, and he wants to build something with me—'

'Why the hell are you here then?' Cameron snapped. 'Why sit with me when you can be at home with your perfect fucking boyfriend?'

'Because I don't love him!' Anika screamed, silencing Cameron. They both stared at one another, breathing hard. Anika continued.

'I wish I did. It would be so much easier, but I don't.'

'Who do you love?' Cameron's voice was softer now. Anika shook her head. She meant what she said. She wished her feelings were more straightforward, but they weren't. When Cameron moved closer, she didn't back away, and when his lips met hers, she kissed him back with fervour.

The kiss quickly intensified, any feelings of guilt extinguished as Cameron climbed on top of her on the sofa, pulling up her skirt and kissing her neck. When he slid inside her, she dug her nails into his back, wrapping her legs around his waist as he drove into her. As the pleasure intensified, she closed her eyes, savouring the ferocious climax that Cameron gifted her.

A little while later, the pair climbed into bed. Cameron wrapped his arm around Anika, a smile on his face. She traced patterns across his chest, her guilt beginning to return in the aftermath of what she had done. Spence didn't deserve this, yet a major part of her believed what she had done was right. The only thing she remained unsure about was what would happen going forward. She thought she had come to see Cameron for closure, yet she'd quickly fallen into bed with him.

'Cam?' She asked.

'You should jet soon. Spence is working, but he might drop in on you. See what you're doing.'

'Spence isn't like that. He trusts me.' Anika felt almost sick saying it. He did trust her. Not once did he ever question what she was doing, or who she was around. She had betrayed that trust in the worst way possible.

'Still, you don't wanna make him suspicious. Might make it harder to get away next time.'

'Next time?' She glanced up at him, irked by the smirk on his face.

'Yes, next time. Save all the hard-to-get shit. You loved what we did. You came like four times,' said Cameron.

'Just because I enjoyed having sex with you, doesn't mean anything has been resolved between us. What is it that you want from me, Cam? Do you want me to stay with Spence?'

'Do you want to?'

Anika didn't reply immediately. She didn't know what to say. She'd wanted closure, and now that the sex had finished, she felt used. Cameron wasn't giving her anything, and his deflections only worsened things. He hadn't even given her an honest answer about whether he loved her.

'Spence cares about me,' she repeated. She felt Cameron shift, but he didn't snort this time.

'Is caring enough?'

'Can you offer me something more?'

Cameron shrugged.

'I don't know. I guess I'd like to, but that doesn't mean I can.'

Anika appreciated the honesty, but wasn't sure that was enough. Without a word, she slid from the bed and began getting her things together.

'Nika?'

She glanced at Cameron. He had his arms behind his head, gazing at her.

'I'm glad you took a chance with me.'

CHAPTER THIRTEEN

DAYS LATER, Natty and Elijah arranged a meeting with Warren. Even with Elijah having connections in Warren's circle, it still took a while to set up.

Making concessions, they agreed to meet on Warren's turf, at a terraced house on Carlton Carr in Little London. Natty and Elijah climbed from their ride, glancing around and noting a pub at the top of the street. The pair were attending the meeting without backup, not wanting to send the wrong message.

A slim, pale woman with mousy hair and jittery features answered the door, her eyes darting between Natty and Elijah. Without a word, she led them to a small kitchen. It reeked of takeaways, but was relatively tidy, mostly taken up by a circular brown table and spindly chairs. Elijah took a seat, but Natty remained on his feet, glancing around, frowning.

'You good?' Elijah asked.

'If this isn't a massive setup, at least we can go to the pub afterwards and get drunk,' joked Natty. Elijah grinned.

Minutes passed. They heard random shuffles and noises, but no sign of Warren.

Natty ignored the growing anxiety he felt. They were in enemy territory, unarmed with no ready backup. Rubbing his jaw, he was about to tell Elijah they were leaving, when he heard heavy footsteps approaching.

A powerfully built man stomped into the room. He wore a black t-shirt, a hooded zip top, and some bottoms. He had a weapon in plain sight, jammed down the front of his trousers. Glaring at the pair, he subtly adjusted his waistband to draw their attention to it.

Natty kept his face neutral, but he already had a bad feeling.

'You must be Warren. Take a seat,' said Elijah, motioning to several seats at the other side of the table. Warren shook his head, his eyes hard.

'This is my meeting. I'm good standing.'

Sitting next to Elijah, Natty kept his eyes on Warren, not liking the hostile vibe he brought to the room. Before the meeting, Natty gave it 50/50 that they would come to an agreement. After this opening, he revised it to 20/80. Elijah took a deep breath, ready to speak.

'Who the hell are you, and what do you want?' Warren got right to the point. His eyes seared into Elijah's, his interruption working perfectly.

Elijah's eyes flashed, but he swallowed down the anger, seeing the disrespect as a cost of doing business. He filed it away, vowing to revisit it at a later time.

'We've been doing business in Little London for a while, and we think there's a way we can do some together,' he said, keeping his words soft.

'Who the hell are you, though? You didn't answer my question.'

Elijah didn't respond. Natty leant forward.

'You wouldn't be meeting us if you didn't know who we were. Let's cut the shit.'

Warren kept his eyes on Elijah for a lingering moment, before switching to look at Natty.

'Just because I know your names, doesn't mean shit. You lot reached out to me. Recognise that.'

'Despite that, we can all do good business.' Elijah paused, catching Natty's eye, willing him to keep his cool.

'What can you lot do for me that I can't do for myself?' Warren demanded.

'Your supplier is ripping you off. Our product is stronger. It's a big part of why we're doing well here. If you come on board with us, it only benefits everyone,' said Elijah.

'Come on board with you how?' Warren snorted.

'Start taking our product. We can get you what you need. You keep putting it out, and we all get paid together. You pay us two grand less than you're paying now, per box.'

Warren's eyes flitted between the pair of them. He folded his arms, his eyes lingering on Natty a second longer, his jaw tightening. Natty returned the look, not backing down. He'd seen this look all too often before; fists clenching, muscles tensing, eyes locked. It appeared Warren was preparing to fight. Natty shifted his weight slightly in his chair, clenching his fist, but concealing it out of sight. His eyes flicked to the weapon hidden in Warren's waistband. It was a problem, but it wouldn't be a factor if he jumped him before he could get to it.

'You lot look like dickheads. I don't trust you, or like the look of you, so why would I work with you?' said Warren.

'Well . . .' Elijah started.

'Nah, I'm not done talking. You could have spoken to me before you moved into my ends, but you didn't. So, here's how we're gonna do it. Pack up your people and move out. If you don't, we're gonna get down to it.'

'Get down to what?' Elijah's voice had cooled, and Natty could tell even he knew the meeting was over.

Warren pulled the gun but didn't aim it. His finger caressed the trigger, both men's eyes glued to the motion.

'I could take you both out right now. Carry on the way you're going on, and it'll happen. Get the fuck out of here, and take your runners with you.'

Natty held Warren's glare. Warren was stupid enough to shoot them in cold blood, with no provocation. Elijah stood, but Natty remained seated, still looking at Warren. Elijah tugged Natty's top, breaking the stare and prompting him to stand. Elijah left the room, his eyes on the door, but Natty's eyes followed Warren until he was past him.

'That's right. Don't even come around my ends talking shit, you pair of pussies. Little London is mine, and I ain't sharing with anyone, let alone you lot.'

Natty's eyes flicked to Elijah's. Subtly, Elijah shook his head, and they both looked forward, continuing toward the door. Natty loathed that Warren was talking to them like they were idiots, but now wasn't the time.

'I'm surprised you kept your cool,' Elijah said to Natty as they climbed in Elijah's car and drove away.

Natty took a deep breath, closing his eyes and trying to calm down.

Despite his outward showing, his blood boiled. He wanted to smash Warren's face in. There was no deal to be made from the start. Warren had no intention of dealing with them. He had wanted to try to make an example of them. Natty guessed he would spread the story of how he had punked them, and wondered how much traction it would get.

'He had a gun.'

Elijah glanced at Natty as they turned a corner onto another street.

'Do you think he really would have used it?'

'I wasn't going to risk my life finding out.'

Neither man spoke after that. The meeting had gone badly, and they had a problem on their hands with Warren. Threats had been made, and Warren had proved himself unwilling to do business.

They would have to get deep, deal with him, and prevent an all-out war in Little London.

* * *

CAMERON WAS at the spot with the youngsters, taking calls on the trap line and directing runners to meet with sales. He'd had some food earlier — chicken and dumplings from Dutch Pot — and was content. When he heard Spence enter, he attempted and failed to swallow down the wave of nervousness that spread through his body.

He couldn't let Spence find out what had happened with Anika.

Spence appeared unruffled in that calm, understated manner of his. The youths flocked towards him, greeting him and slapping his hand as he checked how they all were.

Cameron remained seated until Spence came to greet him.

'*Boss*, how's it going?' He said, noticing Spence's face tighten.

'You tell me. How are things?'

'C'mon, Spence,' Cameron waved his hand, 'we all know the play here. Things are going well.'

Spence looked to the youths, who had returned to what they were doing, then sat alongside Cameron.

'I've noticed takings in the middle shift have been consistently down for the past two weeks.'

'That happens sometimes. Things can be hit or miss, plus sometimes we don't clip the same level of fiends. You know that,' he said to Spence.

'I think someone is stealing.'

'That's nonsense. Our team doesn't get down like that,' said Cameron, his expression darkening.

'I want to set a trap and prove that.'

Cameron shook his head. 'Seems like a lot of trouble for nothing. Just give everyone a warning and see what happens.'

'It won't help us get to the root of the issue. We can use it to send a message and show people that we're on top of things.'

Cameron shrugged. 'If you wanna waste your time over pennies, go for it.'

Spence scowled at Cameron, tired of his friend's attitude. Spence was running the show, and the fact Cameron didn't respect that, was frustrating. His blasé attitude when it came to somebody skimming the profits stood out more than anything. Spence quickly came to a decision.

'Good. We'll go for it. Not only that, you're going to contribute.' He locked eyes with his friend, expecting resistance. Cameron swallowed down his annoyance at Spence, and nodded.

'Cool, bro. No problem.'

Cameron felt the guilt from earlier leaving him. He would let Spence go on his power trip, and focus elsewhere.

* * *

NATTY AND ELIJAH knew they would have to deal with Warren sooner than later, but they were wary about how to do it. The last thing they wanted was an all-out battle that would draw more eyes and attention to what they were doing in the area.

Elijah reached out to his contacts for more information about Warren, and spoke of organising safe-houses and putting a shooter on standby near the area, just in case.

As far as Natty was concerned, Julie and the other locals he had spoken to had given him a solid understanding of what Warren was about. The meeting had validated that understanding. He'd come armed, and Natty knew it wouldn't have taken much for him to pull out his gun and start shooting.

* * *

GAVIN THOMAS WAS an ex-baller who'd suffered a severe injury shortly after going pro. He'd tried to go legitimate after several comeback attempts, working some security jobs; but ultimately hated the 9-5 life. The lure of easy money drew him back to the streets. Gavin had charisma in spades, and had plenty of old tales about his football days, and the players he'd hung out with, that the youths around them ate up. Most of it was bullshit, but it sounded good.

He'd hit upon his scheme shortly after Natty ceded control to Spence. Cameron was in charge of the shifts most times and wasn't the most diligent of people. Gavin had started holding back his total profit and even taking drugs directly to sell on the side. Cameron and Spence were Natty's stooges. When Natty was around, he was on point, but he didn't believe he would have any trouble with his friends. He plied Cameron with spliffs and bottles of liquor, massaging his ego, keeping him distracted.

Gavin repeated his tricks until it was almost muscle memory. Time erased the nerves, providing reassurance. When more resources became accessible, his instincts abandoned him. Hungry for more, he feasted.

On the Friday of that week, he was on an early shift with Cameron and a few youths, when Spence entered, looking oddly serious.

'Gavin, how's it going?' He asked.

'Hey, Spence. It's going good, fam. Just telling these lot about the time I met Beckham and he bought me champagne.'

Spence nodded. 'That's cool. Everything good, though? How's your mum?'

Gavin's eyes narrowed. 'Why are you asking about my mum?'

'She was ill, wasn't she? I heard she had flu or something last week,' replied Spence.

Gavin relaxed. He'd fed this story to Cameron last week, giving him ample time to quietly sell his drugs on the side.

'She's fine. On the mend, but she's getting there.'

Spence smiled. 'That's good to hear. Turn out your pockets, please.'

The room fell silent, everyone facing Spence.

'What?' stammered Gavin, eyes flickering towards the door. Spence gave one of the larger youths a look, and he went to block the door, cutting off a potential escape route. Cameron looked around, noticing that a circle had been formed around Gavin, not enough to crowd him, but enough to let him know escape was futile.

'You heard what I said.'

'Cam . . .' Gavin turned to Cameron, who cleared his throat.

'Yo, Spence —'

'This is the last time I'm going to ask you,' said Spence, ignoring Cameron.

Gavin swallowed, seeing Spence was serious. Heart pounding, he did as he was told, several shots and bundles of cash tumbling onto the nearby coffee table. He heard the angry mumbles of the crew, and knew he'd messed up big time. Spence's face showed no reaction, though, and Gavin wasn't sure if this was better or worse.

'Yo, Spence, look, I know it looks bad, but I forgot I had it on me. I was gonna check it with everything else later. Same with the drugs. It's not what it looks like,' he tried. Spence held a hand up.

Cameron's fists clenched. Gavin had played him for an idiot. He knew it would look bad that all of this had happened on his watch. Before Gavin could say anything else, he drew back his fist, crashing it into the side of Gavin's face. For all Gavin's big talk, he wasn't a fighter, and the first blow folded him. He stumbled from the sofa to the floor, and Cameron continued to hit him.

'Fucking punk. Think you can steal from me and get away with it? Huh?' He signalled to the rest of the crew to get involved, but only two of them did, the rest taking their cues from Spence and remaining where they were. When the two that joined in realised this, they too stopped.

'Cam, that's enough,' said Spence after a few moments. Cameron cocked his arm back, but faltered. Leering down at the whimpering mess beneath him for a moment, he whirled around, turning his attention to Spence.

'What? After what he did? We need to send a message on this,' he snarled, breathing hard.

'He needs to make back what he stole. He can't do that if you break all his bones and kill him.'

'He fucked up good and proper. He needs to do more than just pay it back. What if someone else tries it?'

'Look around you, Cam. None of them are going to try it. They know we're on top of it, and that they will be caught just like Gavin was.' Spence motioned to the beaten man.

'That's not good enough. He made me look like a right dickhead, and I'm not standing for it.'

Spence's expression hardened.

'I'm in charge. This is the direction we're going in, and it's non-negotiable.'

Silence ensued, the two friends staring one another down. The entire crew held their breath, wondering how this would play out. They had noticed the growing tension between Cameron and Spence, and were ready for blows to get thrown. Gavin's cries of pain occasionally punctuated the silence. He crawled toward the door, but it was still blocked.

Cameron glared at Spence, furious that he was being belittled in front of people. Disagreeing with him was one thing. Ordering him around in front of everyone like he was disposable was another. He looked at each man in the room, then back to Spence, his nostrils flaring. Taking a moment, he smiled.

'Fine,' he said with a nod. 'You're in charge.'

When Gavin had been dragged to his feet, and led away by some of the team, Spence turned to Cameron.

'Thank you, Cam,' he started. 'I appreciate you listening to me, and going along with me on this. I know you had your doubts, but we're better when we work together, bro. Always have been.'

Cameron nodded, smiling. 'No problem at all, mate.' When Spence left the room, Cameron took out his phone and texted Anika.

Where are you at?

* * *

AFTER LEAVING Spence and the crew behind, Cameron headed home, pouring himself a straight glass of white rum and downing it.

He couldn't believe how things had turned out. Spence had been down with him and Natty for years, but Cameron had always seen himself as a step above the younger man. Now, Spence was showing he was a natural leader, and his treatment of Gavin exemplified that. Gavin had played Cameron, stealing money whilst smiling in his face and complimenting him, and he was furious that not only had he fallen for it, but that Spence's hunch was correct.

When Natty, Rudy and the others heard about this, they would look down on Cameron, and he couldn't accept that.

He was amid his brooding when there was a knock at his door. He went to let Anika in, not even offering her a drink as he stormed back to the sofa and sat down.

'You're in a good mood, I see,' she said, entering the room, watching Cameron slump onto the sofa. 'How come you invited me if you're angry?'

'What the hell do you care? You came, didn't you?'

'I can leave just as quickly if you don't change your attitude.' Anika's nostrils flared.

'Go then. See if I care.'

Anika stomped for the door, then turned at the last second to scowl at Cameron. He wasn't looking at her, but she noticed his shoulders shaking, awkwardly wondering if he would cry.

'I thought you were leaving?' Cameron said a second later.

'I'm still wondering why you invited me over here. What if I was with Spence?'

'Spence is working. He's got his little fucking promotion, remember?'

'Is that why you're angry?' Anika's eyebrow rose.

'It doesn't matter.' Cameron stood and approached Anika, backing her into the wall. Her chest heaved, breathing intensifying as she looked up at him. With no more words, he kissed her hard, instantly feeling her responding, a feeling of power returning. Cameron decided that Spence could take all the nonsense plaudits he wanted as the kissing intensified. In return, he would keep taking the love of his life.

* * *

THE NIGHT after his meeting with Warren, Natty went to Lorraine's, seeking a distraction.

She answered the door, her face drawn, her hair wrapped. She gave him a brief hug and let him in.

'Jaden's already in bed,' she said, collapsing onto the sofa with a sigh and getting her phone.

'How's your practising going?' He asked. He'd stayed away to allow her to concentrate, telling her to contact him if she needed him to look after Jaden. Despite that, Lorraine's eyes widened.

'You remembered?'

'Course I did.'

Lorraine sighed again, closing her eyes.

'Up and down, but mostly up,' she admitted. 'I've found some great resources online that are helping.

'That's great. I'm glad to hear it,' Natty replied. 'I've no doubt you'll do whatever you want.'

Lorraine's eyes flitted open, and she beamed at Natty.

'I appreciate the faith you have in me, Nat. Where have you been lately, by the way?'

'I told you to contact me if you needed me. I've been doing some work in Little London.' He scratched his chin. 'What do you think of Elijah?'

Lorraine blinked, clearly surprised.

'Why do you ask?'

'I'm doing some work with him.'

'Really?'

Natty nodded.

'Does that work involve Raider?' Her tone lowered.

'No. I made sure of that.'

Lorraine looked visibly relieved at his words.

'Elijah's nice,' she said. 'Polite, and seems to mean it. Doesn't really seem to fit in, though. I always wondered if he had a dark side.'

'Why?' Natty was intrigued.

'He just seems too kind. Figured there had to be a reason he had guys like Raider working for him.' She assessed Natty, staring intensely into his eyes. 'Be careful in Little London, Nat.'

Natty sat next to Lorraine, holding her close enough to feel her pounding heart. He swallowed, inhaling her scent.

'I'm always careful,' he replied softly. 'I appreciate you caring, still.' He remembered his previous thoughts from Julie's. 'Have you ever wanted more kids?'

'Are you offering?' Lorraine teased. Natty poked her in the side, and she giggled.

'I used to,' she admitted, once she'd calmed down. 'I wish Jaden had brothers and sisters to play with. What about you? Ever thought of having any?'

'Sometimes,' Natty replied, his thoughts on Jaden. Neither spoke after that, enjoying the tranquil vibe.

CHAPTER FOURTEEN

BIRDY and his friend Jack walked along Well Close Rise in Little London. Having finished serving some customers, they were strolling back to their base.

'When we clock off, there's a party we can hit,' said Jack. He was nineteen, dark-skinned with pale brown eyes and pockmarked skin. 'There's gonna be loads of girls there.'

Birdy stared at his phone, half-listening to Jack. He was a fair-skinned twenty-year-old with lank brown hair cut low around the sides, and dark eyes. He had a small amount of stubble around his jaw. Both were dressed similarly in bomber jackets over t-shirts and jeans.

They had been working the Little London patch for a few weeks, and so far, it had been easy money. They had the locals mostly sewn up, and both believed things would only improve.

'I'm tired,' Birdy finally replied. 'I can't be arsed with a big party.'

'Suck it up, bro. Have a line, or a Red Bull if you need to sharpen up. We can get some pussy.'

Before Birdy could reply, a tinted blue Audi sharply pulled to a stop next to them. Without communication, both men instantly began running. Jack was faster, charging up Carlton Hill, past several graffiti-ridden buildings. He didn't know the area too well but figured they could lose them nearby. This idea quickly evaporated as Birdy lost his balance and tumbled to the ground. Jack stopped to haul him to his feet as they again began pounding the concrete. The engine revving and yells of those inside the car grew ever closer.

At the end of the road was a locked gate leading to a building. They were about to take a left, when the click of a gun froze them.

Panting, they turned around, watching as four men approached, one of them still holding the gun. He was dressed in black, with a thin, ratty face and slim build. By contrast, his compatriots loomed, also dressed in black, but far more muscular.

Jack swallowed, hearing Birdy squirming next to him.

'Give it up,' the gunman said. The men behind him watched with angry expressions, breathing hard. Jack and Birdy handed over the money they had on them, their drugs, and their phones. One of the men moved forward and began patting them down, relieving Jack of a butterfly knife he hadn't time to pull earlier. Fear glissaded through his body. He was too scared to even look at Birdy.

'You little shits,' the gunman continued. 'I should blow both your heads off right here. Your bosses were warned, and you lot still thought you could do what you wanted.'

'We didn't—' Panicking, Jack tried to speak, but the gunman aimed the gun at him, and he fell silent, still trembling. He heard Birdy sniffing next to him.

'Don't try to explain it now. You're gonna have to pay the cost for their mistakes. This is Warren's turf, and he ain't giving it up.' He signalled for the others, and they swarmed the duo, beating them down. Jack and Birdy landed one hit apiece before being over-whelmed, falling unconscious after several punches and kicks to the chest and face.

* * *

NATTY SMOKED A CIGARETTE, staring at his phone. It had never been one of his vices, but that had changed recently. What started as a means to take the edge off the stress of the streets was quickly becoming a habit.

The kids that had been beaten up were okay, just bruised and a little shaken up. Tapping his phone screen, he took a deep breath, furious at the situation. He finished his cigarette and disposed of the remains. They needed to sort out the situation quickly, or people would be scared to work in Little London. The streets were watching.

He called Elijah.

'Is this important? I'm in the thick of it here.' Elijah's voice was harried, but Natty pushed past it.

'We need to regroup and get something going. If we let him get too much momentum, we're done,' said Natty, avoiding using names.

Elijah sighed. Natty sensed his exhaustion through the phone.

'I'll pick you up from Jukie's in an hour. We can talk on the move.'

Natty agreed, ending the call just as a text message came through. Scanning it, his eyes widened.

Another of their dealers had been attacked. He'd attempted to fight back, ended up getting stabbed, and bled out on the streets.

* * *

FOR THE THIRD time in three days, Natty and Elijah met. Neither was taking any chances. The Chapeltown safe house they were in was heavily protected, with several men around the perimeter, and another sitting in a car up the street, just in case.

The safe house had the basics: a small television and Kodi stick, cheap coffee table, and two hideous brown sofas in the surprisingly spacious living room.

Natty paced the living room, floorboards creaking under his heavy feet. He needed to keep moving, to work off the excess energy this situation was causing. Usually, he would work it out in the gym, but he'd found little time for it recently. He was running low on cigarettes, and though he hated himself for the smoking, he couldn't turn it off right now.

Elijah was seated, eyes glued to his mobile phone.

'These news stories are getting worse,' he said, eyes narrowing. 'They've got an interview with the police. They're promising to *crack down on a growing gang presence in the local Leeds area.*'

Natty snorted, still pacing. It was the last thing on his mind right now. One of their people had been killed, and they had yet to do anything to combat that.

'Things are going to get even harder now, Natty. Everyone has eyes on us.'

Natty stopped, assessing Elijah.

'We need to show them something then, don't we? We have people in place, so we need to hit back. Hard.'

Elijah blew out a breath, the bags under his eyes suddenly noticeable.

'There are multiple angles to consider.'

Natty shook his head.

'Warren's made it clear that he will not work with us. Either we fight back, or we leave Little London for good, and then how do we look?'

Elijah rubbed his eyebrow.

'We need to think about the politics of the situation,' he replied.

Natty smirked, letting out a harsh bark of laughter.

'Did you consider these politics *before* deciding to move into Little London?'

Elijah shot him a dirty look, but didn't reply.

'Look,' continued Natty, 'we have to do something. You wanted this alliance for a reason, right? We need to clap back. Like you said . . . *people are watching.*'

Before Elijah could respond, Natty's phone rang. He squinted at the screen. It was Junior, one of their people in Little London.

'Yeah?' He answered.

'One of the spots just got licked.'

'For real?' Natty's nostrils flared. A police raid was the last thing they needed. 'What did they get?'

'I can't get close enough to get a proper look, but they arrested two people.'

'Fuck. Right, don't say anything else. I'll ring you later, and we'll talk in person.'

'Cool.'

Natty hung up, stowing his phone. He rubbed his eyes, aware of an impending headache. From Natty's tone and demeanour, Elijah looked up, knowing it wasn't good.

'Police raided one of the spots. Make some calls, and get them to temporarily clear out of the other ones. I'm gonna speak with Rudy, and then we need to collaborate and properly sort our next move.'

Elijah nodded, knowing he couldn't argue.

* * *

NATTY MET with Rudy at Delores's. She was out, but Rudy made them cups of coffee, and they lit cigarettes, enjoying the quiet.

'You look like you need that.' Rudy motioned to the cigarette.

'I need more than that, boss. Shit is out of control. Warren needs dealing with.'

'What's Elijah said about it?'

'He's too busy trying to be the fucking UN. We've done decent work until now, but this isn't negotiation time. We already tried that shit, and he punked us. He's still punking us.' Natty's frustration from the past few days spilt out.

Rudy let him finish, sipping his drink and watching the younger man's reactions.

Eventually, Natty deeply exhaled.

'What do I do?' He asked.

'What do you think you should do?'

'Rudy, I know you mean well, but why can't you just tell me the answer? It's obvious there's something you want me to do.'

'I want you to think. You're the point man, so I want to know what you think is the best course of action.'

'Warren needs to go. That's the only way things go back to normal. He's not playing ball and is out there trying to kill my people. There's no going back from that.'

Rudy surveyed Natty, inhaling the smoke from his cigarette, savouring the nicotine.

'Are you the person to finish him?'

Natty looked away for a moment. He had considered this, and in the middle of the night, after several glasses of Hennessy, had considered going out and tracking Warren down himself.

'I'm the point man over there. Like you said.'

'You are, but that doesn't mean *you* need to rush out and get yourself in trouble. That's how your father did things.'

Natty glared at Rudy, remembering their argument in the pub a while back. Rudy shook his head.

'We're not going to have a repeat of last time, but I knew him well, Nathaniel. He was a good man, and like I said before, If I made you feel I thought otherwise, then I apologise. Your old man was a friend of mine, and he was one hell of a soldier. The last thing we want are special task forces and drug squads camped out in our backyards. Whatever happens, you need to distance yourself from the conflict.'

'That's weak.' Despite the words, Natty's tone was solemn. He knew Rudy was right, and it stung.

'It's smart. You're not a little runner anymore. You're not some crew chief either. For all intents and purposes, what happens in Little London is down to you. You're responsible for the area, but you need to think about the best ways to do things.'

Natty was conflicted. He understood what Rudy was saying, and liked the respect he'd shown his dad, but his father had truly lived the life. He had put people in the ground, and his reputation was top tier.

Natty thought about all the times his mum had brought up his dad. Sometimes, she sounded proud of his accomplishments, telling Natty his father had been a man among men, and someone that always handled his business.

At other times, she admonished him, saying he'd left her with nothing but a son, and that he was hot-headed and bloodthirsty, yet Natty was compared to him at every opportunity.

For a man trying to find his place in the world, that was confusing.

He put those thoughts to the side, stubbing out his cigarette in the ashtray in the middle of the coffee table.

'Warren started this,' he reminded Rudy. 'Not retaliating is a bad move.'

Rudy smiled. 'I'm not saying that you shouldn't retaliate. I'm saying there are numerous ways to handle the situation, and that you don't have to get your hands dirty.'

* * *

NATTY RETURNED HOME after his conversation with Rudy. He'd smoked several cigarettes, still on edge, waiting for any further news about Little London.

The talk with Rudy remained at the forefront of his mind. He'd absorbed what Rudy said, yet still felt the team needed to be more forceful in retaliating. That was the only thing Warren understood, and they needed to stop him before he gained too much momentum.

The longer the situation went on, the worse it would get for them.

Natty lit another cigarette, tempted to make a phone call, get some guns, and do the job himself. He sighed, cycling through numbers in his contacts, deciding who would be the best fit. Rather than call, Natty stubbed out the cigarette and stood, stretching. Rudy had more experience than he did — along with his uncle's ear. Natty would give him a chance, and not jump the gun.

With another sigh, he hoped this choice wouldn't lead to more bloodshed in Little London.

CHAPTER FIFTEEN

SPENCE SAT in a spot on Bankside Street near Roundhay Road. It was a quiet little area tucked away in a cul-de-sac. Around him, people came and went. Spence barely noticed, half-staring at an iPad, looking over his investment portfolio online.

In the corner of the room, a *younger* counted and banded money. Despite the turnover of people, no one made much noise. It was well known that Spence liked a quiet atmosphere.

Rubbing his stomach, Spence inwardly regretted the Caribbean takeaway he'd had earlier. As penance, he planned to go on an intense morning run to burn it off. Natty had contacted him earlier, but they hadn't spoken for long.

The situation in Little London was heating up, and Natty was right in the middle. Spence had heard through the grapevine about the kid dying from being stabbed. He wasn't happy that a young life had been snuffed out over something trivial. He'd popped in to see his dad earlier, who had tried pumping him for information about the conflict. He wanted Spence to get involved, stating it was an opportunity to grow.

Spence respected his dad's opinion, but had no intention of getting involved unless Natty dictated. It hadn't gone down well. Despite being a legal worker now, his dad had been heavily involved in the streets when Spence was younger, and had taught him numerous skills, including how to cut drugs and cook crack.

Still, despite his dad's experience, it didn't make him right, and Spence trusted Natty to get the right outcome.

Seeking a distraction, Spence closed the page he'd been perusing, checking Anika's Instagram page. He stopped at a photo of them from a new year's party, smiling and happy. He stared at it for a long moment. Anika had seemed distracted lately. Spence knew he had been working more, but wasn't sure if that was the cause of her moodiness. They hadn't argued, but she had given him the silent treatment multiple times. It never lasted long, but he'd considered addressing it with her, not wanting things to fester.

On the business front, Cameron had stayed out of his way, manning another spot near Markham Avenue, still embarrassed at Gavin's exposure. By all accounts, he seemed to now be taking things seriously. Spence hoped it lasted.

His phone beeped as he looked through more Instagram pages. He glanced at the screen, eyes widening when he saw it was from Rosie. He gawped at the message for a long moment, strangely giddy despite the platonic tones. Spence had known Rosie for a long time through Lorraine and her association with Natty. He'd had a massive crush on her back in the day, but she was always unavailable, having an ongoing relationship with an amateur boxer named Kyle. Kyle was currently locked up, having gotten caught up in an extortion scam.

Reading the message twice, Spence politely responded, wondering why Rosie had started texting him out of the blue. She'd had his number for years, and they had always been polite. The silly part of his brain wondered if she was after something more between them, then he immediately felt guilty when he thought about Anika.

Despite any issues they might have, he still loved her, and wanted the best for them.

Standing, he decided to go for a walk to clear his head, nodding at the diligent youngster still counting. After a moment's hesitation, he rooted around a nearby cupboard, taking out a small knife to carry, recognising they were going through tense times.

GOOD DEED, BAD DEEDS

* * *

DESPITE THE DRAMA, Little London was still surprisingly quiet just after 11 pm. On Fieldhead Terrace, there were a selection of newer model flats, with very few lights on at this time. A car drove down the road, stopping in front of a house on the street. After a moment, the windows wound down, and multiple shots were fired, finding homes in the brickwork, windows, and gardens.

Immediately, the car screeched away, leaving screams and panic in its wake.

* * *

THE NEXT DAY, police were on the scene canvassing, neighbours hanging as close to the scene as they dared. The bullet holes in the flat could clearly be seen, and the area was taped off whilst the investigation was ongoing.

Nearby, Natty sat in the passenger seat of a BMW, glaring at the scene. His nostrils flared, showcasing his anger. They weren't doing enough, and the fact Warren could shoot at one of their spots with impunity, was a telling sign.

'Our people already cleared out, right?' He said to the driver, who nodded.

'The day before yesterday. Warren's people must not have up-to-date info.'

'They're not gonna stop either way. They've already killed someone, and we look weak just sitting here,' snapped Natty, eyes narrowing. 'We're gonna need to pull people out if things continue to escalate.'

The driver didn't respond, likely not wanting to piss off Natty further. Natty considered some of the basic information Elijah had provided about Warren, namely about his personality, and the fact he was a loose cannon. A lot of the info Elijah collated was information Natty already had, just by doing the rounds and speaking to people in the area. It was a sign that Elijah was too far removed from the situation, and that needed to change.

To Natty, it seemed Elijah and Rudy were too passive to do what needed to be done.

Yet, they ranked him. They seemed to be on the same page and had a similar rapport, whereas Natty felt he came across as an aggressive outlier, which wasn't true. Either way, he wanted the situation handled.

'C'mon, let's go,' he finally ordered the driver, who pulled away from the scene.

* * *

ANIKA WAS HOME AFTER WORK, watching television while Spence cooked in the kitchen. She could hear him singing along to the rap songs he was playing, and despite her ever-switching mood, it still made her smile. Picking up her phone, she scrolled through her social media sites when she saw something that made her pause.

Cameron had been tagged in some photos. In several of them, he was all over a trashy-looking brunette in a short, tight dress with a truckload of makeup on her pointed face. Anika's eyes blurred as she glared at the picture. She didn't recognise the woman, but her blood boiled at the sight of Cameron kissing her neck.

Locking her phone, she wiped her eyes as Spence came into the room smiling. When he saw the expression on Anika's face, he paused.

'Are you okay?'

Anika nodded.

'It looks like you've been crying. Are you sure?'

'I said I'm fine. Just leave it,' snapped Anika. Spence stared her down, his jaw tightening.

'Don't speak to me like that. I was checking if you were okay, because you looked sad, and you've been moody lately. I won't bother next time.' He returned to the kitchen, leaving a guilty Anika staring after him. It wasn't his fault she felt this way. The last thing she needed to do was take out her anger with Cameron on her boyfriend.

After a moment, she followed Spence, putting her arms around him as he stood over the kitchen sink, his back and shoulders tense.

'I'm sorry, babe. I didn't mean to snap at you. It's just silly social media stuff, that's all. Nothing worth worrying over.'

Visibly relaxing, Spence turned, taking Anika in his arms and hugging her closely.

'You can talk to me anytime, Nika. Don't feel you have to hold things in.'

Anika gave him a watery smile, and then buried her head against his firm chest.

'I'll bear that in mind,' she murmured, her thoughts back on Cameron and his mystery woman.

SPENCE WASN'T WORKING the next day, nipping into the city centre to do some shopping. As he browsed running shoes in a sports store, he remembered the altercation he and Anika had the night before. He'd slept on it, but still didn't like the fact she had snapped at him, especially over something so trivial as social media drama. Something didn't sit right, but he wasn't sure what it was.

As he chose and paid for a pair of shoes, he headed to an outlet store, looking for some new shirts. Whatever stresses Anika was going through, he hoped she would eventually let him in. He wondered for a moment if it was work-related, but dismissed this, knowing she wouldn't lie if that was the case.

Spence was lost in his thoughts, sifting through shirts, when someone called his name. He turned, recognising the voice, his stomach immediately fluttering when he saw Rosie heading towards him, a broad smile on her face that he returned.

'Hey, Spence. What are you doing around here?' She asked, trailed by two women Spence didn't recognise. He nodded, trying not to focus on how good Rosie looked. She wore a light blue sundress that hugged her body nicely, her toned arms on full display. Her brown eyes were bright and intense, and she had a chiselled bone structure. He audibly swallowed, knowing he couldn't get caught up. Clutching his shopping bag ever tighter, he responded.

'Just doing some quick shopping.' He gestured to his bag. 'What are you doing around here?'

'Same thing. We needed some things, and this place has a great selection. How's Natty? I ran into him in a club a while back.'

'Natty's good. He's just doing his thing,' replied Spence, wondering why Natty hadn't mentioned running into Rosie. Deciding it wasn't important, he focused on Rosie as she took a step closer. He froze as she sniffed him, at the same time inhaling her powerful wildflowers scent.

'You smell good. What aftershave is that?'

'Just some Zara stuff,' Spence replied, his mouth dry. Rosie was gorgeous and had a presence. She had to know what she was doing to him, he mused, resisting the urge to step even closer to her.

'It suits you.' Her eyes roved over his frame. Behind her, one of her friends coughed, the pair having watched the exchange with amused grins. 'Looks like I need to go, but it was good running into you.' She put her arms around him, clutching him for a long moment before pulling away. 'We should hang out sometime. We can talk about investments or whatever.' She held his stare for a second, then gave him a wave and left with her friends.

Spence remained in the same spot staring after her, his cheeks hot and his heart pounding.

He wasn't quite sure what had just transpired. He'd known Rosie for a long time, but had never seen her so flirtatious. He blew out a breath, returning to his shopping, dropping Natty a quick text message. He knew his friend was busy, but this was Natty's domain, and he needed his advice.

* * *

NATTY WALKED into the Bankside hangout spot with a smile on his face. It wasn't often Spence reached out for help, and he figured this would be a good distraction from the mounting problems in Little London.

Several workers were dotted around, and they greeted Natty with hand slaps and grins. He made small talk, then sought out Spence, who was in the kitchen, pottering around the kettle. He motioned to the kettle, and Natty nodded. Spence fixed him a coffee, and Natty took it with thanks, remaining on his feet as Spence collapsed into a chair, sipping his own.

'You probably need that with everything going on,' said Spence, referring to Little London.

'We can talk about that later. What's on your mind.'

Spence simply said, 'Rosie.'

Natty chuckled.

'I need more than that to go on, bro.' Inwardly, he recalled Rosie asking about Spence, when he'd seen her in the club. It still tickled him.

Women were interesting, he mused.

'I don't even know what to say. She sent me a few text messages recently, then earlier today I ran into her in town, and she was just . . .'

'Just what . . .' Natty prompted.

'*On*. I dunno. She was really flirty, and she said we should chill sometime.' Spence sighed, taking another sip of his hot drink. Natty followed suit, surveying Spence with amusement. He was the last person Natty thought would ever go through woman drama.

'What exactly do you want to happen?' Natty asked.

'What do you mean?'

'Do you want something to happen with Rosie?'

Spence shot Natty a look, warming his hands on the coffee mug. 'I have a girl.'

'I'm aware of that. We both know if it was that simple, you wouldn't have reached out to me.'

'I love Anika,' Spence replied. Natty didn't respond. There was no need. After a long moment, Spence sighed.

'I used to like Rosie. A lot. You know that. I guess the problem is that I'm not sure of her intentions, and I get the impression pursuing a friendship would be dangerous.'

Natty nodded, finishing his coffee, enjoying the burn in his throat and chest. He placed the cup in the sink before he responded.

'Rosie's fine as hell. I get it. I bumped into her a while back, and she asked about you. She definitely has you on her mind.'

Spence rubbed his eyes, then finished his coffee. Natty surveyed him, again liking that this situation kept him from overthinking his own issues.

'Bro, I don't know what you want me to say,' he went on. 'You're a good guy, and you'll do the right thing. If you don't want anything to happen, then it won't.'

Spence nodded.

'I appreciate you listening, Nat. Keep this to yourself, please. I don't need Cam to jump on this and start his shit again.'

'I won't say anything,' Natty assured him. Both men mulled the situation in silence for a few minutes.

'What would you do if you were me?' Spence finally asked.

'I'd sleep with Rosie.'

Spence's eyebrow rose.

'Just like that?'

Natty nodded again.

'What if it was Lorraine instead of Anika? Would you do the same thing then?'

Natty flinched.

'What's that got to do with anything?'

'You already know.'

'Me and Lorraine are just cool. There's nothing like that going on.' Natty looked away.

'I don't believe you, and you know that. There are feelings there, and I don't think you would want to hurt her by cheating,' said Spence.

'I've cheated before,' Natty reminded him.

'Yes, when you were young and dumb. You've changed, even if you don't want to see it. Lorraine is different.'

'Whatever,' said Natty, waving him off. The last thing he needed was to get caught up thinking about Lorraine.

'Fine. We can leave that for now. Guess I've got some thinking to do. In the meantime, what's going on with your situation?'

Natty rubbed his forehead.

'I don't even know what to tell you. We're losing face in Little London, and it seems like no one else wants to do anything about it.'

'Who are we talking about? Rudy? Elijah?'

'Both of them. They're happy to sit around and do nothing while Warren shoots at and stabs my people. I don't think it's the right move.'

'What are you going to?'

Natty didn't immediately respond. He still wanted to get a gun and do the job himself. At the same time, he wasn't a killer. He'd never shot anyone before, and the murder of a known criminal would catapult him into the police spotlight.

'There's nothing to do for now. I'm gonna listen to Rudy and maintain my position.'

Spence smiled.

'I wasn't expecting that. I thought you'd wanna charge in and do damage.'

Natty chuckled, despite his thoughts.

'I'm trying my hardest not to.'

* * *

TWO DAYS LATER, Anika flounced into Cameron's place, plopping on the sofa and crossing her legs, arms folded as she glared at him. Cameron chuckled.

'You look happy.'

'How am I supposed to look?' She snapped.

'What's happened? Spence pissed you off?'

'It's not about Spence,' she replied. 'It's about you.'

'What about me?' Cameron mockingly covered his mouth in shock.

'What the hell were you doing in town with that little slut?'

Cameron frowned. 'Have you been spying on me?'

'What? Course I haven't. You were tagged in a picture, and it popped up on my feed. Stop avoiding the question.'

'I don't need to avoid the question. You know exactly what I was doing.'

Anika shook her head. 'I can't believe you.'

'Why not?'

'We're supposed to have something. Why else would you stalk me in the club, mentioning *Fiji*, seeking me out?'

Cameron chuckled, the fact he wasn't taking her seriously only making her angrier. She didn't know what it would take to get him to understand how she was feeling.

She was sharply reminded of how things had been back in the day for them. Cameron had a wandering eye and would often flirt with girls around her and either play dumb, or downplay it later. She wondered what she expected from him, and why she was so surprised that he couldn't change.

'Don't laugh. It's not funny.' Anika threw up her hands.

'Depends where you're sitting, I guess. I think it's hilarious.'

Anika scowled. 'Did you sleep with her?'

'Does it matter if I did or not?'

'That's a *yes* then,' scoffed Anika.

'It doesn't matter to you if I did or not. You have a man. You're living with one of my best friends. Are you really going to pretend nothing is going on with you? Are you going to lie and say you're not grinding Spence?'

Anika's mouth fell open at the sight of Cameron's outburst. She wondered just how affected he was at the fact she was in a relationship with Spence. She started to think he had been hiding his feelings for a long time, and that the truth was slipping out.

'You approached me, Cam. Not the other way around. I didn't tell you to come up to me in the club and try sweet-talking me, did I?'

'You were fucking eager for it, though. You have been all along, because you knew we had unfinished business. That unfinished business had you coming all over my dick, didn't it?'

'Is that all it was about? Sex?'

'No, but we *did* have sex. You *did* cheat on your man, and now you're acting all confused and mad, but if you're really serious . . . if you're really about it, then break up with him.'

'What?' Anika gasped.

'Don't act like you didn't hear me. Dump him. Tell him you don't love him, move out of the spot, because I know it's all in his name, and move on.'

'Move on with you?'

Cameron shook his head. 'This ain't about me. This is about you.

There's a connection with us. Fucking lights up every time we're around one another, but I can't be your excuse to do what it is you wanna do in life. Have you ever actually been single?'

'What does that have to do with anything?'

'It has everything to do with everything. You just don't see it. We're not a couple, so you can't get mad at me for being around other women, especially ones that I *may* or *may not* fuck. That's none of your business, so figure your shit out and don't try to take it out on me.'

Anika's mouth opened and closed, unable to believe the way Cameron had sounded off on her. The worst thing was that he was right about everything.

Anika was confused about many things she wanted from life, but she was sure about one thing: she didn't want to be alone. Spence loved her and provided, and he was the ideal partner. She wished she felt the same way about him, but she didn't, and that hurt. She had allowed her emotions to override her logic. She couldn't demand anything of Cameron.

The smart thing to do would be to simply leave; to walk away from the good sex and the mind games, and the lack of respect, and go home to the relationship, and the arms of a man that she never had to doubt loved her.

Shooting to her feet, she headed for the door. Cameron watched. As she grasped the handle, he spoke.

'Fine. Walk out on me. I knew you didn't care.'

Anika whirled round, eyes blazing.

'Can you stop? You don't give a fuck about anything but yourself. How dare you try and guilt trip me after the way you've acted?'

Cameron sighed.

'Just go, Anika. I won't try to stop you.'

The pair stared at one another, Anika's heart crashing against her chest. She knew the sensible thing to do was to walk away from Cameron, but that didn't make it any easier.

She didn't know much about Cameron's life or upbringing and wanted to learn more.

What made him tick? What caused his issues with women, and why had he never been able to give himself to her?

Her head and heart once again battled for supremacy, and once again, her heart won. She sat back down, and Cameron sat next to her. He reached out to put his arm around her, but she resisted, shifting out of reach. Cameron nudged himself closer to her once more. He looked her in the eyes and kissed her on the cheek, heating the area. She melted into his arms, and he kissed her, working her neck as the intensity grew.

Before long, Anika was naked. Placing her hand on Cameron's chest, she pushed him down onto the sofa, climbing on top of him, slowly moving her hips backwards and forwards. Cameron reared up, digging his fingers into her back and placing his mouth around her nipple, biting so hard that Anika hissed. As her climax neared, her pace quickened. Cameron reciprocated, driving into her, urging her to finish. When it came, she threw her head back as she let everything go, the climax washing over her body, leaving her shuddering and twitching against him as he held her tightly.

'You'll never forget what I can do to you,' he mumbled against her ear. He gave her a few seconds of recovery, then chased his own finish.

Anika panted afterwards, trying to catch her breath. She met Cameron's eyes and shook her head, feeling like shit, but not immediately regretting what they had done.

Cameron had controlled her body. He'd given her an intense climax and taken what he wanted in return.

A wave of overwhelming guilt cascaded through her. Spence didn't deserve this. He deserved something better, and she thought about what Cameron had said; the possibility of breaking up with Spence.

She couldn't imagine being on her own, though.

Anika wondered if Cameron would even want her if she broke up with Spence, and it disgusted her that she didn't know the answer. Cameron had a friendship with Spence, and they were all in business together. She couldn't imagine him doing anything that would piss off Natty — knowing Natty was the glue that held their clique together. She recalled the suspicion in his eyes when she'd stupidly asked him if he was happy.

If Natty spoke up, would either of them even keep her around?

It was a terrifying thought, and she hated herself a little more for being so selfish.

Cameron stood and left the room, still naked. He didn't seem particularly bothered or chastened by what had happened. She looked down, realising she needed to clean herself up, deciding she would get a shower, whether Cameron said it was okay or not.

CHAPTER SIXTEEN

WARREN SAT UP IN BED, smoking a spliff, content and mellow. His woman of the hour lay next to him, rolled on her side, hair splayed over the pillow. He looked at her with a little smirk, satisfied with his surroundings. He was in a shithole spot, but it had three of his most trusted people watching downstairs, all armed.

Warren was ready to escalate things further. He knew of Natty and Elijah's plans to carve up Little London. Even before they reached out for a meeting, he'd heard all about their people sniffing around the area. He was pleased with how he'd handled them, and had no intention of working with them. It was a simple situation, and he had absolutely nothing to lose.

Warren knew Natty and Elijah's reputations were solid, but they tended to keep themselves out of the limelight. Knowing he had solidified his reputation, he hoped that meant theirs had taken a hit in the process.

The woman climbed from the bed, sashaying toward the bathroom. Warren watched her as she walked. She was better than his usual sort, with a slim build, dark hair, and Mediterranean features. Fuelled by drugs and drink, she'd given him the best sex of his life. He'd even ignored some of his regulars, making more time for the one woman who could give him what the others couldn't. If needed, he could get them back later.

If you had enough cash and reputation, women were easy.

Killing the spliff, he messed around on his phone. When she came out of the bathroom, he glared at her.

'What the hell were you doing in there?' His voice was low, and his eyes searching. He expected her to shy away as his women often did when they saw him flip the switch, but instead, she shrugged, fixing her hair, which she'd put into a simple ponytail.

'I wanted to look nice.'

Grumbling, Warren pushed past her and left the room to go to the bathroom. He washed his hands when he was done, looking at his face in the mirror with distaste. He needed to get a few good nights' sleep. He was slacking and didn't want to get caught unprepared.

Maybe he needed to take this girl away; leave the streets in the hands of his people. It wasn't like Natty or Elijah were making any moves against him.

After a few minutes, he re-entered the bedroom, ready for another round. His girl was gone, though. Frowning, Warren glanced around the bedroom, but saw no sign of her things. Collapsing back on the bed, he closed his eyes, choosing to push the sight out of his mind. She was pretty, but high maintenance. If she wanted to cut out, he wouldn't chase her.

He messed around on his phone and took a call from one of his youngsters. They were all armed with knives, just in case Natty and Elijah got cute and retaliated.

'What's going on out there?' He asked.

'It's quiet. Few fiends around, but no one from the other side.'

'Make sure you keep your eyes peeled. They might come for you at any time.'

'Can't I get any backup?'

'You don't need backup. Those lot are soft. Give it a few more days and they'll be out of here.'

The youth didn't speak. Warren's eyes narrowed. He could sense fear, and he hated it. Fear was weakness. Worse than fear, though, was insubordination.

'You wanna come and speak to me face-to-face?'

His voice was as low and dangerous as it had been with his girl. The youth folded.

'Nah, Warren. I've got it covered. You don't need to worry about me.'

'I better not have to. I'm gonna send someone out later to check on you, and you better be where you're supposed to, or we'll have that face-to-face. Understand?'

'Yeah, boss. I understand.'

Warren ended the call. Clambering to his feet, he went to go and see what his crew was doing. They would have seen her go, and he wanted to know if she had said anything first.

'Oi,' he said, traipsing down the creaky stairs, 'where did that girl go?' No one responded. He'd spoken clearly enough for them to hear him over the television, and they'd ignored him. 'Oi, don't fucking ignore me,' he snapped, storming into the room. 'Yo—'

Warren froze. His team slumped in their seats, bullet holes in their heads. They had been shot and left where they were.

Warren's eyes widened, his pulse racing. His mouth fell open, unable to comprehend what had happened. Coming to his senses he turned on his heel and rushed upstairs, adrenaline surging. He dove under the bed and pulled up with his gun in his hand. He made sure it was loaded, then ran back downstairs, gun at the ready, willing to shoot whoever had invaded his spot. He hadn't heard a thing.

How had this happened?

The television was loud, but this kind of commotion should have cut through.

He checked the remaining downstairs rooms, glancing around the kitchen, but nothing was out of the ordinary. He was amped. It had to be Natty and Elijah. They hadn't had the guts to come for him, instead cowardly taking out his people.

Deep in his thoughts, he heard a creak from behind. Instincts kicking in, he whirled around, but he wasn't quick enough. He saw a movement and felt immense pain as something sliced into his throat. Instinctively, he pulled the trigger, missing the woman. She rubbed her ears as he slid to the floor. He tried to lift the gun, but he was fading.

The last thing he saw before the end, was her calmly watching him bleed out.

The killer waited over a minute, watching Warren twitch. Her ears still rang from the sound of the blast, but that was her fault for being sloppy. She'd had the drop on him all night, and had played with him rather than finishing him straight away. Clarke would be annoyed, but she could deal with that.

Putting the knife away, she stepped over Warren and left the house, keeping her head down to prevent identification. Not that she was worried. Warren and his people hadn't known much about her, and she wouldn't get a pull from the authorities. She was two streets away before she made the call to get picked up.

* * *

NEWS OF WARREN'S murder spread through Little London and the Hood, sending a message to everyone, his crew included. The viciousness of the murder gripped the streets, and everyone had a theory about who was responsible.

Natty's name seemed to be brought up regularly. People were aware of the beef they'd had, and it didn't surprise him when police picked him up within a couple of days of the murder.

After having his belongings taken, he was sent to a cell after the custody sergeant was made aware of the charge. He stewed there, with his own theories over what had transpired.

The level of destruction involved and the lack of physical evidence suggested it was one of his uncle's killers. Natty recalled the expression Rudy had worn when speaking of Natty not getting his hands dirty. He had arranged this and used it to send the message. It was spectacular work, but Natty only hoped it wasn't the catalyst for him going to jail.

After a few hours, he was taken to an interview room. His solicitor was with him by now, and had been made aware of the facts of the case. As Natty entered the room, he thought about the last time he had been in one. Years ago, he and Cameron had been arrested on suspicion of assault. They were guilty, but the charges had been dropped, and they'd left without issue.

The room had beige walls, with a sturdy dark brown table, a recording device on said table, and metal chairs in the middle of the room. It reeked of cleaning solution and a lingering cigarette smell that made Natty's eyes narrow. He didn't understand how it could still smell of cigarettes, as smoking indoors hadn't been permitted in years. Despite the stale odour, he wished he had one.

Two officers entered the room — a man and a woman. Natty kept his eyes on the man — on the slight side, with receding, strawberry blond hair, and pockmarked skin. He maintained his cool, knowing he couldn't flinch or show weakness. Glancing at his solicitor, his gaze flitted back to the officers.

'Interview commencing at four twelve pm, present are myself, DS Lowther, DS Calrick, the suspect, Nathaniel Dunn, and his legal counsel,' said the woman — DS Lowther, after turning on the tape recorder. She had a slight hunch, dark brown hair, and visible crow's feet, wearing a blue blouse and dark trousers. Calrick sat in the corner, keeping his eyes on Natty.

'Nathaniel, you have already been informed that you are being held in connection with the murder of Warren Bull, which took place on Friday, 10 April 2020.'

Natty didn't react. He focused on Calrick, whose eyes bore into his, probably hoping to intimidate him.

'We are aware of the problems between yourself and Warren Bull. There was known bad blood, and we also know threats were made on both sides.'

'I'd suggest you ask a question, rather than speculating,' Natty's solicitor interjected.

'Did you know Mr Bull, Nathaniel?' Lowther didn't miss a beat.

'No comment,' replied Natty.

'Where were you on the night of Friday, 10 April 2020?'

'No comment.'

Lowther and Calrick shared a look. Lowther wiped a lock of hair from her face.

'Can anyone confirm your whereabouts on the night in question?'

'Which night again?' Asked Natty.

'The night of Friday 10 April 2020,' repeated Lowther.

Natty paused, eyes again flitting between the pair. He opened his mouth, then closed it. Lowther leant forward in her seat.

'Mr Dunn?'

Natty's eyes locked on hers, and he replied, 'no comment.'

Lowther slammed down her notebook and shot to her feet. Natty's solicitor leaned back in his chair, eyes glittering.

'Is that all, officers?'

Without directly responding, Lowther turned off the recorder.

'Interview terminated at four-twenty pm.'

'Thank you for your time and patience, officers,' said Natty's solicitor, his tone smug. 'Ensure that any further contact or questions are directed to my office. Please and thank you.'

* * *

NATTY GAVE it a day for things to cool off before he reached out to Rudy, who predictably already knew about his arrest. They met in public this time, returning to the pub Rudy had previously taken him to. It was midday, and they forwent pints, Rudy settling for a coke, Natty a lemonade.

'How are you?' Rudy got to the point after a cursory glance around the pub. Several regulars were in, making a lot of noise with their loud conversations.

'I'm good. Got a bit worried for a minute after what happened.'

Rudy's eyebrow rose. 'Why were you worried? You didn't do anything.'

'Wouldn't be the first time the feds have locked up the wrong person. Can't believe you handled it like that, though.'

'How did you expect it to be handled?'

Natty shrugged, sipping his drink. 'Guess I just thought you'd be more subtle about it, not be dropping bodies and knifing people.'

'The message is important.'

Natty met his eyes. 'Do you think I could have sent the same message?'

'Did you want to?'

Making a noise, Natty looked away. Rudy had a knack for getting under his skin, and he swore he did it on purpose.

'Nathaniel, I wanted you removed from the situation. I made that clear. And now, you've been picked up, and they know you had nothing to do with it. You were protected from the outcome.'

'Was it always the plan to deal with him like that?'

Rudy nodded.

'Did Elijah know?'

Rudy again nodded. As much as Natty wanted to flip out, he kept his composure. He wasn't going to storm out like he had the last time.

'What is the point in me being the guy over in Little London if I'm left out of the decisions? You could have asked me for my opinion.'

'If I had, you would have insisted that you do it.'

'So what if I had? Do you not think I'm capable?'

'I don't *want* you to be capable.' Rudy's voice remained level, but his eyes blazed. 'Don't you get that? I don't want you to do that sort of stuff. You don't need to.'

'What does my Unc think?'

Rudy picked up his drink, avoiding the question. Natty sighed. Rudy was hard work.

'What did Elijah think?' Natty tried again.

'He knew we could get it done.'

'Is that it?' Natty's brow furrowed. Elijah was a boss and, outside of Little London, had a solid reputation and a lot of weight. He couldn't imagine him simply going along with the plan.

Rudy shook his head.

'Son, you need to learn to see beyond the obvious. Elijah is successful because he knows when to be involved and delegate. Why piss all over the territory if you know someone you're in business with can do something better? He doesn't want the attention. He wants the business.'

'So, you want me to be thinking like Elijah?' Natty took a sip of his drink.

'I want you to go far beyond Elijah, and beyond me. Learn to use your reputation to work for you, instead of feeling you have to do things for the sake of it. You're doing great work, and I'm seeing the moves you're making. Just take it easy.'

Natty nodded, still annoyed, but at least understanding Rudy's position.

'Who did it?'

'We have people to handle wet work. Heed my words, Nathaniel . . . you don't need to do that.'

Both men silently mulled over the conversation. Natty considered the situation. He'd wanted to go right at Warren, but struggled to piece a plan together because he couldn't get to him — he was too well guarded. The murder was methodical; within days, someone had managed to infiltrate and systematically eliminate everyone in the spot. It showed how a professional truly worked.

Natty wondered about that. Initially, he felt inadequate that he couldn't get the job done. Despite that, it wasn't his skill set. Rudy wanted him to distance himself, and he could accept that was the right decision.

Natty rubbed his eyebrow, deciding to move past it. It had happened; a major pain had been removed. The police would move on, and Little London would now be theirs with little issue.

Natty wondered what was next for the coalition, and what plans the bigwigs were cooking up. He decided not to ask Rudy directly, instead wondering why he seemed so determined to protect him. Rudy was involved with his mum, but it wasn't like he needed Natty's approval. He'd schooled him from an early age, and even when Natty's dad had been alive, Rudy would see him on the streets, give him money, and tell him to stay in school.

Amid his musings, he thought about his uncle, and his lack of involvement in proceedings. Despite Rudy avoiding the question, Natty knew his uncle had given the order, and that he'd likely dictated how he wanted the murders to go down. Rudy had indicated his uncle knew of his movements, but Natty didn't know if that was a good or a bad thing, nor what his uncle's intentions for him were, other than to bring in as much money as possible.

Natty took a deep breath, inwardly calming himself. His job was to make money and elevate his people, so he would focus on that. He had work to do, and decided he would speak with Elijah later, then get started in Little London again.

With a plan in place, Natty found he felt much better, and he and Rudy eventually went for lunch, business talk finished for the time being.

* * *

NATTY WAS home after his conversation with Rudy, staring aimlessly at the television. He'd received a few text messages from acquaintances, trying to pump him for information about the Warren murder. Natty had ignored the majority, and downplayed it with the few he responded to. He wasn't going to fuel any gossip, or attempts at gaining clout from his name.

Warren was gone, and Natty needed to think about his next move.

Dozing off, he was awoken by a loud banging at the front door. Tensing, he hurried to his feet, moving swiftly to the door. Cameron stood there with a big smile on his face. They touched fists, and Natty stepped aside.

'Heard you've had a busy time,' he said.

Natty chuckled.

'That's one way to describe it.'

'What happened? You should have reached out.'

'Wasn't time. Whatever happened to Warren, I wasn't involved,' explained Natty.

Cameron's eyes narrowed.

'Little London is your thing, though. You're the guy down there. How could you not be involved?'

As Cameron was talking, it struck Natty just how long it had been since he'd chilled with his friend. A lot had happened, and they hadn't hung out as much since Natty had become the point man. He sat on the sofa, rubbing his eyes. Cameron sat on a nearby chair, hands behind his head, waiting for Natty to talk.

'Rudy wanted me to stay out of it, probably so that if I was picked up, I wouldn't know anything, which is exactly what happened.'

'And you don't know who dropped Warren?'

Natty shook his head. He wasn't on first-name terms with any of the killers his uncle had on the payroll, and figured it was best that way.

'It could have been you, though. Your name would have been ringing out if you'd done it.'

'My name was already ringing out,' Natty dryly responded. 'The Feds picked me up, remember? They thought I was the one who did it.'

'You should have called me, bro. I would have done it for you.'

'Just like that?' Natty raised an eyebrow, watching Cameron emphatically nod and puff out his chest.

'Course.'

Natty again thought to when he'd wanted to directly attack Warren. Ultimately, he was glad he hadn't.

'I don't think it would be as easy as you think. Warren had like six people guarding him, and they all got killed too. I don't know anyone that could get in and out like that unharmed.'

Cameron scratched his chin. 'Maybe . . . still, would have been a great way to prove myself.'

'Prove yourself to who? Rudy?' Natty asked. 'The bosses like things quiet. That's what I've learnt.'

'How can you say that? You just said they dropped Warren and all his people. What's quiet about that?'

'Warren had his chances to back away, and he didn't. I guess a message needed to be sent.'

'Exactly. And I could have been the one to send it.' Cameron's nostrils flared. Natty finally realised just how annoyed Cameron was about the situation. He didn't understand.

'You have enough to think about, without trying to become a shooter,' he said.

'What do you mean by that?' Cameron visibly flinched, eyes widening for a moment. Natty noticed, but didn't comment.

'I heard about the situation with Gavin.'

Cameron scowled.

'Spence been telling tales, has he?'

'No. There was a room full of people when you confronted him, Cam. Spence doesn't have to run and tell me anything.'

'It doesn't matter.' Cameron waved a hand. 'He violated and got dealt with.'

'He violated on *your* watch. You wanted to step up. You sulked because I picked Spence, and then you're letting people rob the team right in front of you?'

'It wasn't like that. He was sneaky.' Cameron's jaw jutted.

'Doesn't matter. The fact is, it makes us look bad. You're talking about the message, and how people see us . . . how they see you. You can't let things like that happen again.'

Cameron looked away, breathing hard. Natty assessed him, wondering if Cameron could have pulled the trigger, the way he seemed to think. He wasn't sure. Cameron had heart, but he was often led by emotion. Natty couldn't see him executing a plan to take out a room full of people by himself, nor did he think that was bad.

Natty rubbed his cheek, thinking of the difference that had cropped up between them. He hadn't wanted to take out Warren for the name. He'd seen it as the only viable way to resolve the situation.

'Let's just forget it. It's done. Warren is gone, and you lot sorted Gav.' He climbed to his feet. 'Let's get a drink. We haven't chilled in time.'

* * *

WITH WARREN and most of his team out of the way, business went on. The police continued half-heartedly searching for the killers, widening their list of suspects, with several dumb outfits claiming credit for the job.

After laying low for a few days, Natty put it behind him and visited Julie in Little London again, holding a football. She noticed, but didn't comment. The interior was unchanged from his last visit, just as untidy, with the kids making as much noise as ever. He declined Julie offering him a drink.

'See! When I offer you a drink, you don't take one. Don't talk to me about *dehydration* this time.' Julie's eyes twinkled as she grinned. Natty laughed.

'What's the word on what happened to Warren?'

Julie smiled.

'Apparently, he got too big for his boots and tried it on with the wrong people. No one's crying about what happened, let's put it that way.'

Natty nodded.

'He messed with a lot of people, but we move on. Are you ready to go to work?'

'Yeah, I've got some others interested now too.' She handed Natty a piece of paper with several addresses hastily written down. Natty pocketed it, leaving two twenty-pound notes on the table. Julie raised an eyebrow.

'Business drying up or something?' She said.

Smirking, Natty put a couple more twenties down. He liked the fact she had come out of her shell.

'Someone will visit you every week with your wages. I'm gonna give you the number of your contact. You see or hear anything, contact them,' he told her.

Julie ran a hand through her hair.

'Won't you be coming around anymore?'

Natty hid his distaste. Julie sounded almost sad, and he hoped she didn't imagine something would happen between them. Nonetheless, he gave her a little smile. If it kept her motivated, he was all for it.

'I'm sure I'll be stopping by now and then, but I want to make us all as much money as possible. The team does better, then we all do better. Stack some money, and then maybe you can see about moving into a better spot. For now, keep working and let your kids play out. Give them this.' He handed her the football.

CHAPTER SEVENTEEN

THE DAY after hanging out with Cameron, Natty's mind was back on Spence and his dilemma with Rosie. Warren's murder had taken precedence, but with normality restored, he wondered what his friend would do. As Natty had said, the fact Spence needed Natty's advice, despite being in a relationship, was a sign he was conflicted about how to move.

If Natty was honest, he wanted it to happen. His instincts told him there was something wrong with Spence's relationship with Anika. He wasn't against it for the same reasons as Cameron. He didn't think it had changed Spence or made him soft, but he didn't think his friend was being honest about his feelings.

Natty wasn't a fan of Anika. He could get along with her for Spence's sake, but he'd never forgiven her for hopping from Cameron to Spence. At the same time, he was equally as bad because he'd never told Spence, and now, over a year later, he had to live with the same lie.

Rosie was cool. He knew her well through Lorraine, and the pair had a solid friendship. She was refreshing, spoke her mind, and seemed to have more energy than Anika, who seemed disengaged most of the time.

As he made himself a drink, he considered how complex the situation was. Spence had liked Rosie for the longest, then he'd got a girlfriend, and now she was chasing after him. If it was another woman, he'd think they were messing around just to disrupt the situation, but Natty didn't think Rosie was like that and was prepared to listen to his instincts.

He wondered what Spence would do about Rosie, if anything.

After finishing his drink and making a few phone calls, Natty called Lorraine. He would need to go down and sort a few loose ends in Little London now that things were dying down, but he wanted to talk to her.

'Hey Natty,' she said, upon picking up. 'How are you?'

'I'm good,' he replied, gratified that she seemed happy to hear from him. 'This is gonna sound weird, but has Rosie said anything to you about Spence?'

When Lorraine started giggling, Natty had his answer.

'Next time you stop by, we can talk about it.'

'What are you doing now?'

* * *

BEFORE LONG, Natty was camped on Lorraine's sofa. Jaden was staying at a friend's house, and consequently, Lorraine seemed more relaxed. She was casually dressed in a vest top and leggings. Whilst Natty built a spliff, she went to make drinks.

Soon, *Maxwell* played in the background. Lorraine had lit some incense, the vibe extremely mellow. They took turns with the joint, Natty laughing as Lorraine coughed when she first inhaled. He leant back on the sofa after a while, realising that just being in the house and being around Lorraine, had drastically improved his mood. For the time being, his troubles had vanished.

'How have you been?' He asked. 'I know I haven't checked you in a while, but it's been hectic.'

Lorraine smiled, nodding. 'I get that. I've been good, but I've missed you. Guess sometimes I forget just how used I am to you being around.'

Natty grinned at her words.

'I'll be around a lot more. Things were going on that have mostly been sorted out now.'

'I heard you got arrested.'

Natty wasn't shocked. The tale had done the rounds, especially immediately after Warren's murder.

'I got questioned about something that happened, but they let me go.'

Lorraine didn't delve any deeper, which Natty was thankful for.

'Jaden will be happy you're going to be around more,' she remarked.

Natty felt a rush of warm energy seeping through his body, happy that Jaden and Lorraine wanted him around, and privately resolving to do something nice for the kid.

'What are you saying about Rosie, though?'

Lorraine coyly smiled, then sipped her drink. Natty followed suit. He didn't enjoy the taste of green tea, but wouldn't make a fuss.

'She didn't see what was right in front of her.'

'Meaning Spence?' Natty pressed. Lorraine nodded.

'You know about her situation back then. Kyle made it hard for her to be around anyone, even me.'

Natty tensed. He'd never liked Rosie's ex. Kyle had a woman-beating reputation for years that no one ever called him out on. Natty had fought him at a party over ten years ago. He didn't remember why, but recalled it getting broken up before he could hurt him too badly.

'Do you think she's only interested because Spence has a girl?'

Instantly, Lorraine shook her head, adjusting her position on the sofa. Natty fought to remain looking at her face, not wanting to be distracted by her cleavage peeking out of her top.

'Rosie isn't like that. She's had a thing for Spence for a while. I don't think him getting with his partner has anything to do with that. They just click, and she thought it would go away, but I guess her feelings have only grown stronger. She mentioned running into him in town recently and said there was chemistry between them.'

Natty mulled over what Lorraine had said. They killed the spliff and sipped their drinks, the silence comforting.

'He's loyal to Anika. I can't see him straying, even for someone as fine as Rosie,' Natty finally replied.

Lorraine elbowed him, rolling her eyes.

'You're shameless.'

'Don't get me wrong, I'd still rather have you,' said Natty. Lorraine couldn't hide the smile that appeared on her face. With all their ups and downs, there was no denying the good times she and Natty had shared. Especially in the older, pre-Jaden days.

Natty always had a presence about him, and the chemistry between the pair was palpable. They were more like friends nowadays, but the feelings were still there.

Lorraine wasn't sure they would ever go away.

'Can I ask you something?' Lorraine finally said.

'Of course.'

'Do you like Spence's girl? I know you've mentioned Cam seems to have a problem with her in the past, but you've never said how you feel.'

Natty didn't hesitate to respond.

'I don't like her,' he said, thinking back to his earlier thoughts, and the effect he felt she had on Spence. Lorraine's eyes widened.

'Just like that?'

'I don't trust her, and I'm not sure she has Spence's best interests at heart.'

'Why don't you tell him that?'

'It's not a conversation you can have with your boy. Not without being able to back it up with anything.' Natty blew out a breath. 'What do you think Rosie is going to do? I heard she was talking about them wanting to chill.'

Lorraine smirked.

'Rosie's not going to back down. I don't know her plan, but I'm sure about that. Spence needs to watch himself around her if the chemistry is there like she says it is.'

* * *

THAT NIGHT, Spence cooked for Anika. When they'd finished eating, he gathered the plates and cutlery to wash up. Anika went to take a shower.

Spence took his time, enjoying the mundane act. It allowed him time to think, and he liked the solitude. He was almost finished when his phone buzzed. Anika entered the kitchen as he was reading the message. Her hair was wrapped in a towel, and she wore a red dressing gown. She grabbed a teabag and plopped it into a cup.

'Who's texting you?'

Spence didn't lie.

'Rosie.'

Anika's eyes narrowed, forgetting about her drink.

'*Rosie* who?'

'She's a friend of Lorraine's. I knew her from back in the day,' said Spence.

'Back in the day before me?'

Spence nodded.

'I'm not sure why that matters, but yeah.'

Anika folded her arms, her cup abandoned on the table.

'Why is she texting you?'

'She was seeing what I was doing. I ran into her in town, and she mentioned we should chill sometime.'

'*She wants you to chill with her . . .*' Anika's voice was cool. Too cool.

'We have things in common. Like investments,' Spence said, knowing from Anika's demeanour that she was close to exploding. Though he didn't say it out loud, he realised it was the most emotion he had seen from her in a while.

Anika shook her head. 'You can't be serious. You're standing there telling me about some woman you used to know texting you, wanting to chill with you, and that's all you have to say?'

'You asked, and I answered, Nika. I don't get why you're reacting like this, but you know me. I'm not like that.'

'Does she know you have a girlfriend?' Anika ignored Spence's comments.

'Yes. Of course she does. Would you like to read the messages?'

Even in her rapidly angered state, Anika recognised how petty it would be to say *yes*.

'Just do what you want, Spence. If you want to hang out with some random girl, just do it. See if I care.'

'What is your problem? I didn't say I was going to hang out with her. I was just telling you what she said.'

'Like I said. Do what you want,' said Anika venomously. She went to leave.

'Get back in here.'

Something in Spence's tone stalled Anika. She turned to look at him, taken aback by the fury lining Spence's face. Anika had never seen him like this before, and was unprepared.

'I . . .'

'It's my turn to speak —' Spence cut her off. 'You asked who texted me. I told you. I was honest about the conversation, so don't you dare try to turn this on me and invent a scenario where there isn't one. Have I ever given you any reason not to trust me? Am I the one that doesn't want to have certain conversations, or is that you?'

Anika's mouth fell open, still unable to deal with Spence's anger. The fact he was still speaking in a quiet tone somehow made his words even more effective.

'I'm sorry,' she said after a moment, moving towards him, taking his hands in hers. 'I didn't mean to overreact. I just got jealous at the thought of some other woman being around you.'

Spence sighed, his anger dissipating. He hadn't meant to lose his temper with Anika, and now that he had, he wondered why, and if this was brought on by the fact he felt something for Rosie and liked talking to her. Not wanting to think about it anymore, he brought Anika in for a hug, clutching her tightly in the middle of the kitchen.

* * *

PUTTING his conversation with Lorraine about Spence and Rosie aside for now, Natty sewed up the business in Little London. The police presence had dissipated, and Natty took full advantage, reaching out to several smaller gangs, who came under the umbrella of Natty and Elijah in exchange for a discount on product.

With the streets working in tandem, the money quickly shot up for Natty, and within a month, he was earning far more than he'd ever made in his previous role.

* * *

SPENCE PULLED to a stop outside Cameron's house, yawning as he killed the engine. The last month had been interesting. When the tension died down, and the dust settled, Spence and Anika spoke openly about his friendship with Rosie.

Since then, he'd hung out with Rosie several times. Though there was evident sexual tension, nothing untoward had happened with them. Rosie was well learned and funny, and they always seemed to have something new to talk about. The conversation never felt forced, and they had history they could fall back on.

Spence had considered introducing her to Anika, but had decided against it.

Cameron let him in, and they touched fists. Spence entered Cameron's living room. It had been a while since he'd visited, but the large new television encompassing most of the wall caught his eye. He glanced at Cameron, taking in what looked like a brand-new black Gucci sweatsuit. Spence didn't comment. What Cameron did with his money was his business.

'Here you go,' Cameron handed Spence a packet of money. 'I was gonna have one of the youngers drop it off tomorrow.'

'It's fine,' replied Spence. Cameron disappeared into the kitchen, returning with a bottle of Courvoisier, motioning to Spence.

'Fancy a drink? We haven't chilled in a while.'

'Sounds good,' said Spence, privately unable to remember the last time the pair had hung out without Natty being present. Cameron poured them glasses of brandy, and they clinked glasses and drank, Spence savouring his, whilst Cameron downed his own. The brandy burnt his throat, but he enjoyed the feeling, allowing Cameron to top his glass up before he'd even finished.

'That's my lot. I'm driving.'

'We'll see,' replied Cameron, smirking. 'How've you been?'

'Everything is golden right now. Business is booming, and we're all making more money. The other gangs don't want any static, so there's no major drama.'

Cameron nodded. 'You're right. The other spots are clicking. What about your missus? Everything good?' Usually, he wouldn't bring up Anika around Spence unless he was teasing him, but he hadn't seen much of Anika since she had confronted him about the girl he'd been caught in the picture with.

Cameron had seen the girl multiple times since, but in the past month, he had only hooked up with Anika twice, wondering if Spence had something to do with it.

As Cameron sat there, he felt a trickle of guilt. Spence was his closest friend other than Natty, and he'd willingly sought out and slept with a woman he knew Spence was in love with. He swallowed his conflicting feelings, pouring himself a small glass of vodka from a nearby bottle.

'How's Anika doing with your promotion?'

Spence surveyed Cameron for a long moment, trying to work out if he was being funny. He shrugged.

'She's up and down about it. One minute she seems happy, and the next, she's miserable. I'm not sure what else I can do, but sometimes things just feel wrong.'

'Wrong how?'

'It doesn't always feel like she's invested in the relationship.'

Cameron was surprised to find his heart beating faster at these words.

'Have you considered ending it?'

Spence's eyes narrowed.

'Why would I?'

It was Cameron's turn to shrug.

'If you think she's not feeling it, and this is your life, then I dunno . . .' he trailed off.

Spence rubbed his chin.

'We've both sacrificed for the relationship. If I can fix it, I will.'

Spence hesitated, debating whether to share what had happened with Anika last month. He regretted speaking to her about Rosie. They'd gone back to normal, but there was a barrier in place, and Spence wasn't sure who'd erected it.

'We argued a while back,' he finally said.

'Who did?'

'Me and Anika.'

Cameron fought down his glee. Anika hadn't said anything to him.

Other than sex and a little pillow talk, they hadn't delved into the parameters of their situation, which Cameron was glad for.

'What did you argue about?'

Spence rubbed his forehead. 'I told her that I was thinking of chilling with Rosie.'

'Which Rosie? Lorraine's Rosie?'

Spence nodded.

Cameron sniggered. 'Bet that went down well.'

'She flipped out, then I got annoyed and snapped back at her.'

'Then what happened?' Cameron leant forward. He couldn't imagine Spence standing up to Anika.

'We just kinda squashed it.'

Cameron scratched his chin. 'Can't say I blame you. Rosie's fucking sexy. I've moved to her a few times, and she wasn't having any of it.'

Spence didn't let on, but he knew all about this. Rosie had mentioned during a recent conversation that Cameron had come onto her multiple times, at one time getting quite aggressive when she'd said no. Spence offered to force him to apologise, but Rosie hadn't wanted to make a big deal of it.

'Tell you what . . . I'd move to Lorraine if Natty wasn't all over her,' Cameron went on.

'That definitely wouldn't be a good idea,' said Spence. No matter how vehemently Natty insisted nothing was going on between him and Lorraine, Spence knew it would start a war if Cameron made a play for her.

'I know. Natty's funny like that. Think they'll ever get together?'

'I'm not sure,' admitted Spence. He thought they were a good match, but wasn't sure Natty would ever take the risk.

'He's doing well in Little London. He's raking it in down there. Think he'll bring us in on it?'

Spence shrugged. 'It's not really up to him. Guessing Rudy would have the final decision. Or Nat's uncle.'

'Mitch won't care,' grumbled Cameron. 'Neither will Rudy. Natty's running shit. Both of you are. It's only me that's still doing the same stuff.' His face darkened.

'Do you want me to talk to Natty for you?'

'He's my boy too. I can talk to him myself,' snapped Cameron. He took a deep breath. 'Sorry. Just stresses me out. You lot are stepping up. Guess I just want the chance to do the same.' He glared down at his drink.

Not knowing what to say, Spence finished his drink in silence, lost in his thoughts.

CHAPTER EIGHTEEN

NATTY DROVE INTO LITTLE LONDON, window wound down, allowing him to feel the heat of the warm summer day. To combat this, he wore a white t-shirt, grey shorts, and pristine designer trainers.

Driving up Meanwood Road, he turned onto Oatland Road, taking in the various terraced houses, a mix of red and pale-bricked spots, some newer looking than others. Kids rode around on bikes, a few children kicking a football to one another, mindful of the busy road. Natty grinned, reminded of Jaden.

'Are you staying in the car?' Carlton asked. Natty nodded.

'No need for me to go in there.'

Shortly afterwards, they parked on Carlton Place, a few streets away from where Julie lived. Natty wondered if she had been letting her kids play out after their last talk. His people knew to leave her children alone, even when they were patterning youths to come and work for them. Again, Natty thought of Jaden, remembering Lorraine's passion about her son never being like him.

Shaking off the thoughts, Natty glanced at the black Vauxhall Corsa parked next to him as Carlton climbed from the car and headed into a nearby house. Despite things being relatively peaceful, Natty kept his eyes on his mirrors, not wanting to be caught slipping in what had formerly been enemy territory.

After a few minutes, Carlton strolled out. He climbed back in, showing Natty the stack of money he held.

'They had four grand,' he said.

Nodding, Natty pulled away. A group of students walked by, outfitted with backpacks and strategically ripped clothing, talking over one another in loud voices.

The pair drove to various areas, collecting large amounts of money.

'Gotta say, boss; I thought the money would have slowed down by now,' Carlton admitted, a grin on his face as he looked at the stacks bundled into a black sports bag.

'Just make sure everyone remains on point,' replied Natty. 'No one should be slipping up.'

Carlton nodded. 'Got it.'

Natty eventually dropped off Carlton, driving through the Hood, ensuring he wasn't being followed. Gathering the sports bag, he took it into a house on Francis Street. A group of men sat in the living, which reeked of cigarette smoke. The whirring of money-counting machines permeated the room. Noticing Natty, one of them grinned and offered him a cigarette, but Natty shook his head.

'Latest takings,' he announced, dropping the bag on the floor. 'Just under forty bags, give or take. Wonder will probably do some more drops later.'

'We know the drill, Bossman,' the same man that had offered the cigarette, replied. Natty hung around for a few more minutes, then left. Approaching his car, he stifled a yawn, deciding to take a break to go and see Lorraine and Jaden, hoping she would cook for him. It had been a long day, and he hadn't eaten.

When he arrived, she gave him a quick hug and let him in, a harried expression on her face.

'Hey Nat, where are you coming from?'

'All over, handling business. What's up with you?'

'Trying to study, but Jaden is doing my head in. I might have to move it to when he's asleep, but I concentrate more during the day,' she said. 'Plus, it's kicking my arse.'

'How so?' Natty braced himself for more complex computer talk.

'I need to apply what I'm studying, and use it. That involves trawling different sites, watching videos, and searching forums to learn how to solve certain problems.'

'Sounds tough,' replied Natty. Lorraine nodded, rubbing her eyes.

'It is. My laptop's a piece of shit too. It's not powerful enough to run the programs I use, so it takes me twice as long. I keep meaning to buy a new one.' She shook her head. 'Forget it. Jaden will be happy to see you.'

Jaden leapt to his feet when Natty entered the living room. Natty hugged him and rubbed the top of his messy head.

'Yes, little man. You need a haircut,' he said, his heart warm at the sight of the kid. He beamed down at him, missing the smile on Lorraine's face.

'No, I don't. *You* need a haircut,' retorted Jaden, though he was grinning too. 'Will you play my game with me? We can play Fifa.'

'Jaden, darling, Natty is busy,' said Lorraine.

The sight of Jaden's head lowering broke Natty. He had love for Jaden, and didn't ever want to be responsible for seeing such a look on his face. He didn't have any plans, and made a split-second decision.

'Course I will, little man. Get the game ready, and I'll make a drink and talk to your mum for a minute.'

'Okay.' Jaden beamed and went to change the game. Shaking her head, Lorraine followed Natty into the kitchen.

'You don't have to stay with him, Nat. He'll sulk for a bit, but he'll get over it.'

'I want to spend time with him. Don't worry about it. Use this time to get your studying done, and I'll look after him. I might take him for a walk or something.'

Lorraine tilted her head, eyes slightly widening.

'Are you sure?'

Natty grinned.

'Wouldn't say it if I wasn't. Get set up, and I'll make you some of that green tea crap you like.'

'Oi, don't knock it. It's good for you.'

'Everything horrible is good for you.' Natty winked and busied himself with the kettle. When he'd made Lorraine's drink, he smiled at her, slapped his hands together, and walked into the living room.

'Right, I hope you're ready to get beat!'

Lorraine's eyes lingered on the spot Natty had disappeared from, a slight smile on her face. She shook her head, smiled a little wider, then returned to her laptop.

* * *

NATTY AND JADEN had three games on *Fifa*, with Natty winning one of the three. Jaden was putting in the time and was getting a lot better at the game, meaning Natty could play properly and didn't have to let him win anymore.

After playing, they got ready and headed to the park on Reginald Terrace. It always amazed Natty just how much the local area had changed. When he was younger, the park was far more haphazard, containing a rough concrete square where kids would play football. It was a battleground of broken glass, with the odd syringe. That had been scrubbed away, though. Now, there was a neat and well-kept park. It made Natty wonder what his life could have been like if he'd had a well-kept park when he was growing up. He glanced at Jaden, vowing to make sure Jaden's future was more positive than his.

Natty looked around the park some more. He'd heard rumours of several Chapeltown heavyweights banding together to pay for some of the development, but didn't know how true that was.

As Jaden ran around and exhausted himself, Natty watched from a bench, wishing he'd taken the cigarette he'd been offered earlier. He didn't like smoking around Jaden, and had warned him not to do it when he was older. It didn't stop him from wanting one now, though.

He thought about the moves he was making, and how things were going. With Warren out of the way, Little London was easy pickings, and the money they were making was a sign of that. That being said, he didn't feel he was moving quickly enough.

Thinking of the heavyweights of old made him anxious. Chapeltown had numerous legends that had the world at their feet; some had even reigned when they were younger than Natty. What made him more nervous was how few of those heavyweights lived to enjoy the life they'd forged. A couple had, but they were the exception to the rule. Only the truly elite had managed to cut and run at the right time.

Natty had a long way to go.

Eventually, Jaden wanted Natty to play with him, so they had to run around the park. It knackered Natty, and he was now happy he hadn't smoked earlier, meaning his lungs were clear for the unexpected exercise. Still, he liked seeing Jaden happy.

After a while, Jaden was ready to go, and Natty was ready to sleep forever. It struck him that he couldn't remember the last time he'd been to the gym. As they returned to the house, he placed his hand on Jaden's shoulder.

'Natty, can I ask you something?' Jaden looked uncharacteristically serious, and that drew his attention.

'Course, little man. What's up?'

'Do you know my dad?'

Natty glanced at him, tensing.

'I do.'

Jaden nodded.

'I don't know much about him, other than when he's come to the house, and that's mostly to see mummy. What's he like?'

Natty was tempted to let Jaden know the truth. He was an eight-year-old kid, though. He had all the time in the world to grow up and see how life really worked. Natty wanted to protect him, and also keep it real.

He settled for a safe response.

'I don't really know him that well.'

'Why doesn't he live with mummy and me?' Jaden kept up the questions. Natty stepped aside so a couple could walk by, the move giving him critical seconds to formulate his answers.

'It's just like that sometimes,' he finally mumbled. Jaden didn't respond, and Natty felt terrible. He was out of his depth and didn't know how to relate to the kid when he started asking about Raider.

'Look, J,' he continued, 'I get it. My dad died when I was young — not much older than you, actually. I'll always miss him, and it's tough even now with him not being here.'

'How did he die?' Jaden asked.

Natty had a flashback to his younger days, standing in a cemetery, staring at his father's headstone. His fists instinctively clenched, and he felt a wave of anger that he had to force away. Luckily, Jaden didn't notice.

'Let's play another game of *Fifa* when we get back. Bagsy PSG!' He said, and Jaden immediately forgot about the conversation in protest.

* * *

BACK HOME, Lorraine was still in the kitchen, poring over her laptop. Jaden kissed her on the cheek and then bounded back into the living room. Lorraine surveyed Natty.

'You look wiped out,' she said.

'Your son is better than any exercise bike,' he admitted. 'He's killing me.'

Lorraine laughed, closing the laptop.

'How's it going?' He asked.

Lorraine nodded. 'I've managed to focus, which is good. Still got a lot of work to do, so I hope I'm taking it all in.'

'You're the sharpest person I know,' said Natty. 'I know I've said it before, but I do think what you're doing is great. You're amazing.'

Eyes widening, Lorraine opened her mouth to speak, but they were interrupted by Jaden.

'C'mon, Nat! The teams are ready. You said we'd play!' He whined, pulling Natty toward the room.

'Duty calls,' said Natty. He made a crying face. 'If you're making coffee . . . mine is three sugars.'

When he left the room, Lorraine chuckled. She stood and added some water to the kettle. Switching it on, she stared straight ahead with a smile.

'Three sugars . . .' she repeated a moment later, realising how ridiculous the request was.

* * *

AFTER PLAYING, Natty made food for the three of them. Lorraine had finished her studying by now, and looked exhausted. Lorraine thanked him for cooking, and after eating, she went to make Jaden take a bath and get him ready for bed.

Natty made a few phone calls, checking in. Wonder had indeed done his drop-offs. Natty would need to speak with Elijah later and see if there were any further steps to take in the streets. On the other side, Spence was still handling the old crew. Natty didn't tell him he was with Lorraine, but was sure that Spence knew.

Lorraine collapsed on the sofa next to him, blowing out a breath. Despite her bedraggled state, she still looked gorgeous, and Natty felt the familiar stirrings. He tried his hardest not to put Lorraine in the category of a woman he just wanted to have sex with, but she made it incredibly difficult at times.

They sat quietly for a while, and the vibe was nice. He liked that she was comfortable enough just having him in the house around her son, and felt like he had earned it.

Natty cared about her and Jaden. It didn't make his feelings — if that's what they were — any less confusing.

'Tell me some more about your studying,' he said.

Lorraine smiled. 'What do you want to know?'

'You were saying last time that you were learning how to *code*. What does that mean?'

Lorraine gazed at him for a moment.

'It's software engineering.' Natty's face remained blank. 'Computer programming; the thing that makes that phone in your hand work.'

Natty looked slowly from the phone back to Lorraine, his mouth wide open. She continued.

'I like computers, and I want to learn to understand them, and parlay that into a job.'

'That's amazing.' Natty meant it. He had a laptop and tech devices like everyone else he knew, but he didn't know of anyone with a genuine interest in computers. He blinked, amazed at how her face had come alive when she talked about it.

'It really is. To most people, a laptop or a phone is just a thing to use, to do what they want with. With coding, the machine becomes a partner, working together on whatever venture they choose.'

Natty did his best to keep up, but when she started using words like *SQL* and *Python*, they turned his head to mush. He loved her passion, though; despite supporting her, it made him feel almost insecure. He'd never felt that passion for anything of substance, mainly just women and trying to look good. He did not doubt that Lorraine would achieve her dreams, but he had to wonder what his own were.

Natty recalled some time back, when Lorraine had asked him what he wanted from life. He'd been unable to answer then, and he wasn't sure that he had the answer even now.

'Thank you for looking after Jaden,' Lorraine said, pulling him from his thoughts. 'And for cooking. You didn't have to.'

'Jaden's my little guy,' he replied, not using the word *soldier* anymore. 'I love spending time with him.' Remembering their trip to the park, he asked her, 'does Jaden ever mention Raider?'

Lorraine sat up.

'Why?'

'He was asking me about him today. Wanted to know if I knew him, and what he was like.'

'What did you say?'

'I said I didn't know him so well.'

Lorraine seemed satisfied with that. She sighed, wiping her hair from her eyes.

'He used to ask about him when he was younger, but not so much anymore. I try to avoid it. When he's older, it's going to be so awkward if he wants to know where things went wrong.'

Natty shook his head. 'You've raised him properly. When he's older, he's only going to remember just who was there for him.'

Lorraine gave Natty a sad smile, snuggling close to him.

'You're there for him too, Nat, and I really do appreciate it.'

The pair shared a light, almost chaste kiss, then watched television in comfortable silence, with no more conversation needed.

CHAPTER NINETEEN

A FEW DAYS after spending time with Jaden, Natty was drawn back to the park. He sat on a bench, smoking a cigarette, thinking about life and what his future might hold. He didn't know what it was about the park that made him so introspective, but he enjoyed the insight it helped to unlock.

Natty was making more money, essentially running Little London, but it wasn't his. He didn't have anything of his own, feeling chafed under the rule of others. Natty saw how seriously Spence took his investing, Lorraine's passion for software development. He wanted something of his own.

The major problem was that all Natty knew was crime. Even as a child, being a gangster on the streets was his biggest dream and outside of hustling, he didn't know how to define himself.

Natty was tempted to approach Rudy, but wasn't sure what he would say to him. Instead, he contacted Elijah and arranged for the two to talk.

* * *

'WHAT'S UP THEN?' Elijah asked, shaking hands with Natty as he climbed into Elijah's BMW. 'Do you wanna go somewhere?'

'Here is cool,' replied Natty, formulating his words. 'I've been thinking lately that I want more, and I thought you'd be a good person to speak to. You mentioned before that I should go out on my own.'

'More what? Money?'

'I want something of my own. Guess I'm wondering how you managed to establish yourself. You're with me in Little London, but you have your own thing too.'

Elijah nodded, scratching his chin.

'It wasn't easy. I saw how the people that came before us did it, and I tried to learn from their mistakes. What is it that you actually want?'

'More,' replied Natty.

* * *

A FEW DAYS LATER, Natty went shopping with Cameron, watching as his friend went from shop to shop, burning money.

'Where'd you get so much money from?' Natty asked. He knew what Cameron earned selling drugs, but he'd spent thousands without batting an eyelid.

'Don't worry about that. I've been saving.' Cameron gripped a shopping bag containing the new designer trainers he'd just bought, along with several other bags.

'Saving?' Natty frowned.

'Yes. Saving. Why aren't you buying anything? You're paid now. Treat yourself.'

Natty shook his head. 'I don't need anything.'

Cameron sniggered.

'Bro, you're a boss, and you're not even stepping your game up. Buy a watch or something. Look at what you're wearing; my clothes and trainers are more expensive than yours.'

Natty took the taunting in his stride. Once upon a time, he'd have bitten, and bought something expensive just to shut Cameron up, but he didn't need to.

They went to a Japanese restaurant for lunch. After they placed their orders, Natty turned to Cameron.

'I'll pay,' he said. Cameron smirked.

'Oh, so you actually bought your bank card then?' He joked.

Cameron devoured the food like he was dying, likely because Natty was paying. When they finished eating, Natty paid for the meal. The pair stood.

'I've gotta shoot off,' said Cameron. 'Are you gonna look for anything?'

Natty looked past him, noting someone with a laptop bag being shown to a seat.

'Yeah. There's one more place I need to go.'

After saying his goodbyes, he headed off in the direction of the nearest Apple shop.

* * *

ANIKA STEPPED OUT OF AN UBER, looking behind her before she entered Cameron's garden. He let her in and made them both drinks, just like last time. He popped a pill and washed it down, but didn't offer her one.

'I was chilling with your hubby the other day,' he said.

Anika shrugged.

'You're friends. Of course you were chilling,' she said. She didn't want to talk about Spence when she was with Cameron. Their argument about the girl he wanted to hang out with still irritated her, but she'd done her best to let it go.

'We don't really chill one-on-one anymore,' said Cameron. 'I heard about your little talk.'

'I don't want to talk about it,' said Anika.

Cameron sipped his drink. 'Fine. Rosie's harmless, anyway.'

'How do you know?' Anika's eyes narrowed.

'I've been around them before. Lorraine and Natty are always eyefucking and sliding around each other. Rosie is always sniffing after Spence, but he never did anything.'

'Seriously?' Anika didn't like the sound of this, and it added credence to her initial response. Spence wanted to spend time with a woman who clearly wanted him, but she didn't know how he felt about her. 'Do you think she'd try something?'

'Fuck knows. Look.' Cameron took out his phone and loaded Rosie's page on Instagram.

Anika's stomach twisted when she looked at the woman. She was beautiful and clearly energetic. Her page was full of affirmations, and numerous photos of her out with friends, even a few of Lorraine, who Anika had always thought was stunning. She didn't understand why Natty wouldn't date her, but admitted there were bits about the situation that she wasn't privy to.

'She's pretty,' she said through clenched teeth. Cameron slyly smiled.

'I can't believe you're jealous, even though you've been banging me . . .'

'Fuck you, Cam.'

'Fuck you right back. Don't get mad because I'm right. Is that why you're here now? Revenge?'

'I'm here because . . .' Anika trailed off.

'It doesn't even matter. I'm proud of Spence, though. We don't always click, but I'm glad he stood up to you.'

Anika cut her eyes to Cameron. 'You don't think it's a little fucked up that this girl wants to hang out with him?'

'I think it's a little fucked up that he thought he had to tell you. He has his own life, and shouldn't need to check in with you all the time. I'm always telling him this, so deep down, maybe he's listening.'

Anika didn't like what she was hearing, and disliked that Cameron wasn't taking her seriously. He seemed to find the whole thing a joke, which she supposed was because he was getting what he wanted from the situation. He had co-opted her and seduced her. Now, he had her here, and he hadn't even had to try. She wondered if she could even trust the things he was saying, or if he was trying to manipulate her and keep her divided.

'You're a piece of shit. I don't even know why I'm here.'

'You're here because you like getting fucked, and you want to do it again. Stop trying to front and overthink it.' Cameron smirked.

Anika scoffed. 'You're so cocky.'

'Cockiness has nothing to do with it, Nika. We have a connection, and we're both here. Doesn't matter what Spence does in the end, if you're here with me. You must see that.'

Anika turned away, sipping her drink. She tensed when she felt Cameron standing behind her. He squeezed her shoulders, rubbing at the nape of her neck, and though she didn't want to do it, Anika leaned into his touch, feeling the security she craved.

'Nika, I know that things are fucked, and I know you're confused, but I'm glad you're here with me. Even if we don't do anything else and hang out like this, I'm good.'

'You mean that?' Anika looked up at him, shocked at what he was saying.

Cameron nodded.

'I do what I do, but there aren't many girls I know that I can just chill with like this.'

'You say that, but things never worked out with us,' said Anika, trying to believe in what Cameron was saying, despite what her gut screamed at her.

'People change. We were young, and you remember what it was like back then. Everyone and everything was wild. I was a kid on a money mission, and then I had this girl I didn't know what to do with.'

'You let me go.'

'Yeah. And you went, so don't act like it was all some one-way shit. We had something, and then we didn't, and we moved on, but that doesn't mean there aren't still feelings involved.' Cameron kept up his massaging. Anika closed her eyes.

'And for you, those feelings go beyond sex?'

'Where do they go for you? Don't forget, you're the one that's fucking my boy.'

'I'm in a relationship with Spence.'

'Yes, you are, but you're with me. Like I said, this thing between us, it's 50-50. Maybe you need to believe otherwise to alleviate that guilt you're probably feeling, but that's on you.' Giving her one last rub, Cameron sat down.

Anika didn't respond. The truth was that Cameron was right. She was here with him despite knowing she shouldn't be. Despite how awful she felt, being with Cameron was the only time she felt at least a little whole. They had never gotten over one another, and those feelings had influenced her relationship with Spence. She figured that was why she couldn't settle into the relationship, and why his attempts to get closer to her only seemed to make her more distant.

She went to sit with Cameron, and gripped his face, kissing him tightly. Cameron made no attempt to resist. He deepened the kiss, and before long, she was trailing behind Cameron, holding his hand as he led her up the stairs.

* * *

SPENCE SAT in Rosie's place, surveying the room as always. She lived in Oakwood, having grown up in Moor Allerton, despite having connections in the Hood.

Spence was especially fond of Rosie's living room. Her home, in general, had a comfortable feel, reeking of independence. She had a walnut Bornholm coffee table, various bookshelves, and a yoga mat in the corner of the room. Fresh white oriental lilies rested on the table, and the smoke grey sofas were adorned with throw pillows.

Sipping his drink, Spence delved into his thoughts. He and Anika remained up and down. After their argument, things had picked up for a few weeks, and Anika had seemed more engaged. Gradually, she became withdrawn again, and his attempts to discuss it with her had been rebuffed.

As Spence had left to go to Rosie's, Anika had been dressed to go out, wearing a short grey dress and high heels, her face heavily made up. She was meeting her friend Carmen and going somewhere, but Spence hadn't asked questions.

Rosie crossed her legs on the sofa nearby, sipping a glass of white wine.

'Even now, you always seem nervous around me,' she remarked.

Spence smiled, shaking his head.

'I have a few things I'm mentally trying to work out.'

'Anika?' Rosie asked.

'Sort of. We argued a while back about me wanting to spend time with you.'

'You spoke to her about it?'

'She came in the room when you messaged me, and I didn't have anything to hide, so I told her then. It didn't go too well at first,' said Spence.

'Why? You and I are just friends, right?' Rosie met his eyes. Spence fought to maintain his composure under her intense gaze. It was a habit of hers.

'I used to like you, so I guess that came across when I was talking to her.'

Rosie's eyes widened.

'When did you like me?'

'I liked you for years,' he admitted.

'Why didn't you say anything?'

Spence shrugged. 'You were never available, and after a while, I just stopped watching. After that, I fell for Anika.' Even after the brief conversation, he felt much better. Talking about what was on his mind was good for clearing his headspace, and Rosie was a good listener.

Rosie sighed. 'I guess I can understand that. I want to be friends, but sometimes I wonder if we're more than that.' Again, her eyes surveyed him. 'I think if we're being honest, there's something more here.'

The pair locked eyes. Without breaking eye contact, Rosie shifted closer to Spence. His heart pounded, and he fought to keep his expression neutral.

'It's not fair that we missed one another,' Rosie whispered. Spence's heart felt like it would burst from his chest, temptation surging throughout his body. Rosie smelled as wonderful as always, seeming even sexier and more alluring in her space. Spence's mouth was dry, and he yearned for her in a way he knew was wrong. With a deep breath, he pulled back.

'It's not fair, but it's the way it is,' he said, thankful that his words sounded firm. Rosie nodded, giving him a small smile.

'Let me get you another drink,' she said, grabbing his glass and sashaying to the kitchen as Spence let out a deep sigh of relief.

CHAPTER TWENTY

NATTY DROVE into Little London to get an update on the latest figures, reflecting on the brief conversation he'd shared with Elijah. Elijah hadn't given him much, other than stating he'd just gone for it, something Natty was thinking about more and more in his free time.

He didn't know how his uncle would take it, nor Rudy, but the idea of having something of his own fuelled him, and he felt it would be worth making less money short term, to properly benefit long term.

Natty knew what he wanted and knew who he'd take with him.

At the same time, there was always the possibility that his uncle wouldn't allow him to walk away, and if he did, that he wouldn't let people go with him. If he did that, Natty wouldn't be able to fight it. He didn't have the power to go up against the whole organisation, and the murder of Warren and his associates was a gruesome reminder that his uncle played for keeps.

Pulling up outside the main spot, he tensed when he saw Raider standing outside, talking with one of Elijah's people.

Immediately, they exchanged hard glares as Natty climbed from the car. He felt his fists clench and saw Raider's jaw reciprocate. The man he'd been talking to looked between them in alarm, giving Natty a tentative nod. Raider was physically imposing, and as much as Natty disliked him, he couldn't doubt this. Despite being an inch or two shorter than Natty, he was broader, with sharp features and a thick neck and shoulders. He wore a black coat, jeans, and high-top trainers.

'Elijah's doing well around here,' he said as Natty grew closer. Natty ignored the slight.

'I didn't know he'd given you permission to come around here,' he replied, watching Raider's face contort and twist with anger.

'You're lucky you're useful, Dunn. Keep running your mouth, though, and we'll see what happens. How's my girl? People tell me you're still sniffing around her, even after all these years.'

It was Natty's turn to react. He had expected it, but he still didn't like Raider bringing up Lorraine.

'Are *people* also telling you about the son you abandoned?'

The man Raider had been talking to, shook his head, walking away. He headed indoors as quickly as possible, away from the storm. Raider took a step towards Natty, his features hardening. Natty held his ground.

'You shouldn't talk about things you don't understand. Lorraine talks shit, and whatever you've heard, doesn't make it your business. Understand?'

'I understand that you're a deadbeat. Do you even know when your son's birthday is?' He interjected as Raider opened his mouth. 'You can come with all the big talk you want, but at the end of the day, you're a joke, and you always will be.'

Raider grabbed for Natty, and the pair tussled. Before they could get into it, several workers hurried outside to separate them. Not resisting, Natty headed inside with a smile as a fuming Raider left, feeling he'd won the exchange. He'd wanted to fight, but getting under his skin was the next best thing.

'Are you okay?' One of the workers asked, having followed Natty inside. They heard the distant sounds of tire screeches as a car drove away.

Natty headed to the fridge to get a bottle of Ribena. He turned, looking out to the room, noting that all eyes were on him. Opening the drink, he took a long swig.

'Ahhhh . . . refreshing.' He wiped his mouth on his sleeve and smiled, before finally replying to the worker, 'I couldn't be better. Now, tell me how much money we're making.'

* * *

LATER THAT NIGHT, Spence came to Natty's house. He handed him an envelope with the latest takings, and accepted the drink Natty gave him.

'Any issues?' Natty asked, as they sat outside.

'Not on my end. I was going to ask you the same thing.'

'What do you mean?'

'Everyone's talking about you and Raider getting into it. Was that smart?'

Natty snorted.

'He sought me out, not the other way around. I'm not gonna let him punk me out.'

'Is that what it's about?' Spence asked. Natty frowned.

'What do you mean?'

'I mean that you both have Lorraine and Jaden in common, and it's clear that's the problem. You said there's nothing between you and Lorraine, though, so you need to avoid becoming entangled. Fighting over a woman that isn't yours . . . that's not practical, fam.'

Natty stared down Spence.

'The shit with Raider is deeper than that. We've never gotten along, and he's not even supposed to be down with our thing.'

Spence nodded. 'I understand it's personal, but you need to rise above that, and you know it. You're killing it with everything you're doing now, and that should be your focus.'

Natty grinned, his mood improving. Spence loved to lecture him, but Natty never doubted it was coming from a place of love. The pair touched fists, finishing their drinks in silence. Natty appreciated the warning, but the streets were torrid at the best of times. The success simply didn't mean much if people didn't respect him. He was making more money, but was still seen as a little guy to people. No matter what, he would change that perception.

'What's on your mind?' Spence asked. 'You've been quiet lately.'

'I've been thinking about my future. Lately, I've kinda wanted to branch out and do my own thing.'

Spence's eyes widened in surprise.

'I wasn't expecting that. What's brought that on?'

'Everyone keeps telling me that I'm killing it in Little London. I got myself out there, built alliances, and got people working together, but ultimately, it hasn't got me anywhere. I figured my unc would do something else with me, maybe bump me up to a new position, but he hasn't. Seems he's happy to keep me at this level, but I'm not happy being here.'

'You've definitely been giving it some thought then,' said Spence, nodding his head in approval. After hearing about the exchange with Raider, he'd been worried, but Natty was definitely in a different place. When Natty was locked onto something, he found a way to make it happen.

'I have. I'd want you there alongside me. Me, you and Cam, working this thing by ourselves, with more money and responsibility in the long term.'

'Do you think that could work?'

Natty nodded. 'We clash, but we balance one another out. We always have.'

Spence patted him on the shoulder.

'I'm with you, Nat.'

Natty grinned, shocked at his friend putting it out like that.

'Really?'

'Course. I think you can do it, and if there's a proper plan in place, then I'm in. I can't speak for Cam, but I can't see him saying no either.'

Natty's grin widened. Spence's endorsement meant a lot. He was a serious thinker, and the fact he'd committed so quickly was a sign to Natty that his plan was fruitful.

'I'm glad to hear that. I'll keep you updated. There's a lot I still need to consider. Other than business, how are things with you?'

Spence scratched his eyelid, blowing out a breath.

'Rosie,' was all he said in reply. Natty chuckled.

'What happened?'

'We were chilling together, and there was a moment.'

'What did you do?'

'Nothing,' Spence quickly said, running through the situation, and the talk they'd had on her sofa. When he finished, Natty again chuckled.

'It's a messy situation, but you didn't do anything wrong. Sounds like you resisted her basically laying out for you what she wanted to happen.'

Spence nodded, his shoulders sagging. 'It was one of the hardest things I've ever done, Nat. Things with Rosie are easy. We clicked, and it seemed like she was saying she liked me too.'

'And Anika? Are things easy with her?'

Spence lowered his head. 'We're like strangers sometimes. She goes out a lot nowadays. Says she doesn't like being home by herself.'

Natty's eyes narrowed, not liking what he was hearing.

'Where does she go?'

'I don't know,' said Spence. 'I'm guessing she goes to Carmen's, as she's always getting dressed up. Carmen is her usual partner for going clubbing.'

Natty didn't respond, mulling over what Spence had said, his uneasy feeling growing. He didn't know much about Carmen, but knew she was engaged and lived with her fiancé. He didn't understand why Anika would get dolled up to hang out with them, but he intended to find out.

* * *

After his conversation with Spence, Natty found himself mulling over Spence's relationship with Anika. He wasn't surprised Spence had told her about Rosie, but something about her reaction, and the behaviour Spence described, worried him. The more he thought about it, the more he reached a horrible conclusion. She seemed to be judging him by a standard that wasn't appropriate for Spence. He loved Anika and had been nothing but loyal.

Maybe she was judging him by her own standard.

Natty didn't think this lightly, but Spence had commented on her growing distance. He remembered her strange words to him when he'd gone looking for Spence; she'd enquired whether he was happy, and even now, he still thought it was a random question to ask.

It was apparent to Natty that she had checked out of the relationship. The only thing to consider now was what to do about it.

Natty had several options. He could speak with Spence, share his feelings, and allow his friend to talk it out with his partner. Or, he could confront Anika himself.

Natty knew which option he would pick. He felt he and Anika were long overdue a conversation. Even though her past with Cameron hadn't gone anywhere, it had somewhat sullied her in his eyes, especially when she'd never mentioned to Spence that she had been involved with one of his closest friends. He'd given her the benefit of the doubt in the past because Spence seemed happy, but now that was no longer the case, and all bets were off.

With this in mind, Natty grabbed his keys and left the house. He drove to Spence's place, knowing his friend was working, wanting to catch Anika alone.

The area was relatively quiet, with a few of Spence's neighbours pottering around. They recognised Natty, greeting him with warm smiles that he returned. Spence was good to his neighbours, especially the older ones. He'd help them with shopping and take in parcels on their behalf if he was home. He always had a kind word for them, and they loved him. Natty wasn't sure Anika inspired such loyalty.

Knocking hard on the door, Natty waited for her to answer. When he received no response, he waited almost a minute before trying again. Still no response.

'She's not in.'

Natty almost jumped at the sound of the voice. Spence's neighbour directly opposite was a middle-aged woman. She was on the heavy side, and had a kind, moon-shaped face.

'Excuse me?'

'Anika isn't in. Neither is Spence, but Anika left a short while ago,' said the neighbour.

'Do you know where she went?'

'I don't, I'm sorry. Looked dressed up, though. I assumed she was going to see some friends.'

Or she was going to see someone else, Natty thought darkly, his desire to confront Anika growing.

'Thanks.' He gave the woman a slight smile that he knew hadn't reached his eyes.

'Do you want me to tell them you stopped by?'

Natty thought for a moment longer than he needed to.

'No,' he replied. 'It's not important.'

* * *

WHEN NATTY RETURNED HOME, he trawled over Anika's social media accounts, but couldn't find any clue where she was. He knew a few of her friends, but their online profiles were equally bereft of information.

Slumping back on the sofa, he rubbed his forehead, wondering again if he should try speaking to Spence. He dismissed this. There was the possibility Spence would react badly if he accused Anika of cheating on him, especially without tangible proof. Despite her supposed faults, Spence loved her and wanted to build a life with her. That counted for a lot.

He called Cameron, wondering if he could share some insight, but his phone was off.

Closing his eyes, Natty soon dozed off, exhausted from the day.

* * *

PUSHING his worries about Spence and Anika to one side, Natty drove to see his mum the next day, already wary about how the conversation would go. Since their argument a while back, he'd stopped in on her sparingly, mainly at the behest of Rudy, who constantly insisted that his mum loved him and looked forward to his visits. She never showed that to Natty, though. Things between them had never been as straightforward as Rudy would have liked.

When Natty entered, his mum was sat in the living room, *Judge Judy* on the television. She glanced up when she saw Natty, her face noncommittal. Approaching, he gave her a light kiss on the cheek and sat next to her.

'How are you doing?'

'My hip hurts,' she responded.

'Is there anything I can do?' He asked. Rudy hadn't said anything about her hip the last time they'd spoken.

'No. I probably just slept on it funny. Don't need a big fuss made. How are you doing?'

'I'm doing well,' replied Natty. His mum scrutinised his appearance.

'You look well,' she agreed, the words bereft of joy. She almost sounded annoyed.

'Yep, things are good right now,' replied Natty, skipping past her demeanour. She folded her arms, staring at the screen. Natty didn't doubt she'd likely seen the same episode dozens of times. After all, she'd been watching the show since Natty was a child.

'That's good. Rudy still treating you well?'

'He is,' replied Natty.

'Do you want some tea?'

'Sure.'

Soon, he sipped the steaming tea. It was slightly watery, but he didn't comment.

'Make sure Rudy treats you right,' his mum said, as if they were mid-conversation. Natty wasn't sure how to take the comment, seeing as his mum was in a relationship with Rudy.

'I will.'

His mum sipped her tea, still eyeing him.

'He mentioned you had a girlfriend.'

Natty's stomach lurched, and he sipped the weak tea to distract himself.

'She's not my girlfriend,' he finally said. His mum nodded.

'Good. You shouldn't be raising some other man's kid.'

Natty felt the words needling away at him, which he was sure was his mum's intent. Pushing away his irritation, he responded.

'Is that how Rudy feels about me? You two are together, after all.'

The words had the effect he wanted. His mum gave a start, spilling some of her drink and cursing, hastening to clear the mess. Her eyes bore into Natty's, her demeanour unfriendly.

'You're a grown man,' she snapped. 'Rudy respects that, and our relationship is none of your business.'

'That goes both ways.'

Her mouth pursed.

'Watch how you speak to me.'

Shrugging, Natty again sipped his drink, eyes now on the television. The judge was laying into some poor fool, and he watched with a smile, appreciating the fact he'd survived a tongue lashing from his mum without snapping.

'Are you hungry?' His mum eventually asked. 'I'll make you something.'

'I could eat. Are you sure you can manage with your hip and all?'

'I'll be fine,' she responded, though Natty was sure that her limp on the way to the kitchen was for his benefit. He placed his empty cup on the coffee table, grinning as he hummed a tune.

* * *

THAT EVENING, Anika was in her living room, sipping wine and staring at her phone, ignoring the television playing in the background. A sharp knock at the door startled her, and she hastened to answer, her eyebrows raised when she saw Natty standing there.

'Hey Nat, are you looking for Spence? He's not here.' She smiled at him, startled when he didn't return it.

'Oh. I must have missed him,' he said. 'Sorry for disturbing you.'

'It's fine. I wasn't up to much. How have you been?'

'I'm good. What about you? Are you *happy?*'

The way Natty phrased his second question made Anika's insides turn to ice. Something was going on here, and she wasn't sure what it was. She wondered if Cameron had spoken to Natty about them, but couldn't think why he would.

'Why are you asking me that?'

'I'm just taking an interest,' said Natty blandly. 'After all, you're with one of my best friends. I want to make sure everything is good between you.'

Anika flinched. Natty zeroed in on this, surer than ever that something was going down.

'I'm fine, Nat. You just surprised me, that's all. Spence and I are busy all the time, and I guess that leads to stress. I am happy, though,' she insisted, heart hammering as Natty continued to survey her. Finally, he smiled, and she felt herself relaxing.

'Good to hear, love. I'll catch Spence later. Run a bath or something; keep those stress levels down.'

Anika returned his smile, though she still felt uneasy.

'I think I'll do that.'

* * *

CAMERON HESITATED. He stood on a street, looking at a house, taking deep breaths, trying to psych himself up. Rudy had again reached out, offering Cameron the chance to improve his standing by eliminating a problem. It was a clear test, and he felt the nerves settling in despite being eager to take it at the time.

After a minute, Cameron glanced around, checking no one was watching. He'd dressed in all black to blend in with the night. Finally, he entered the garden and knocked on the door.

Christian answered, warily staring out at Cameron. Cameron gave him a small smile. After the beating he'd given Christian and his girl, he'd collected from him again afterwards with no problems.

That was then, and this was now. Christian had messed up big time.

'Are you gonna let me in? You don't want your neighbours to hear our chat, right?' said Cameron. Christian swallowed, then nodded. The living room was unchanged from the last time Cameron had visited. An Xbox One controller rested on the sofa — the video game Christian had been playing currently paused.

Christian remained on his feet, surveying Cameron.

'Do you want a drink?'

Cameron shook his head. He felt calmer than he had outside. Something about Christian's nervousness relaxed him.

'I'm good. How have you been?'

Christian's eyebrow rose.

'Why are you asking me that?'

'We used to be cool before that bullshit you pulled. You paid for it, so no reason for me to hold a grudge,' he replied.

'I'm fine.'

'How's your girl?'

Christian scowled, folding his arms.

'We're on a break. She cheated on me.'

Cameron couldn't hide his smirk. Christian noticed.

'It's not funny, mate. I did everything for her, and she violated.'

'It happens. You can't trust women. Next time, you'll know to pick better.' Cameron's thoughts shifted to Anika for a moment. He didn't know what was happening with them, or what he wanted to happen. 'Anyway, how's business?'

'It's picking up. I've kept my head down, staying out of the mix.'

Cameron scratched his chin.

'Yeah?'

'Yeah,' replied Christian. 'I've just been stacking my money. I wanna get out of Leeds as soon as I can.'

Cameron didn't speak for a moment. He cleared his throat.

'You know what, I will have a drink after all.'

'What do you want?'

'Cup of tea. Milk and four sugars.'

Christian headed to the kitchen. Cameron could hear him pottering around, grabbing a cup. He took another deep breath, pulling out a gun, keeping it by his side. Christian had his back to Cameron, humming a tune. Cameron stepped towards him.

He must have been noisier than he thought, because Christian turned, eyes widening when he saw Cameron. He flung the cup at him, and despite Cameron avoiding the object, it allowed Christian to charge, slapping the gun from his hand. Christian dove for it, but Cameron kicked him in the side, then punched him twice, his fist crashing against the side of Christian's head. Despite clearly being stunned, Christian let out a roar and charged Cameron, slamming him into a nearby table. They fell to the floor, Christian mounting Cameron, hitting him twice. Cameron rolled over, overpowering Christian, hands wrapping around his throat. His teeth gritted, watching him attempt to break free. Tighter, he squeezed, wanting it to end.

Christian attempted to claw Cameron's face, trying to break free, but he held on tightly, feeling Christian's strength fade. After a few more seconds, he let go, crawling for the gun. Clambering to his feet, he pointed the gun at Christian's head, hesitating for only a moment before pulling the trigger three times.

Glancing at the dead body for only a moment, Cameron hurried from the house, gun by his side. He kept his head down, striding down the road, taking a left onto the street where he'd parked a stolen getaway car. Climbing in, he drove away at moderate speed.

After five minutes, he stopped the car, opened the door, and threw up.

When he was finished, he carried on driving.

* * *

CAMERON DIDN'T REPORT for work the next day. He told Spence he didn't feel well, and spent the day drinking alone, thinking about what he'd done.

Cameron was a career criminal and had sold drugs for longer than he could remember. He'd beaten people up, threatened them, and committed numerous robberies.

He'd never killed anyone. Until now.

In the past, he'd talked with Natty, bragging that he would have the guts to pull the trigger and feel nothing, but he'd lied to himself, because he'd struggled to sleep last night, seeing Christian's lifeless body. He wondered how Christian's ex would react to the killing; whether she would care, or regret cheating on him.

Snorting a line of cocaine, Cameron tried centring his thoughts. He'd stepped up and done the job, and Rudy had paid him well for it. No one else would know what he had done, and he had shown the higher-ups that he could be trusted to do the job. It didn't matter that he'd failed to sneak up on Christian, nor did it matter he had lost his weapon. The job was done, and he would eventually get over the feeling of wrongness permeating his body.

Pulling out his phone, Cameron debated trying Anika. After a few seconds, he scrolled further down his contacts list, calling another woman instead.

CHAPTER TWENTY-ONE

ON THE DAY of Jaden's tenth birthday, Natty straightened himself and knocked at the door, before walking in, ready to join the after-party — if a child ever needed such a thing. Natty had skipped the first part of Jaden's birthday, not fancying being surrounded by screaming kids in public.

When Natty entered the living room, he saw people milled around, before something slammed into his legs, making him stumble.

'Natty! You're here.' Jaden's eyes shone as he looked up at Natty. Natty lifted him off the ground with one arm, feigning a groan.

'I can barely lift you. You're gonna be bigger than me soon,' he joked.

'Really?' said Jaden, continuing before Natty could speak. 'What did you get me for my birthday?'

'Jaden!' Lorraine scolded him, having approached.

'Here. This is for you.' Natty set him down and handed him a carrier bag. As Jaden thanked him and fawned over the trainers and tracksuit, Natty said his hellos to the others in the room. Lorraine grinned at him, shaking her head.

'You spoil him,' she said, giving Natty a brief hug. Natty clutched her tightly, happy to see her smiling.

'He deserves it. He's the best kid in the world,' said Natty, watching Jaden showing off his new clothes to several of his cousins in attendance.

'What else did you get him?' Lorraine noticed Natty still held a bag. 'You've already given him enough.'

Natty smiled, his stomach fluttering.

'This is for you. Come with me.'

Natty led Lorraine to the kitchen. It looked like a bomb site, with children's coats strewn over the kitchen table and surrounding chairs. Numerous half-full juice glasses were on the kitchen counter, along with several unfinished packets of crisps.

Lorraine faced Natty, her eyes on the bag. Steeling himself against his nerves, Natty handed it to her. Keeping eye contact with him now, Lorraine opened it, eyebrow raised. When she saw what was within, her mouth fell open.

'You . . .' She shook her head, looking down at the brand new MacBook Pro, then back to Natty.

'The dude in the Apple shop said it was the best model,' Natty mumbled, pleased his voice hadn't cracked. 'Said you can easily install coding software, and that it's got some chip that makes it super-fast.'

'I can't believe you did this . . . why?' Lorraine remained at a loss for words. Natty rubbed the back of his head.

'You said a while back that yours was slow . . . I wanted to help so you could study,' he said, his face warm.

'I can't believe you,' Lorraine replied, hugging him. Natty again held her tightly.

'Are you sure? They're so expensive . . . I shouldn't take it,' she said weakly. Natty waved off the protests, noting a tear in Lorraine's eye. He glanced away.

'You're gonna take it, and you're gonna keep working hard, because it's going to pay off,' he said.

Lorraine nodded. Wiping her eyes, she composed herself, then took the MacBook and left the kitchen.

Natty waited another minute, buoyed that she'd liked his gift. By the time he left the kitchen, the MacBook had vanished, and Lorraine was talking to another woman. She was smiling widely and gesturing in the direction of the kitchen. Natty leant against the doorframe, grinning. Lorraine and her friend glanced over, Lorraine and Natty sharing another moment, the friend looking between them.

Natty spoke with a few more people, his eyes never straying far from Jaden and Lorraine.

His thoughts were interrupted by Lorraine's mum approaching. She wore a small smile, but her eyes were hard as she surveyed him.

'It's good to see you, Nathaniel. Jaden was worried you wouldn't show,' she said.

'I'd never let Jaden down like that,' Natty replied. The woman nodded, glancing in her grandson's direction a moment.

'I hope not.'

Natty didn't respond, used to her blunt ways after the years he'd known her. When he first started hanging around Lorraine, she'd hated him, thinking he was a bad influence. He couldn't say for sure what she thought of him now, but figured it was more positive. Natty had nothing but respect for her. She was tough, rarely minced words, and despite several hardships, had eventually carved out a successful catering business.

'It's good you came with presents too. He seems to like your taste.'

'We've been shopping before,' said Natty. 'He's not shy about telling me what he likes.'

'My daughter trusts you.'

Natty waited for her to continue, but she didn't. Without another word, she left. Lorraine glanced from her retreating mother to him, likely wondering what they'd been talking about. Natty gave her a small smile and kept it moving. After they cut the cake, he hugged a corner, happy to watch the proceedings as he scarfed down the chocolate sponge.

'Nat, good to see you, bro.' Lorraine's older brother Tommy approached. The pair slapped hands. He'd known Tommy longer than he had known Lorraine. At one point, Tommy had been knee-deep in the streets, but after a few prison sentences, he'd slowed down and seen the writing on the wall. Nowadays, he co-owned a local gym, and also held workout sessions for all groups in Potternewton Park.

'You too. Your kids are getting big,' said Natty, nodding to Tommy's children, running around after Jaden.

'Can I have a chat?'

Natty's eyebrow arched. Tommy's tone was oddly serious. Nonetheless, he nodded, and they went to stand outside.

They stood in silence for almost a minute. Natty surveyed Tommy. His jaw was tight, but he had his hands in the pockets of his jeans. Taking a pack of cigarettes from his pocket, he offered one to Tommy, who shook his head.

Tommy was old school and a proponent of the old school dress code. He refused to wear skinny or slim jeans, and tended to wear baggier clothing. Nonetheless, he had the build of a man who took his weight training seriously, similar to how Natty used to. He and Lorraine didn't look alike other than their colouring. Tommy's features were harsher, his nose and lips broader.

'I'll get right to it. What's going on with you and my sister?'

'We're cool,' Natty replied, confused by the question. He and Tommy had been friends back in the day, and other than threatening to kill him if he ever hurt his sister, they'd never discussed his and Lorraine's involvement. Tommy shook his head.

'I'm not an idiot, Natty. I was in the room before. You two are closer than cool. I've seen the way you look at each other.'

'What are you trying to say, Tom? Whatever it is, talk your talk.'

'Fine. Jaden's getting big now. You've seen him in there, running around with his family. Soon, he's gonna be grown, and he needs some structure. That means you and my sister need to be honest about what you both want.'

'What if I just wanted to screw your sis? Would that be okay?' Natty replied, annoyed by the conversation. Whatever was going on with him and Lorraine — and he still didn't know what that was — it wasn't any of Tommy's business. Tommy sized him up for a long moment, and Natty wondered if he was going to swing. Despite Tommy's reputation back in the day, he was sure he could take him if it came to it.

Silently, Tommy continued to stare him down. He held out his hand, and after a moment, Natty offered him the cigarette he'd turned down earlier. Lighting it, Tommy took a long drag, exhaling before he responded.

'Jaden looks up to you. He talks about you all the time. He wants to be just like you, and I don't think you'd be putting in the hours playing with him and taking him places, if all you wanted was to grind my sister. Fact is, Jaden needs a father figure he can look up to.'

Natty respected Tommy's approach, but the whole conversation made him nervous. He wasn't sure he was ready to tackle it, but it kept surfacing in his mind.

He knew he couldn't avoid it forever.

'It's not that simple,' he replied, his stomach lurching.

'Make it simple.'

The air around the pair seemed to cool, and Natty's eyes narrowed, not liking Tommy's tone.

'Don't threaten me.'

Tommy shook his head, taking another deep burn of the cigarette.

'I walked that same path you're on, Nat. Never forget that. The world is bigger than these streets, though, and I'm speaking to you as a man — one I think is good enough for my sister.'

Another silence ensued, but it differed from the others. There was a newfound respect between the pair, who shared a long look, clearly understanding where the other was coming from.

'Am I too late for the party?'

Both men whirled around, and Natty's hands immediately balled into fists. Raider stood there, a bag in his hand. His eyes locked onto Natty, who awaited Raider making the first move. Instead, Raider greeted Tommy, then walked by without acknowledging Natty. As he entered the house, Natty and Tommy glanced at one another again.

'Did you know he was coming?'

'I knew he was invited. I don't think he replied to Lorraine, though,' said Tommy, staring at the door Raider had just walked through. They headed inside, expecting to hear some shouting, or an argument. Instead, Jaden was talking with Raider, smiling as he stared at the present his dad had bought him.

'Thank you,' he said, holding up another pair of trainers — expensive Jordan 4's.

'You're welcome, J. Sorry I couldn't get here earlier, but look how big you're getting! You're almost a proper man.'

Natty grit his teeth, Raider's words almost echoing his own from earlier. The longer he watched them spending time together, the more jealous he grew. Raider could turn up out of the blue and get all of the plaudits, despite being absent for years. Natty didn't get it. Lorraine approached the pair with a wide smile, gushing over the trainers and handing Raider a beer. He took it with a smile, his eyes roving over her curvy frame.

Natty turned away, Tommy still watching him, as was Lorraine's mum. Not knowing what to say to either, he stayed silent, getting a drink of his own, watching the proceedings from the corner. The thought of Raider picking up right where he left off made him want to hit something — namely Raider. He hadn't forgotten the last time they had spoken; his words to Raider about not looking after his child. Clearly, they had been taken to heart.

Not everyone was as enamoured as Lorraine and Jaden. Lorraine's mum was guardedly polite when she addressed Raider, and Tommy found his way over to Natty's corner after a while.

'I can tell by your face you feel the same way as me,' he said.

'It's nothing to do with me,' replied Natty.

'Don't give me that shit. I saw the look in your eyes outside. You were ready to fight when you saw him.'

Natty said nothing.

'I don't blame you, but I'm glad you held it down. As nice as it would be to beat some manners into him, Jaden's the one that would be hurt. As it is, he's gonna be hurt anyway, because we both know Raider ain't sticking around.'

Natty didn't respond, but agreed with Tommy. He had wanted to fight Raider. He still did. Turning away before he hit him with a bottle, he sipped his drink as a distraction. Tommy patted him on the shoulder, then went to stand with his kids. Lorraine had stepped back, her eyes on Raider and Jaden, who were still talking at length. Steeling himself, Natty went to stand next to her.

'Hey, Nat. Are you having a good time? I know we haven't spoken much,' she said, wiping a stray lock of hair from her face.

'It's cool. This is Jaden's day. This is a nice turnout.'

'It is. I still think he got too much stuff, but I can't blame people for wanting to spoil him.' Lorraine's eyes hadn't left her son and baby father. Natty took a deep breath.

'Lorraine?'

'Don't, Natty.'

'Don't what?' He replied, frowning.

'Whatever you're about to say about Raider, just don't. Please.'

Natty didn't know how she knew, but he pushed ahead anyway.

'Look, I know you don't want to hear it, but you need to be careful around him.'

Lorraine shook her head.

'Natty, it's Jaden's day. I don't want to do this right now, so leave it.'

'I'm only looking out for you both,' Natty said thickly, stung by her response.

'Look, he's happy to see his dad. So please, for Jaden, don't start anything. Okay?'

Natty scowled. Sighing, Lorraine moved away. Again, Natty felt Tommy's eyes on him. Whether he agreed with Lorraine, she was right about it being Jaden's day. As much as he wanted to, he wasn't going to do anything to ruin it for him. He finished his drink, and then said his goodbyes. Still busy with his dad, Jaden barely gave him a wave, and Lorraine's goodbye was perfunctory. Raider smirked his way, then winked.

As Natty left, Raider shifted closer to Lorraine, his arm already around his son.

CHAPTER TWENTY-TWO

NEEDING a distraction from thinking about his plans, or overthinking about Lorraine and Raider, Natty stepped up his investigation into Anika. He'd wondered if he would hear from Spence about turning up at his house, but either Anika hadn't said anything, or Spence was keeping it to himself.

Either way, Natty had someone else to speak to.

Carmen was Anika's closest friend. Natty followed her on Instagram through a burner account, and it was easy to find her in town after checking her story. She was walking out of a nail salon when Natty accidentally crossed her path.

'Natty?' She said, recognising him immediately. Natty stopped short, smiling at her.

'Carmen. How are you doing, babe? You look good as hell.'

Carmen preened, a flush appearing across her pretty face. She had curly blonde hair, pale green eyes, thin lips, and a slender figure.

'Don't start, Natty. You know that I'm taken,' she said, giggling. Natty held up his hands in mock surrender.

'I'm just telling you the truth. Your fella is truly a lucky guy.' Natty surveyed the gleam in Carmen's eyes. If he pursued her, he was sure he could make it pay off, but he had work to do, and the last thing he needed was more female drama. 'Seriously . . . how's everything going? I saw Anika the other day. Her and Spence seem well.' He watched Carmen closely for any sort of reaction.

'I assume she's doing well. I mean, we text every now and then, but I haven't properly hung out with her since my birthday. She's always busy with work, but we're definitely due a messy night out.'

Natty smiled at Carmen's words, more convinced than ever Anika was cheating. Spence had mentioned her getting dressed up to go to Carmen's, meaning she'd lied.

'You should definitely ring her and sort something out. She's her own boss, so she should be able to make the time for her best friend.' Natty glanced around. 'I'm gonna let you get back to your man, anyway. You can show him how pretty your nails look.'

Natty was ready to leave, but Carmen surprised him by hugging him. He held her tightly for a moment and went to move away, but she held on a second longer, biting her lip and looking up at him, her face flushed.

'It was nice running into you, Natty. Maybe I'll see you again soon,' she said, walking away. Natty watched her leave, amused at her antics. Turning away, he forced Carmen from his mind, already coming up with a plan for dealing with Anika. He considered going to Spence with what he knew, but he wanted more proof. It was the least his friend deserved.

* * *

NATTY'S DETERMINATION TO expose Anika led to him waiting on Spence's street the same night. Spence was working, and he wanted to see where Anika went, or if anyone suspicious came to the house. He parked across the road, no music playing, staring at the house, hoping nothing untoward happened, yet preparing for the worst.

The lights were on, but there was no movement so far.

As Natty stifled a yawn a while later, a taxi pulled up. Natty straightened in his seat as the Uber stopped outside Spence's. After a few minutes, Anika sauntered from the house, looking in far better spirits than the last time Natty had spoken to her. She wore a red vest top and tight white trousers with heels. Her hair was elaborately teased into curls, dark red lipstick adorning her mouth. She climbed into the back of the taxi, which drove away.

Natty pulled out after a few seconds, following at a distance, keeping a car between them. His heart raced as he gripped the steering wheel. Carmen had said they weren't spending much time together, and she was Anika's closest friend.

They drove toward the Hood, Natty's suspicion ever increasing. Whoever Anika was creeping with was going to get a beating. There was no way around it. He continued the steady pursuit, driving past the Northern Dance School and further up Chapeltown Road. He slowed at some traffic lights, mimicking the car in front, but cursed when Anika's taxi zoomed through the amber light. Natty turned onto Cowper Street and pulled up after the light's turned green, unsure where the taxi had gone.

Natty pulled out his phone and called Cameron, hoping he was home and could do a search for the taxi. It rang through to voicemail. Kissing his teeth, Natty tried again, still receiving no answer. He tossed the phone onto the passenger seat and drove home, his mind buzzing.

* * *

NATTY MULLED over the situation with Spence and Anika for the rest of the night, irritated that he still didn't have adequate proof about Anika. His gut told him she was up to no good, but that wasn't enough. He wondered if he could discreetly put the word out. If she was messing around with a guy in the Hood, someone had to know about it.

Natty called Carlton. He worked with Natty in Little London, but moved between their teams. He could do the rounds on Natty's behalf and get more information on Anika's Hood link.

'Yes, boss. What's good?' said Carlton.

In an instant, Natty changed his mind, not wanting to involve more people than necessary in Spence's business.

'Just checking in. Everything good?'

'Better than good, bro. The numbers are high.'

'That's what I like to hear. Listen, I'll check in on you soon. Shout me if you need anything.'

Natty hung up, still holding his phone. Lately, he had dedicated a lot of time to this task. Things in Little London were running smoothly, but Natty needed to be able to handle both.

Again, his plans were at the forefront of his mind. He called another person.

'Rudy,' he said when the man answered. 'Fancy a drink tomorrow?'

* * *

THE NEXT NIGHT, Natty and Rudy went for drinks at another pub — this time in Headingley. After paying for their drinks, they sat outside. Natty surveyed the woman arrayed around the spot. The weather hadn't cooled yet, and his eyes lingered on the shapely ones wearing sundresses and floaty skirts. He felt young and carefree for a moment, but wondered when life had grown so tough.

'How are you getting on?' Rudy asked after a moment. He sipped his beer, his eyes on Natty.

'I'm not sure.'

Rudy frowned.

'I don't understand. You're doing extremely well in Little London. You've made a name for yourself out there. You're making more money . . .'

'True. I want more.'

'More money will come, Nathaniel. You're making the right moves, and your name is in the right circles. What you need to do is stop wasting the money you have. Keep hold of it, because you never know when you might need it.'

Natty scowled, annoyed at Rudy's assumptions. The fact was, he'd saved up a decent amount of money. He wasn't going out as much, nor was he spending silly money on clothes and jewellery he didn't need.

Until now, he hadn't considered why.

'Money isn't a problem, Rudy. I want more responsibility.'

Rudy took another sip.

'I'll relay this back to your uncle, but I'm not promising anything.'

'Why can't I speak to him myself?' Natty's drink remained untouched.

'I can't stop you speaking to your family, Nathaniel. You have his number, but we both know your uncle respects structure. He won't appreciate you calling about business. I think you know that.'

Natty rubbed his forehead with his free hand. He hated that he had to go through so many hoops, comparing this talk to the time he and Rudy had gone to the pub after his argument with Elijah's team. He'd asked what he had to do to step up, and had been annoyed by Rudy's answers then. Still, he'd kept his head down and did what he needed to do.

Now, he was in the same position.

'Are you still getting along with Elijah?' Rudy asked after a long moment. Natty simply nodded. 'What about that girl you like? Anything going on there?'

Startled, Natty glowered at Rudy, surprised he would bring up Lorraine.

'We're friends,' he said, not mentioning that he hadn't seen her in a while. Finishing his drink, Rudy said no more.

* * *

AFTER LEAVING RUDY, Natty stewed at home, unsatisfied by the meeting. He'd kept his temper and avoided saying something he couldn't take back, but he wasn't sure how much longer he could carry on at his level. The money in Little London was good, and for what he needed to do there, extremely easy. It wasn't enough, though. Not anymore. He was thinking deeply about his future, and the logical next steps he could take.

Natty's thoughts slipped to Anika and Spence, irritated he hadn't gotten anywhere. He considered reaching out to Cameron. He hadn't seen his friend much lately, and Cameron knew about Anika — he could give some insight into what was going on, or who she could be hooking up with. His phone buzzed, drawing his attention.

Natty's stomach fluttered when he saw a message from Lorraine, asking how he was.

Staring down at the message, Natty locked his phone, clambering to his feet and shuffling off to bed. He wasn't tired, but wanted to try to get some sleep regardless.

* * *

LORRAINE SAT in her living room, her hair wrapped, legs curled under her as she typed on her MacBook. She'd been working steadily for over an hour, and when she grabbed her cup of tea, she frowned when she realised it had gone cold. Taking a short break, she poured the remains down the sink and made a new one.

As she waited for the kettle to boil, she glanced at the kitchen table, recalling Natty approaching the first time he'd seen her working. He hadn't cared then, but he'd since shown more of an interest. Lorraine wondered what he was doing. She hadn't heard from him since Jaden's birthday party. It had been nice seeing him there, and she liked that he got along well with her family. Her mum liked him, and so did Tommy — who didn't like many people. Raider included.

Lorraine smiled, thinking of Jaden and his attempts to sleep in the tracksuit Natty had bought him. He wanted to wear it everywhere, and she'd caught him in the mirror, flexing his muscles and trying to smirk and stand like Natty. It warmed her heart.

With a sinking feeling, she realised that the last time she'd spoken with Natty, he'd tried talking to her about Raider, and she'd silenced him, not wanting to have an awkward conversation during the party. Recalling he'd bought her the laptop that she loved, her stomach fluttered, remembering the moment he'd given it to her in the kitchen.

Before she could change her mind, she sent him a text message, to see how he was doing.

Lorraine was unsure of the implications of Raider being back around. Since the party, he'd come over a few times, chilling with Jaden for a while before leaving. There had been no drama, and he hadn't tried it on with her, or asked about Natty.

As the kettle boiled, Lorraine wondered about Raider and whether he wanted to be in Jaden's life full-time. She hoped he did. Whilst she had no desire for any relationship with her son's father, she wanted her son to still have one. After a while, she was back working when there was a loud banging at the door, startling her. She opened the door, and Raider stumbled inside, grinning, eyes red and bloodshot.

'What are you up to?' He slurred, pulling her in for a hug, hands roving over her curves. Lorraine tried to pull away.

'Get off me. Keep the noise down too. Jaden is sleeping.'

'What are you doing? You still ain't answered me.' Ignoring her, Raider pulled her into the living room and flopped on the sofa. 'What do you have to drink?'

Lorraine's lip curled. 'It looks like you've had enough.'

Raider scoffed.

'You're not my mum.' His eyes gleamed as he checked her out. 'I've never gotten over you, Lorraine. We should try again. Things will be different this time.'

Lorraine blinked, unsure where the words were coming from. She folded her arms, thinking of the older days, when her weaker self would have fallen for his shtick.

'I don't think that would be a good idea.'

Raider's eyes narrowed, his drunken grin finally dissipating.

'We could be a family: me, you, Jaden. We could even have another one. You always wanted a little girl, didn't you?'

Lorraine wiped away an angry tear, furious at his attempted emotional manipulation.

'You don't care, do you? You'd really use your son as an excuse to get your leg over?'

'It's not like that, babe. You know how I feel about you,' said Raider.

Lorraine tensed.

'Do *not* call me babe. I know exactly how you feel: entitled; like I belong to you, but I don't, and I never will.'

'What are you trying to say?' Raider's voice was dangerously low, but Lorraine didn't let it affect her.

'I've already told you before. I don't mind if you want to spend time with Jaden, but beyond that, there is nothing further between us.'

Raider gawped at Lorraine, startled she was speaking to him like this. Attempting to swallow down his anger, he spoke again.

'Is this about that prick Natty?'

Lorraine shook her head.

'Natty has nothing to do with this.'

Raider sat up, nostrils flaring.

'Bullshit! You've always been all over him. Even back in the day. When I first wanted to check you, everyone said you were taken, but I was dumb enough to believe you when you said you weren't. Tell me the fucking truth!'

'Keep your voice down,' Lorraine hissed. 'Your son is trying to sleep, or do you no longer care because I won't fuck you?'

'Don't change the subject, Lorraine. You're supposed to be my girl. What was the point in even making a baby if I can't have you?'

'Have me?' Lorraine laughed incredulously. 'It takes two to make a baby, Michael, but you did it because you could. From day one, you've done your best to stay uninvolved, thinking you can pop up for a bit, then disappear again. Also, let's not forget the fact you tried to make me get an abortion.'

Not wanting to admit she was right, Raider pressed on, eyes blazing.

'Fuck that. This isn't even about us. It's about Natty, trying to take something that's mine.'

'No, it isn't about Natty. This is about you and your responsibilities as a father. Responsibilities you've never taken seriously.' Lorraine took a deep breath, feeling a tightness in her chest. 'I want you to leave, Michael. I'm tired of having this conversation. Come back another time if you want to see Jaden.'

'Why are you trying to get rid of me? Who do you have coming round?'

'No one. Please, just leave. Don't wake up your son and let him see you like this,' said Lorraine.

Raider rubbed his forehead.

'I'm sorry, babe. I do care. About you and about Jaden.'

'I said, *don't* call me babe, Michael. Please, just go.' Lorraine had heard all of this before, and it was draining.

Raider ignored her, continuing to stare her down. She could see his muscles trembling, realising he was furious at her defiance. When she didn't see him move, she made a decision.

'Fine, you can deal with Tommy.'

Snarling, Raider leapt to his feet and grabbed her when she went for her phone. Lorraine lashed out, attempting to defend herself. She caught Raider in the face, and he snarled. Slapping her twice in retaliation, he shoved her into the coffee table. Lorraine shrieked when her back slammed into it, pain shooting through her. Raider didn't hesitate, drawing his foot back and kicking her in the ribs. She curled into a ball, gasping for breath.

Raider glared down at her trembling form, breathing hard.

'I'll knock out your brother if he talks shit. He's not in the life anymore, and he's washed up.' He yanked Lorraine by her hair and pulled her up. 'I breeded you, not Natty. Remember your place, or else.' He stormed out, letting her drop to the floor, leaving Lorraine weeping in pain, her ribs almost certainly broken.

CHAPTER TWENTY-THREE

CAMERON SIPPED A GLASS OF BRANDY, staring at his phone. Lately, he found himself staring off into space from time to time.

He was a killer.

The knowledge weighed heavily on him, yet lately, he felt more like his old self.

The word on Christian's death had flittered around the Hood, but he was such a small player that it didn't linger for long. Rudy had hinted at more jobs for him in the future, and despite his mixed thoughts, Cameron liked the idea of being considered important; there was a particular reputation that came with being a shooter, and he was ready to grasp it, no matter who he had to take out.

Cameron's ringing phone took him out of his thoughts. He glanced down at Natty's name, wondering what he could want. Though still close, they hadn't hung out much. Natty was focused on growing the Little London market, and Spence was taking his responsibilities running their crew seriously. They didn't have as much time for Cameron, and he wiped his mouth, unsure whether he was still bitter about this fact. Finally, he answered.

'Yes, Nat. You good?'

'I am, bro. You home? I need to speak to you.'

'Yeah, I'll leave the door unlocked,' said Cameron, a sliver of fear glissading down his spine. 'Everything okay?'

Natty didn't speak for a moment.

'I'll tell you when I get there. I'm on route.'

Natty hung up. Cameron drained his drink, then went to wash his face and sharpen up. He didn't know if Natty had heard about Christian, but he didn't think he could link it to him, regardless.

When he returned downstairs, the door opened, and Natty walked in, nodding at him. He seemed the same as ever, his solid build and height imposing. His eyes seemed different. Sharper somehow, but with small bags underneath, suggesting late nights on little sleep. Cameron knew the feeling.

'You look tired,' he said. Natty grinned his agreement.

'I'll be alright. Pity your shit coffee won't do anything for me.'

Cameron laughed. They went to the living room. Natty glanced at the huge television Cameron had bought, his eyebrows raising.

'When did you get that?' He asked.

'I can't remember. A few weeks ago, I think.'

'You have a family member die or something? You're spending money like you own Amazon.'

Cameron chuckled. 'I'm just being better with my money,' he said easily. 'Maybe Spence is having more of an influence on me than we thought.'

That got a smile out of Natty.

'Maybe. I've noticed I'm not spending as much lately,' he admitted. 'Spence is the reason I'm here, anyway.'

'What's happened?' Cameron asked. He'd finally gotten over the humiliation he felt after Gavin played him. Since then, he'd remained vigilant and was sure that nothing else had got past him.

'Anika.'

Cameron froze, fighting to stay neutral. There was no way Natty could know.

'What about her?' He was pleased his voice sounded normal.

'I think she's creeping.'

The bad feeling in the pit of Cameron's stomach grew. He coughed into his fist.

'I'm thirsty. Do you want a drink?' He asked, motioning to the empty glass on the table.

'I'm good,' Natty replied. Cameron topped up his drink, taking advantage of the moment to formulate his responses. He was prepared to blame it all on Anika if it came up. Natty would be angry, but if Cameron focused his ire on Anika, he could get through it.

'Right,' he started, sipping his brandy to fortify his nerves, 'what were you saying about whatshername?'

Natty kept his eyes on Cameron, arms folded across his chest. His expression was grim, and that made Cameron as nervous as his words.

'Back in the day, you lot had your thing . . .'

'. . . That's old news. What about it?'

'You know her better than I do. What was she like back then?'

Cameron's mind whirred as he formulated a response. Natty knew something. He didn't realise it was Cameron, but he knew Anika was messing around with someone. He could still get out of this if he said the right things.

'What have I missed?' He asked after a moment. Natty continued to stare him down. Cameron fought to stay calm, but with every passing second, his panic grew.

'Back in the day, you lot had your thing. Do you remember her checking for any other guys in the ends?' Natty finally spoke.

Cameron scratched his chin, needing the extra seconds. The time back then was a blur. He remembered randomly meeting Anika in a club, the vibe between them heated from the beginning. She liked to go out and party, occasionally partaking in drugs. Cameron couldn't remember her sniffing around other guys, nor could he think of a patsy he could use to potentially divert suspicion from himself.

'Nah. She liked to go out, and I'm guessing she had connections in the Hood, even back then.'

'What makes you say that?'

'She just seemed comfy,' replied Cameron. 'You know the rep Chapeltown has sometimes. Seems scary to people outside of the bubble, but she was always calm.'

Natty didn't respond, still deep in thought.

'Why do you think she's creeping?' Cameron pressed.

'She's been acting funny for a while. Saying she's going to see friends, but going somewhere else. I caught her leaving the other night. She took a taxi to the Hood, but I lost track of her at some lights.'

'For real? That's mad.' Panic warred with fury in Cameron's mind. He couldn't believe Anika had been so stupid with her excuses and attitude.

Now, Natty and probably Spence were onto her.

'I'm gonna find out who she's dealing with, then I'm gonna deal with them. No one fucks with my people.'

'I get it, Nat,' said Cameron, unease growing at Natty's words. He didn't doubt he meant them. 'What do you need from me?'

'Just keep an eye on things. If anyone says anything about Anika or Spence, I wanna hear about it. If anyone is bragging about a new ting they're banging, I wanna hear about it. Cool?'

'Cool, Nat. Spence is my brother too. We'll deal with this.'

Natty slapped Cameron's hand. They hung for a while longer, talking about general things, before Natty's phone rang, and he left.

Cameron locked the door behind him, remaining standing, breathing deep after the revelation. Natty was relentless when it came to investigating matters like this. He wouldn't stop until he found something, and if he interrogated Anika, it would end badly for both of them. Cameron stomped back to the living room and grabbed his phone, needing to have words with her.

* * *

ANIKA'S MIND whirred as she leaned back in the taxi. Cameron had been contacting her all day, insisting on meeting. It was so against how they usually did things, that she found herself suspicious.

Was he trying to set her up?

Anika dismissed the idea as quickly as it came to her mind. Not because she fully trusted Cameron, but because she knew that he would also be at risk if anyone found out about them. She thought about Natty turning up to see Spence again, flipping her question on her by asking if she was happy. It had baffled her; she'd wondered if he had meant something by it, but couldn't work out what.

Finally, Anika had put it to the back of her mind, not needing more things to worry over.

Anika worried something was broken between her and Spence. She wished she could say it was due to his desire to have a friendship with Rosie, a woman she knew was beautiful. More than this, Anika and Spence seemed to be on opposite sides, like passing ships shuffling around each other. They rarely spent time together, nor did they seem to actively pursue it. Occasionally, one of them would offer to cook, or suggest going out to eat, but these times were few and far between. Further, since their last argument.

Anika had backed down, unwilling to impose her own cheating ways and assumptions on Spence. He had told her of Rosie. He hadn't lied.

He wasn't sleeping with her best friend.

Wiping her cheek, Anika blew out a breath, an action caught by the taxi driver. He shot her a look.

'Everything okay?'

Anika nodded.

When she arrived, she glanced around her, not wanting any of Cameron's neighbours to see her. He'd assured her they were cool, but she wasn't sure what that meant. Luckily, Cameron was quick to answer, all-but dragging her inside and locking the door behind them. She jerked her arm away, glaring.

'What the hell are you doing?'

'I could ask you the same damn question,' Cameron snapped.

'What do you mean?' Anika's brow furrowed. Cameron looked furious, his eyes flashing, mouth set in a hard line. She didn't know what could have caused it.

'Natty came to see me.'

Anika's insides twisted. Natty randomly showing at the house again flashing behind her eyes.

'Why?'

'Because he thinks you're cheating on Spence.'

Anika's knees weakened, nausea swimming around her throat. She took several deep breaths, forcing the bile back down.

'Why does he think that?'

'Because you have no fucking chill,' Cameron snarled. 'What the hell is going on between you and Spence?'

'What do you mean?' Anika repeated.

'Natty says Spence thinks you've changed. He's seen you getting all dressed up, and Natty knows you're not going to your stupid friend's house. He even followed you to the Hood . . . the last time you came here.'

'What?' The words struck Anika like blows. At first, she struggled to comprehend what Cameron was saying. 'How does he know all of that?'

'Because he's smart,' Cameron roared. 'He put it together, and now he's asking me questions about you; about dudes you might know in the Hood.'

'What did you say to him?' Anika's heart leapt in her throat. She couldn't believe this was happening. Natty hadn't come to the house looking for Spence. He'd come to see her, wanting the measure of her, to see how she responded to his riddle of a question.

'What the fuck do you think I said? What was I supposed to say? I said I would ask around.'

Neither spoke for a moment, gathering their thoughts.

'Well?' Cameron finally demanded.

'Well, what?'

'What is going on with you and Spence?'

'Nothing,' she snapped. 'We're barely communicating, but that doesn't mean —'

'What? Doesn't mean he should speak to his friend and tell him you're different? Use your damn brain. Spence is too smart for his own good, and Natty is sharp. He sees the things Spence doesn't.'

Anika took a deep breath, wanting to retort, yet not seeing the point.

'What do we do now?'

Cameron rubbed his forehead, sighing.

'We keep it calm. You need to fix your relationship and stop Spence suspecting anything. Doesn't matter how you do it . . . listen to Spence talk about his day, or sit and watch Netflix. It just needs containing. If that happens, he'll tell Natty it's calm, and things will return to normal.'

'Okay. What happens after that?'

Cameron didn't know what to say. He wondered why he was fighting so hard to keep this going with Anika. He'd gotten her back, even when she was in a serious relationship with his friend. She'd succumbed to him multiple times.

So, why was he continuing it?

* * *

Lorraine lay in a hospital bed, staring up at the ceiling, unable to speak. When she'd recovered some of her strength, she'd called Rosie. Rosie had called Lorraine's mum, who'd stayed with Jaden while she went to get checked out.

Lorraine felt overwhelming emotions over what had happened. Despite how things had been with her and Raider over the years, she never thought he would attack her. He hadn't even cared his son was in the house.

In the afternoon, Rosie entered the room, eyes glistening when she saw her friend's state.

'Raider?' She asked, already knowing the answer. Lorraine nodded. 'Have you called the police yet?'

'I don't want to do that . . . I just want to forget it happened. The doctors said I can go home later. I just want to focus on that.' Lorraine rubbed her arms. She shifted, unable to get comfortable, wincing as she stared straight ahead.

Rosie hated how broken her friend seemed. When Lorraine called, all she'd said was that she'd been hurt, refusing to give any details about the attack to either Rosie or her family. Rosie's veins thrummed with rage at the thought of Raider putting his hands on her best friend.

'You can't let him get away with this. He could have killed you. You're lucky your ribs aren't broken,' she said.

'Trust me, badly bruised ribs aren't that much better,' said Lorraine, wincing as she moved.

'Lorraine . . .'

'It's my life, Rosie. This is my decision to make.'

'Do you remember what I went through with Kyle? How I buried my head in the sand every time he kicked the shit out of me?'

'Do you remember when you wanted to be left alone to deal with it?' Lorraine retorted.

Rosie sighed, trying to calm down.

'I spent more time than I ever wanted in this place. I hate it.' She looked around the boxy, white-walled room, cleaning solution mixed with a putrid *hospital* stench, filling her nostrils. A tear spilt down her face. 'I'm going to have a cig, and when I come back, we can talk about anything you want.'

Lorraine gave Rosie a grateful smile and closed her eyes. When Rosie headed out, Lorraine succumbed to tears, tired of holding it together; reliving the fear she had felt when Raider loomed over her.

His child's mother.

As Rosie headed away, she heard Lorraine's tears, which wrenched her heart. Tears ran freely now, hurting over the pain her friend had suffered. When Rosie reached the exit, She called a number, steeling herself for the person answering.

'Spence? It's Rosie.'

* * *

NATTY AND SPENCE were in the middle of a lazy day. Natty had been running himself ragged in so many different circles that he just wanted to relax. He still felt like he was at the precipice of an important decision, but for once, he didn't want to overwhelm himself with thoughts about his issues.

The pair had eaten lunch in the Hood earlier, now sitting in Spence's garden with cans of ginger beer, and containers of cake and custard. Natty sat on the wall, his snack resting on his lap, enjoying the feel of a gentle breeze on his arms. Times like this, he felt he could stay this way forever.

Spence's garden had a small patch of well-tended grass, surrounded by a concrete square. He wasn't much of a gardener, but they had enough room to sit comfortably. Natty knew Anika was at work — at least, that's what Spence believed. He'd yet to hear anything back from Cameron about men from Anika's past, and his subtle inquiries about recent high-profile hook-ups had gotten him nowhere.

'Feels like we haven't done this in a while,' Natty said after a while.

Spence, resting peacefully against a small brown fence separating his garden from the next, cleared his throat.

'We're busy men these days. I can't remember the last time all three of us kicked it.'

Natty considered this. It had been a while. Since he began overseeing Little London, he couldn't think of a time they had all hung out, hoping it wasn't a sign they were growing apart.

'How has Cam been with you lately?'

'He's doing better, it seems. He's not getting on my back about Nika anymore, and he does his job without issue. That shit with Gavin and the missing product knocked him back.'

'I can see that. Cam's not a guy that likes making those kinds of mistakes.'

'He's learned from it and chilled out by the looks of things. He's not causing drama. In fact, he's not really around.'

'What do you mean?' Natty's ears pricked up.

'Nothing really. He just works and bails. Doesn't hang around like he used to.'

'Why do you think that is?'

Spence shrugged. 'Couldn't tell you. It's not something I've thought about. Do you think something is going on?'

Natty wasn't sure how to answer. It was a change of character for Cameron. He thrived on being seen, and when Natty was previously around the base, Cameron was always around, whether he was working on not.

'He might be freelancing. That, or he's got a girlfriend.'

Spence chuckled.

'Wouldn't that be something? Cam all loved up, after all the shit he gave me?'

Natty too laughed, nearly choking on his drink. He wiped his mouth, deciding to give the matter more thought later.

'How are things with you and Anika lately?'

Spence's jaw tightened, Natty immediately noticing.

'We're fine, I guess.'

'You guess?'

'We argued over Rosie, but that was ages ago. Thought we got past it, but I dunno. Doesn't feel like she's all in.'

Natty mulled the words, combining these with the lack of emotion in his friend's voice. He desperately wanted to mention what he suspected about Anika, but couldn't. Not yet.

'How are you doing with Rosie?' He smirked, noting how flustered Spence was.

'We're fine. Nothing since the last time I thought she was gonna try something.'

Despite Spence's nonchalance about the time he spent with Rosie, Natty knew there was chemistry between them, and couldn't see that changing any time soon.

Before he could question this any further, Spence's phone rang. Spence glanced at the screen, eyes widening before he answered, pressing the phone to his ear.

Natty tuned out while he was talking, thinking about Spence and Rosie. He wished he could speak to Lorraine about it, but he hadn't responded to her last text message, and felt weird trying to start another conversation. The longer it went on, the harder it seemed. They'd worked hard to get past all the nonsense before, and he missed her. And Jaden.

Despite that, he didn't like how she'd responded to Raider at Jaden's party. Draining his drink, he put the can on the wall beside him. Turning to Spence, he frowned when he saw the worried expression on his friend's face.

'Spence? What's up?' Natty's immediate thought was that something had happened with Anika.

Spence took a deep breath.

'Nat, I need you to stay calm. That was Rosie. Something happened to Lorraine.'

'What happened?' Natty felt a weight on his chest, lifting his shoulders, bracing himself.

'Raider attacked her. She's in hospital.'

A great chill overwhelmed Natty as he absorbed what Spence had said. He felt his hands clench and unclench, an edgy, twitchy feeling surging through his body.

'Is she okay?' His voice sounded foreign and far away. He hadn't realised he'd climbed from the wall, the can and container tumbling to the ground. Ignoring them, Natty focused on Spence.

'She's bruised and a bit shook up, but she's fine. I know what you're feeling, Natty, but you need—'

'Is Jaden okay? Did he see anything?'

'Rosie didn't mention him, so I'm guessing he is. He's probably with Lorraine's mum. Nat—'

'Don't, Spence. Don't even try.'

Spence's shoulders slumped. He'd watched Natty's reaction, startled when his friend had leapt from the wall. For a moment, Spence had thought Natty would attack him. He knew exactly how things were going to play out. Natty wouldn't be stopped.

He tried anyway.

'Nat, stay calm. Speak to Elijah; get him to sort it with Raider. Think about the business.'

'Fuck the business,' Natty replied, his voice calm. Spence closed his eyes, acknowledging his friend's words. An angry Natty was hard enough to get through to. It rarely surfaced, but when it did, logical and calculated Natty was terrifying. His mind was made up, and there would be no telling him otherwise.

'Speak to Lorraine, because I guarantee she won't want you getting into trouble over her.'

'She should have come to me. I would have protected her,' replied Natty, pacing on the spot, voice trembling.

'She probably didn't want you to get yourself in trouble, like I said.' Spence tried again.

'Spence, it's already done. You're not gonna talk me out of it.' Natty didn't even look at him.

'Lorraine wouldn't want you to get involved.'

Natty faced him, his eyes locked onto Spence's.

'Not Lorraine. You. *You* don't want me to spoil the flow of money into your fucking pocket, so don't pretend this is about her feelings.'

Spence took a step back, realising he needed to back off. Natty took a deep breath, seemingly calming down.

'Are you at least ready to admit it then?' Spence asked.

'Admit what?'

'That you have serious feelings for Lorraine.'

Natty shook his head.

'It isn't the time for that conversation, Spence.'

'Fine, let's get real. Raider is super-tough. He's a throwback to one of those crazy street dudes from the early two-thousands. Remember the beef he got into with Drakey? He almost killed him.'

'Whatever happens, happens. I'll get with you later, Spence.' Natty left, ignoring the calls of his friend.

* * *

AT HOME, Natty stared at his phone. It had been nearly an hour, and his anger hadn't abated. He wanted to contact Lorraine, but he wasn't supposed to know what happened.

Spence was right about one thing; Lorraine had tried to keep him out of it, but he wasn't going to listen. He was going to handle this, once and for all. He would do it for Jaden and Lorraine. The thought that Jaden might have seen his mum get attacked was too much for Natty to cope with, as was the thought of Jaden potentially receiving the same treatment.

He made a few calls, trying to get Raider's number, his anger growing every time another contact let him down, either unknowing or unwilling to share Raider's number. He tossed his phone aside after trying Rudy and Elijah, nostrils flaring. He needed to find Raider. An alternative was to spin the streets in the Hood, looking for him. Rubbing his knuckles, he pondered the dilemma until an idea came to him. Grabbing the phone, he found a contact a pressed the call button, jamming the phone to his ear.

'Yo,' the person answered.

'It's Natty. You good?'

'Yeah, fam. What's going on? Not like you to reach out,' said Wonder. They'd buried the hatchet a while back, and the few times they'd hung around each other since Ellie's party had been amicable.

'I need Raider's number. Figured you'd have it.'

'What do you need it for?' Wonder's tone had changed, becoming more guarded. Natty couldn't blame him. Everyone knew their issues.

'I wanted to speak to him about burying the beef.'

'Why?'

'Our teams are working well together. Everyone's making more money, so why hold a grudge?'

Wonder didn't respond. Natty's heart thudded as he waited, worried he'd overplayed his hand. If this didn't work, he'd hit the streets, vowing not to rest until he'd found Raider.

'Look,' Wonder finally said, 'I'll give you the number, but don't tell him you got it from me. Raider is funny about people chatting his business.'

Relief flooded Natty.

'I won't say a word, bro. Next time we're out, the drinks are on me.'

Laughing, Wonder relayed the number and hung up. Natty immediately inputted Raider's number and called him, trying to control his roiling emotions. The effort to stay calm during the call with Wonder had tested his resolve, but it was worth it.

'Who's this?' Raider's tone was dismissive, full of malice, and only made Natty angrier.

'You know who this is.'

Raider snorted.

'Guess she told you what happened. Figured she'd go running to her little sideman.'

Natty didn't respond, letting Raider talk.

'What do you want, Dunn? Did you ring me just to hear me breathing? How the fuck did you get my number, anyway?'

'We need to talk.'

Again, Raider snorted.

'Are you sure you wanna do that?'

'We're going to do it. If you're the man you're claiming, you'll do it one-on-one.'

Raider chuckled.

'Okay, fam. You wanna die so badly, you can. I'll be waiting at my spot.'

Raider gave Natty the address, then hung up without waiting for confirmation.

* * *

NATTY DROVE to Raider's place, parking across the road and wondering if he should have brought a weapon. There was always the possibility Raider was setting him up, but Natty decided it wasn't in his nature. Raider wanted this as much as Natty did. This thing between them had festered, reaching its breaking point. There was only one way to resolve it, and Natty recognised that.

Raider stayed on Hamilton Avenue, the terraced spot blending in with the houses around it. It had a black door and a matching black gate with chipped paint. Natty climbed from the car and strode across the road, walking into the living room with his hands down. Raider wasn't going to jump him. He didn't know how he knew, but he did.

Sure enough, Raider stood in the cramped living room. He'd already moved a cheap coffee table to the corner of the room, giving them space. His eyes glittered as he stared down Natty, a smirk gracing his brutal features.

'Should have known she'd go running to you. Where's Tommy? Was he too pussy to come after me himself?'

Natty just watched, heart thudding against his chest. He tried to stay in control. Raider was tough, and this fight was going to take a lot out of him, but there was no way around it. Business or not, this needed to happen. Realising Natty wasn't going to reply, Raider spoke again.

'I dunno what any of them see in you.'

'You shouldn't have put your hands on her.'

Raider shook his head.

'You should have put a baby in her. She'd always have been yours then. Instead, you're fucking hanging around, anyway. Confusing shit.' Raider took a step forward. 'You're the reason she took a beating.'

Both men cautiously moved toward the other. Natty's eyes widened as a fist shot towards his face quicker than expected. He dodged, but it still glanced against his cheek, smarting. Raider chuckled.

'Everyone says you're a badman. Thought you were rougher than this.'

Enraged, Natty lunged in, missing the smirk on Raider's face as he played right into his hands. Grabbing him, Raider slammed his fist several times into Natty's stomach, each blow more punishing than the last. Natty spluttered from the hits, finally managing to get his knee up, breaking the hold. He caught Raider with an elbow. Raider backed away, no longer smiling. He wiped his mouth.

'They all think you're so fucking special, but you're not. Without Rudy and your uncle, you'd be nothing.'

Breathing hard, Natty began circling, putting his hands up. Rushing in before was silly, and he needed to avoid making a similar mistake. Raider was much stronger than he'd expected, but there was no going back now. They were here, and this had to happen. Raider was strong, but emotional. Natty wondered if that was his way in. Either way, he needed to fight carefully. Raider's eyes narrowed.

'What are you waiting for? Fight!'

The fight continued, both men trading blows. Natty got in too close, taking more damage from Raider's solid hits. He was still working out how to defeat Raider; the retaliatory hits his price to pay. He'd realised that when Raider's guard was high, it caused the punches Natty threw to deflect away from his face. After one such barrage, he again backed away.

Raider wiped his mouth, breathing hard.

'You shouldn't have come, Natty. You're a pussy. I don't even need to try against you.'

Losing his composure, Natty again charged, forgetting what had worked for him, taking a vicious knee to the stomach, which drove all the air from him. Raider drilled him in the face with a sharp right, and Natty tumbled to the ground, body screaming in pain. Raider mounted him, punching Natty several times in the face.

'Lorraine is mine,' he hissed. 'I'm gonna pay her a visit, and she's gonna know you died because of her.'

Natty's eyes dimmed, his energy slipping. He was in a precarious position, and knew he wouldn't survive too many more blows. Raider had played it perfectly, using his anger against him, and it surprised Natty. With all the stories he'd heard, he'd assumed Raider was a mindless brute, but he was far more intelligent than expected. As Raider raised his fist to hit him again, Natty thought of Jaden, imagining him scared and worried about his mum. Before Raider could hit him, Natty laughed. Raider's eyes narrowed, startled at the action.

'Y'know,' Natty croaked, 'Lorraine always said I fucked her better.' Raider stilled, and Natty knew he had him. 'She had your son, but her heart and pussy will always belong to me.'

'Fuck you!'

Raider was distracted enough for Natty to push him off. Both men scrambled to their feet. Natty's eyes flickered. He was unsteady on his feet, fighting to keep his guard up. By contrast, Raider was barely scratched. It took only a moment for Natty to work out what he needed to do. He launched forward. Raider's eyes lit up, thinking Natty was making the same mistake he'd made earlier. Raider raised his guard to deflect the blow, but Natty dropped, delivering a shuddering punch to Raider's rib, bending the brute over double. Gripping him, Natty kneed Raider in the face. Forcing him to the floor, Natty climbed on top of him, pounding into his lifeless face.

Natty drew his fist back one more time, but hesitated, staring at Raider's battered face. He dropped his hand, leaning back and sucking in air, adrenaline beginning to ebb as he realised how much trouble he was in.

CHAPTER TWENTY-FOUR

NATTY STEWED AT HOME, going over everything that had transpired. His hand ached, and as he'd calmed down, he considered his next move. There were several ways he could have handled the situation, and now he would have to deal with the politics stemming from his decision.

Spence came over the next day. Natty had called him after leaving Raider. His tense face told the story.

'They found him. Everyone's talking. With Raider's reputation, people are querying who could have beaten him up like that; what they might gain from doing it.'

Natty didn't respond, and after a moment, Spence pressed on.

'How are you feeling?'

'I don't regret it, if that's what you mean. I was reckless, but there was only one way that situation was gonna end.' Natty's vibrating phone stole his attention. He looked at the screen, then dropped it on the sofa.

'They're not going to stop calling, Nat. Rudy and Elijah are gonna wanna speak to you. The streets may be speculating, but it'll be obvious to the higher-ups who did this.'

Again, Natty didn't speak, rubbing his head. Spence was right, and he knew it. The beating Raider had taken, suggested it was a personal attack. Elijah, in particular, knew of the hatred between Natty and Raider.

Spence blew out a breath.

'Do you need anything?'

Natty shook his head.

'Have you spoken to Lorraine yet?'

Natty froze. He'd forgotten to speak to Lorraine in his haste to get back at Raider. The rage had taken over.

'No, I haven't.'

'Maybe you should, bro. Listen, I need to go away for a couple of days. One of my cousins down in Portsmouth died, and me and my pops are gonna go down for the funeral.'

Natty glanced at his friend. 'Sorry to hear that, bro. Do you want me to come with you?'

Spence shook his head.

'I'll be fine, fam. Stay here, and get your shit sorted out. Ring me if you need to talk some more.'

Spence gripped Natty's shoulder, then left him to his musings.

* * *

LATER THAT NIGHT, Natty was in an Uber on the way back from the hospital. When the pain in his hand had grown worse, he'd gone to get it checked out. Several hours later, he'd received some strong painkillers after an examination. His hand was simply sprained and would need a short while to heal. Nothing was broken, which he took as a relief. Hopefully, he wouldn't have to punch anyone soon.

Before going to sleep, Natty sent Lorraine a text message, asking if he could see her the next day. When Lorraine confirmed he could, he read the message several more times, before finally putting his phone away.

After a restless sleep, Natty showered, dressed, then left the house.

* * *

LORRAINE GREETED him at the door with a short hug, wincing, which refuelled Natty's rage. She had bruising on her face and was still moving gingerly. Inwardly, he felt satisfaction over the beating he'd given Raider in her honour.

'Are you okay?' She asked, watching his changing emotions. Natty nodded. Lorraine traced the bruising on his face, eyes widening. 'What happened?'

'Nothing.' Inwardly, he tensed, wishing he'd thought of an explanation for his face. Lorraine didn't respond, but glanced at him a moment longer, before they headed inside.

Jaden beamed when he saw Natty. He was on the sofa, a gaming device in his hands.

'Hey, Natty. Where have you been?'

'Just been busy, little man. How are you doing?' Despite his current problems, Natty smiled at Jaden, his heart lifting at seeing him.

'Fine. Mummy's not well. She fell over and hurt herself.'

Natty looked from Jaden to Lorraine. A long moment passed between them, before Natty cut the conversation with Jaden short, heading into the kitchen to make a drink, trying to keep it together.

'Natty.'

Natty's eyebrow rose when Tommy entered the kitchen. They bumped fists. Tommy grinned.

'Heard what happened to Raider. Glad you handled your business for my sister.' He glanced at the door, then back to Natty. 'Surprised you let him live.'

'I almost didn't,' admitted Natty, making a face. The painkillers he'd taken last night were wearing off, and he hadn't taken any more since waking up. Rooting in Lorraine's drawers, he found some ibuprofen and dry swallowed two tablets.

'What's going on now? The streets are talking. Elijah's gonna be out for blood.'

'What do you want me to say, Tom? I smacked him up, and I'll deal with whatever happens.'

Tommy hung his head. 'She's my little sis. I should have dealt with Raider. Deep down . . . I don't know if I'd have won.'

Natty shrugged, understanding how hard it was for Tommy to admit that.

'It is what it is. You don't need to worry about it now.'

'Nat?'

Lorraine appeared in the doorway, and both men froze, wondering how much she'd heard.

'How are you feeling?' Natty found his voice first, struggling to stay neutral. Lorraine kept her eyes on his.

'I'm fine.' She noticed the pack of painkillers. 'Why do you need those?'

'I had a headache,' said Natty. Lorraine frowned.

'Are you sure you're okay? What are you two talking about?'

'Just street stuff,' Natty replied. He pulled out his phone. 'I need to go.'

'You just got here. I need to talk to you,' protested Lorraine. Natty fought the urge to stay with her, slapping hands with Tommy, then giving Lorraine a short hug.

'I'll come back and see you later.'

Lorraine held her stomach and said, 'Natty, I really need to talk to you.'

Natty's hand rested on the door handle. He locked eyes with Lorraine, both recognising the sadness in the other. After a moment, he turned the handle.

'I know, Lorraine. I'll be back soon. I promise.'

* * *

AFTER LEAVING LORRAINE'S, Natty sat in his car, taking a deep breath. Lorraine didn't know about Raider yet, but it would only be a matter of time, especially if word was out about what had happened to him. Ignoring another call from Rudy, his stomach lurched, wondering how much longer he could get away with it.

Pulling up at Cameron's, he banged on the door, figuring he would need to rouse his friend. Seconds later, Cameron answered with a scowl.

'Couldn't you have called before you turned up?' He said.

'What's the big deal? Are you busy?'

'Nah, nothing like that. You just knock like you're fucking police.'

'Whatever. Move out the way and let me in.'

Chuckling, Cameron did as he was told. Both men headed for the kitchen, and Cameron fixed himself a coffee. He offered to make one for Natty, but he declined.

'Figured I'd hear from you. Streets are saying some shit about Raider. Was that you?'

Natty nodded. Cameron shook his head, laughing.

'You nearly killed him. What made you go off like that on him?'

Natty filled Cameron in. Cameron stopped chuckling, his brow furrowing.

'You're playing a dangerous game, Nat. Raider's a prick, but he's Elijah's boy. He can't lose face on this one. What if he snitches on you?'

'I don't know, Cam.' Natty rubbed his eyes. 'I tried calling Elijah beforehand to get Raider's details, but he didn't answer. I wasn't gonna wait.'

Cameron sipped his drink, his expression surprisingly unreadable.

'I always knew you were whipped over her.'

Both men shared a look, laughing for a moment.

'This isn't about that. He beat her up for no reason, and I wasn't gonna take that.'

'Big difference between smacking someone around and nearly killing them.' The image of Christian slumped on the floor flashed into Cameron's mind. He felt himself flinch.

Again, Natty shrugged. He didn't have the words for Cameron.

'At least you didn't kill him. I'm surprised you didn't.'

Natty frowned at Cameron's words. They weren't killers, but then again, he recognised that he had been angry enough to do it.

If he hadn't pulled his fist back at the last second, he might be sitting there having murdered someone.

'It doesn't matter now. Did you handle that thing?'

'What thing?' Cameron's brow furrowed.

'Anika. Did you learn anything?'

'Oh . . . Nah. If she's creeping with someone in the Hood, she's keeping it lowkey.'

'Spence is out of town, so I figured this would be the time for her to link her dude on the side. If I didn't have all this going on, I'd watch the house to see where she went.'

'Leave it with me, bro,' said Cameron after a moment. 'I'll look into it some more. You've got enough on your plate.'

'Okay. I appreciate it. Ring me if you hear anything.' Natty touched fists with Cameron, then left.

* * *

CAMERON LOCKED the door behind Natty, glad he hadn't stayed longer. With Spence having gone to a funeral, Anika hadn't wanted to stay home alone.

Staring into space for a moment, he gathered himself and headed back upstairs. Anika sat on the edge of the bed, pulling on her clothes. She glanced up at Cameron.

'Who was that?'

'Natty.' Cameron paced the bedroom. 'He was asking about you.'

'He knows I'm here?' Anika jumped to her feet, panicking.

'Course not. If he knew, he'd have dragged you out of the house.'

'And you'd let him do that?'

The pair locked eyes. Cameron weighed up his words, deciding to give it to her straight.

'We need to stop this.'

Anika's mouth fell open. Cameron could see her struggling to compose herself.

'What?'

'It's getting on top now. Natty ain't gonna stop until he finds something, and we're getting sloppy. You should have never stayed the night. We should have done this after he first came to me.'

'You . . . you can't be serious. What about everything we have? Everything you said to me?'

'We got sloppy,' Cameron repeated. 'You have a man, and I'm not waiting around for things to come out. We need to end it now.'

'I can't . . .'

Cameron held up a hand, losing patience with her. Anika wasn't seeing what was right in front of her. She was cheating on her man, and now they were at risk of being discovered.

'It's over. And let me tell you right now, don't let me hear about you saying anything to anyone.'

Anika's eyes widened.

'You're threatening me?'

'Only if you're dumb enough to call my name. Don't put me to the test. Even if anyone says anything, you'd better make something up. Got it?'

Anika stared at him.

'I said, *got it*?' Cameron took a step forward, and Anika flinched, the fear palpable. She nodded. Gathering her things, she hurried from the house without a word. Cameron sighed, knowing he'd done the right thing deep down. He'd allowed himself to get too close, but he had fixed it in the end.

Collapsing onto his sofa, he built a spliff, needing to relax.

* * *

ANIKA KEPT her composure until she reached her car. Before she could start the engine, she burst into tears. There was no going back for her now. Cameron had callously cast her aside, and the worst part was that she should have seen it coming. She had dealt with him when she was younger and stupider, but had learned nothing.

Her shoulders shook as she let go of her emotions. After a few minutes, the tears subsided, but the desolation and awful feelings swirling around her stomach went nowhere.

After several deeper breaths, she came to a decision, one she knew there was no coming back from.

* * *

ANOTHER DAY PASSED, and Natty knew he couldn't avoid Elijah any longer. He finally answered his call as he sat home, ignoring the football highlights on the TV.

'Elijah,' he said by way of greeting.

'Oh, good. That hand's not too injured to answer the phone. I was beginning to worry. Natty, we need to talk.'

Natty didn't hesitate. 'I'll come to you.'

They met at the house of one of Elijah's women. Natty had been there before, both with and without Elijah. The woman was one of his past contacts, a pretty brown-skinned girl called Charlene. She let him in, keeping her face neutral as she led him to Elijah.

'Give us some space, baby.' Elijah stood in the living room, ignoring the television, a cigarette in his hand. Charlene left them alone. Natty, too remained standing. Elijah's posture and demeanour were hard to work out, but that wasn't a surprise. Elijah went to great lengths to stay in control of his emotions. An empty cup rested on the coffee table, alongside two mobile phones. After a moment, Elijah faced Natty, eyes boring into him.

'What the hell were you thinking?'

Natty stayed quiet.

'Raider's in critical condition.' Elijah's eyes narrowed. He looked angrier than Natty had ever seen him. 'Was this your plan all along?'

Natty shook his head.

'He went too far when he beat up Lorraine.'

'That's what this is about? Raider's baby mother? Again?'

Anger flared up in Natty.

'I told you I would keep Raider under control—' Elijah started.

'You didn't, did you? He smacked her around despite your *control*,' snapped Natty.

'Did I know that? Did you speak to me before you went off and nearly killed him? Did you even check if I knew about the situation?'

'I called you. You didn't answer.'

Elijah's eyes widened.

'Once, Natty. Why didn't you try again? Or wait for me to get back to you? It's almost like you didn't want me to answer . . . so you could take it upon yourself to react in the way you wanted to.' Elijah continued to smoke his cigarette, the tension in the room ebbing.

Natty's mind raced. He wondered what Elijah's next move would be. His eyes darted around in anticipation, exploring Elijah's demeanour. Seeing his fist clench, Natty's jaw tightened, and he adjusted his feet slightly.

Finally, Elijah spoke.

'I'll speak with Rudy directly. For now, any business between our crews is on hold. Stay away from Little London for the foreseeable.'

'Excuse me?' Natty gawped. Elijah continued to meet his furious gaze with his own colder one.

'See yourself out.'

Natty stepped forward.

'You need to watch how you talk to me,' he snarled.

Elijah didn't back down. Their eyes locked, neither saying a word. After a few seconds, Natty picked up the pack of cigarettes from the coffee table. Lighting one, he blew the smoke in Elijah's face, then turned and left.

* * *

LORRAINE'S THOUGHTS kept slipping to Natty, and the injuries he was trying to hide when he came to visit. She had finally gone online and had learned about Raider's injuries. People spoke of him being in a bad way, asking for prayers and hope, which made her feel ill. Raider was undeserving of anyone's support. He didn't deserve her sympathy, but she found he had it anyway for a reason she could not work out.

She'd tried speaking with Tommy, but he remained as evasive as ever, retreating when she began probing. Natty's face was bruised, not to mention his damaged hand. Lorraine had seen the ibuprofen he had taken, and all signs pointed towards him being involved in what happened to Raider. She pondered how he could have found out about the assault so quickly, and as Jaden cheered the goal he'd scored on his football game, the answer came to her.

'I'll be back in a minute, baby. I'm just going upstairs,' she said to Jaden.

'Okay, mummy.'

Hurrying up the stairs as fast as her injuries would allow, Lorraine closed her bedroom door behind her and called Rosie.

'Hey, Lo. How are you feeling?'

'Who did you tell about what happened to me?' Lorraine got to the point.

'There was a moment of silence, then a sigh.'

'I told Spence.'

A sharp knocking at the door cut across Lorraine's response. She curtly told her friend she would speak with her later, then shuffled downstairs to answer. Her stomach lurched when she saw the two police officers standing there. One male, one female.

'Lorraine Richards?'

'That's me,' she replied, eyeing the officers, her head flinching slightly.

'Can we come in? We just want to ask you a few questions.'

Lorraine couldn't avoid it. She led them to the kitchen and told Jaden — who looked at the officers with wide eyes — that she wouldn't be long. She sat in the kitchen, waiting for the officers to speak.

'I'll keep this brief,' said the male officer. He was taller than his counterpart, with short hair and a scruffy beard. 'We're investigating a recent attack on Michael Parsons. We understand he is well known to you.'

Lorraine nodded. It wasn't often anyone used Raider's real name.

'He is the father to your son, is that correct?'

'If you want to call him that. He's not the most active participant in his son's life,' replied Lorraine, praying that Jaden didn't walk in on them.

'Mr Parsons suffered serious injuries. He's currently in intensive care, and his condition is touch and go. If there is anything you can tell us about the circumstances, we'd appreciate it.'

Lorraine thought she was going to be sick. She'd read about Raider's injuries, but the police being there made it ever more real.

'I'm sorry, but I don't know anything. Michael and I are not that close.'

'When did you last see him?'

'Several nights ago. He came to the house, and we had a conversation, then he left,' lied Lorraine, jumbling the facts. She wasn't about to tell them about the assault. That would only make things worse and drag her further into the situation. She had Jaden to think about.

'I can't help but notice you're sporting a few injuries,' said the female officer, who'd silently assessed Lorraine as she spoke with her colleague.

'What's your point?' replied Lorraine, clearly rattled.

'Did Mr Parsons cause those injuries?'

Lorraine grit her teeth, her attention flitting to the female officer, who'd hit the nail on the head.

'As I said, we had a conversation, then he left. Now, if you don't mind, I need to return to my son.'

The officers shared a look, and Lorraine's heart raced, wondering if they would arrest her, or interrogate her further. Her shoulders visibly relaxed when the male officer handed her his card.

'Please get in touch if you think of anything else. Any little detail could help us.'

Lorraine saw the police out, locking the door behind them. Her heart hadn't stopped racing as she shuffled back into the living room. Jaden paused his game and looked up at her.

'Are you okay, mummy?'

'I'm fine,' she responded, her mind on Natty, and the conversation they needed to have.

CHAPTER TWENTY-FIVE

NATTY LEFT ELIJAH, still furious with how the conversation had transpired. All the good work they'd done had seemingly vanished, all over someone like Raider. It made him feel sick. When the decision was made, he'd struggled to control himself. Natty felt hurt and disrespected, and, in the life, those feelings almost always led to confrontation.

Pulling up outside his house, he noticed a blacked-out Nissan 4X4 parked nearby. Sighing, he didn't bother going inside, instead walking towards the vehicle and climbing in the back. As soon as the door slammed shut, the car drove off.

Natty recognised the driver as one of Rudy's men and nodded. The man didn't return the gesture, focusing on the road. To Natty's surprise, they didn't drive toward Delores's as he expected, but to another spot.

Anxiety gnawed at him as they eventually reached the destination. There were numerous men posted in and around the spot. It didn't look good, and he started to fear his uncle was behind this. Stories of Warren's murder flashed in his mind. He took a deep breath, trying to calm himself, focusing on what he could say; how he should look. The minor details were necessary, and he needed to ensure he got them right.

Natty followed his escort inside. They headed down to the cellar, and Natty's worry only grew. He glanced around, looking for potential escapes, quickly realising all his possible exits were covered.

Rudy waited in the cellar, which was larger than Natty expected. It was the same size as his living room at home. Rudy smoked a cigarette, face twisted in anger as he scowled at Natty. The men left the cellar without a word, leaving the pair alone. For several minutes, Rudy finished his cigarette, each moment growing more agonisingly tense for Natty. He wanted Rudy to speak, to say something. Anything. Finally, he did.

'What the hell were you thinking?' Rudy started. Natty opened his mouth, but Rudy raised his hand, and Natty immediately fell silent. 'You've jeopardised an alliance, undone months of hard work with your stupid stunt.'

'That wasn't the intention, Rudy. Raider beat up his baby mum, knowing full well what I would do.'

'I don't care about that,' said Rudy, his scowl deepening. 'This is real life. Not television. You involved yourself in a situation you didn't need to be in. You didn't think about the bigger picture; the effects your actions would have on the wider scheme. Now, you've fucked everything up. If Raider doesn't recover, we'll need to make it right with Elijah. He's out for blood.'

Natty listened to Rudy's words, and rather than feel chastened, his annoyance grew.

'You may not care about the situation, and Elijah may not, but *I* do. Raider overstepped the mark, and you lot weren't going to deal with him. So, I did.'

Both men stared at the other, Natty's gaze defiant. Rudy was almost impressed with his demeanour, but shook his head. He stepped closer to Natty, almost nose-to-nose with him, looking him dead in the eye.

'You were doing so well, Nathaniel. For a while, we thought you could do it. We thought you could ascend to that next level, but you've undone all that hard work. You're out.'

Natty frowned.

'Out of what?'

'You're gone from the crew. Effective immediately. We don't want to see you at any of the spots. You'll be paid up to date, and that's it.'

Natty froze, unable to believe what had just happened. He knew he'd messed up, but he had done it for the right reasons. Never did he imagine it would go like this. He cleared his dry throat, thinking of the words to save this.

'I . . . let me talk to my uncle. I can fix this.'

'There's nothing to say, and nothing to fix. The man you came with will escort you out. Goodbye, Nathaniel.'

* * *

AT HOME, Natty sat in stunned shock, still reeling from the meeting and realising it was all over for him. Despite his words at the end, he knew his uncle wouldn't change his mind. Wiping his eyes, he looked down at his phone, seeing missed calls from Lorraine, Tommy, and Spence. He had a quick conversation with Spence, trying to sound calm, telling him he would speak to him when he was back in Leeds.

Next, he spoke to Tommy.

'Tom. What's happening?'

'Just giving you a heads up, fam. Lorraine knows what happened. She's on the warpath.'

Natty closed his eyes. This was the last thing he needed, but there was no way around it.

'Thanks for the warning. I'll handle it.' After a little more conversation, he ended the call.

Looking at his missed calls after hanging up, he saw three of them were from Lorraine. He stared at her name for a few seconds, his finger hovering over her name, considering calling her back rather than facing her. After a few moments, he put his phone away, deciding to speak to her face-to-face. Walking to the door, Natty again took out his phone, checking the temperature, deciding to grab a hooded top. Slowly, he pulled the basic grey hoody over his head and returned to the door. His hand rested on the key, but didn't turn to open the lock. Natty stared at the key, his mind racing. After a few more moments, he shook his head, annoyed. Turning the key, he swung the door open and walked through it, locking it behind him.

Taking a deep breath, he set off.

* * *

SPENCE ARRIVED home after dropping off his dad, his mind whirring with the news about Natty.

Word had spread swiftly about his dismissal from the organisation. Despite the severity of what Natty had done, Spence was still shocked that it had happened. He had always seen Natty as untouchable while he was working for his uncle, and it seemed crazy that anything could have gotten him the sack.

Spence wondered if it was a sign that the alliance between Elijah's crew and their team had grown ever stronger.

Regardless, he wanted to speak with Natty. They would need to discuss a plan. He hoped Natty had money saved. If not, Spence would help him out, knowing Natty wouldn't hesitate to do the same if the situation was reversed.

Spence hummed a tune as he unlocked the door. He hadn't heard from Anika while he'd been away. Locking the front door behind him, he called out for her, leaving his travel bag in the hallway, but heard nothing. Frowning, he went to check upstairs, assuming she had gone to bed early. Entering their room, he froze.

Anika's wardrobes were opened, all her clothing missing. Stomach lurching, Spence noticed her perfumes and jewellery were gone. He swayed on the spot, barely avoiding throwing up. As he systematically searched the house, he tried convincing himself it was a mistake, but by the end, he collapsed onto the sofa in the living room, tears prickling his eyes. If he was being honest, he'd known before the frantic search that he wasn't going to find Anika. The moment he'd seen her clothes were missing, he knew.

The tears streamed down Spence's face, and he angrily wiped them away, not knowing what could have caused this, but blaming himself. He should have probed more, listened to her and got her to admit what was on her mind. Instead, he had let it fester. Frantically, he called her friend Carmen, heart racing as he waited for her to pick up.

'Hey, Spence.'

By Carmen's solemn tone, he knew she was aware of what had transpired.

'Where is she, Carm? Please, don't mess me around.'

'Spence . . .'

'Carm. Please.' Spence's tone hardened.

'I don't know. That's the truth. She said she was sorry, but she couldn't stay. I couldn't get her to tell me where she was going, but she's got family down south. She might have gone there.'

Spence's stomach sank.

'She must have mentioned something when she stopped with you the other night.'

'Spence . . . she never stopped with me. She hasn't for a while now.'

'Is there someone else?' Spence's heart broke anew even uttering the words, but he had to know.

'I don't know. It would explain a lot, but Anika loves you, Spence. This could just be temporary. Hang in there.'

'Hang in there?'

'Spence—'

Spence swallowed the harsh words he'd wanted to unleash on Carmen.

'Yes?'

'She . . . left you a letter. She didn't tell me what was in it. She just said it would be where she stacks all the rest of the post. She said you always hated it when she did that. That you never did manage to tame her messy side.'

Spence stood, arm falling by his side. He noticed a letter atop the stack of post near the door, just where Carmen said it was. He heard Carmen's faint mumblings in the background as he slowly moved toward the letter. When he reached it, he placed his right hand on the note, ending his call with the left.

Opening the letter, he began to read, a tear escaping his eye, tracing down the page.

* * *

Entering Lorraine's, it was clear from the outset that this wouldn't be easy. Jaden was already in bed, unable to distract Lorraine. She glared at Natty as he walked in, and he swallowed down the lump in his throat. Lorraine's eyes flitted to his injured hand.

'How is it?'

Natty's eyebrow rose.

'I'll be fine.'

'What the hell were you thinking?' Lorraine snapped, her manner eerily similar to Rudy's earlier. Natty rubbed his eyes, but met her stare.

'Raider hurt you.'

'Raider is my problem, Nat. I didn't ask for your help. You put yourself at risk with what you did, not to mention that you nearly killed him. How would you have explained it to Jaden if you had?'

'He's never been a dad to Jaden,' Natty snapped, watching Lorraine's eyes flash with anger.

'That doesn't involve you. I . . . appreciate everything you've done for my son and me, but you could have killed Raider, and that's unacceptable.'

'I did it for you.'

Lorraine shook her head.

'Don't even try that shit. You did it for ego. It's always about ego with you. You and Raider, you always want to be the big dicks. You may have convinced yourself that it's about me, but it isn't. Me and Jaden are in the middle, and I won't put up with it anymore.'

With a sinking feeling, Natty again met her eyes.

'What are you saying?'

Lorraine lowered her head for just a moment, eyes glistening with tears.

'I don't want you around my son, Nathaniel. I want you to leave, and I don't want you to wait for me to cool down, or to try to sweet talk your way around me in future. Leave, and don't bother coming back.'

Lorraine's words twisted Natty's stomach in a way he had never experienced. His legs felt heavy, and maintaining his composure was the hardest thing under the weight of her words.

'I *did* do it for you,' he said, knowing that the words would have no effect. 'No matter what you say, this isn't about me.'

Lorraine shook her head, tears streaming down her face.

'If that was the case, you would have spoken to me first. I had you all wrong, and that's something I will need to deal with. You don't respect me, and you didn't consider my feelings.' She took a deep, shuddering breath, pointing to a bag on the sofa. 'I want you to take the laptop back. It wouldn't be right to keep it.'

Natty stared at Lorraine, sadness in his eyes.

'No. It's yours,' he finally replied, heading for the door.

* * *

AFTER LEAVING LORRAINE, Natty once again stewed at home, the pain he felt quickly turning to anger. He'd spoken with Elijah, Rudy, and Lorraine, but none of them truly believed Natty had done what he did for Lorraine. Instead, they thought it was an excuse to get back at Raider, which Natty knew wasn't true. Only Spence seemed to believe him.

Upon entering the house, Natty had tossed his phone on the sofa, grabbed a bottle of brandy from the kitchen, then commenced drinking. Rudy had left him in the lurch, kicking him from the crew and claiming the decision was made by his uncle. As Natty sipped his brandy, he wondered how integral Uncle Mitch was in making the decision, and if Rudy had tried speaking up for him. He imagined he hadn't. Rudy knew better than to speak up against his uncle, especially when it came to protecting someone else.

Through a blurry haze a while later, Natty became aware of a knocking at the door. Stumbling to his feet, he still clutched the bottle, ready to use it as a weapon. When he saw Spence standing there, he let him in, missing the devastated look on his friend's face.

'Have you heard?' Natty said, when they were both in the living room. He collapsed back onto the sofa and took another sip. Spence remained standing, not responding. After a moment, Natty glanced over. His eyes widened as he noticed how unkempt Spence looked. His eyes were swollen and drawn, and his clothing was rumpled. 'What happened?'

'Anika left me.' Spence gnawed his upper lip, cheeks quivering. Natty blew out a breath. He wished he could say it was surprising, but it had been building for a while.

Spence swallowed down a lump in his throat, his voice hoarse.

'She took all her things and left. I tried speaking with Carmen and her friends, but they're not telling me anything. I don't know what to do.'

Natty sat up on the sofa, wiping his mouth. This was the worst time for Spence to be unloading on him. He'd lost a lot in a short time with his demotion and rejection. He had his own issues to deal with. Blinking tightly, Natty tried his best to sober up. Spence needed him.

Spence waited for Natty to respond. After a moment, he spoke again.

'Bro, what am I supposed to do now?'

'Nothing you can do but move on,' said Natty, eyes fixed ahead, thinking of Lorraine, their moment by the door, when he'd walked away.

'How?'

'Don't think about her. Don't let her have that power over you.'

Neither man spoke for a moment.

'I loved her, bro. We were building something, and now she's gone. Just like that. What did I do?'

Natty shook his head. 'You didn't do anything, fam. You were there for her. This isn't on you.'

Spence leant against the wall, sighing. 'Then why do I feel like it is? Why do I think I should have done more?'

'What more could you have done?' Natty thought about his reaction to Lorraine's assault.

He hadn't even checked on her. He'd charged after Raider instead.

'I could have listened more. Could have asked what she wanted, rather than going about by myself; my goals and aspirations.'

Natty took another deep pull of the liquor, wincing as it burned his throat. He wiped his eyes with his free hand.

'Look on the bright side, bro. You're free. We're both single, and ready to move on.' He forced a chuckle, finally glancing at Spence. Spence's laugh was equally forced, and silence ensued again, both men considering their situations. Natty took another sip, then offered the bottle to Spence, who shook his head. Shrugging, Natty took another.

'Bro, you're better off without her. Think about it. You know Rosie likes you, so see what she's saying. She'll be good for you.' Rosie made him think of Lorraine, and his stomach clenched. He took another deep swig. Realising Spence hadn't responded, he glanced at him again, taken aback by the disgust on Spence's face.

'It's that fucking easy for you, isn't it?' he snarled, his lip curling.

Natty's body tensed, his muscles quivering.

'Wait a fucking minute. You've no idea what it's like for me.'

'Don't I? You've told me to move on, and you're already suggesting women I can move on with.'

'That has nothing to do with me. I'm doing it for you; so you can get over that stupid bitch.'

'She's not a stupid bitch,' roared Spence. 'I love her.'

Natty's eyes flashed with anger. Staggering from the sofa, he scowled at Spence.

'Are you really this stupid?'

'What?' Spence was stunned at Natty's change of demeanour.

'I'm saying . . . how could you not see it? All those times you were out working, and she's getting dressed up to chill with her friend, who has a fiancé she's loved up with . . . you can't see it? Where were the photos of the nights out if she was out all the time? Why did she get so fucking camera-shy all of a sudden? She was cheating, and you were too fucking whipped to see it. She was getting fucked in the Hood. I followed her.' Natty's scowl intensified. 'She fucked Cam, you know . . . back in the day. Did she ever tell you that, when you were talking shit about building a future with her?'

Silence ensued. Spence's eyes opened, staring at Natty in horror. Natty breathed hard, hand tightening around the bottle. The moment lingered. Shaking his head, Spence made his way to the door, leaving without saying a word.

CHAPTER TWENTY-SIX

'I'M SORRY ABOUT ANIKA.'

Rosie had never seen Spence looking so dishevelled. They were sat in his living room. Rosie had never been to the house before, and had been surprised when he'd reached out, wondering if he was ready to get something going with them.

Upon arriving, she realised Anika wasn't there, and Spence had quickly told her what happened. Rosie's surprise at being invited turned promptly to shock when she learned the whole story. Anika had apparently been cheating on Spence, and he and Natty had fallen out most explosively.

Spence's demeanour was alarming. His shoulders were slumped, and he looked tired and drawn.

'Are you really?' He replied after a few moments.

'Am I really what?' Rosie blinked, confused.

'Sorry.'

'Yes. It's no secret that I like you, but I wouldn't want you to get hurt so I could get what I wanted.'

Spence sighed, lowering his head.

'I feel like such a fool. I was so focused on bettering myself that I couldn't see what Natty could.'

Rosie cleared her throat. 'Do you know how Natty is doing? Lorraine has fallen out with him. Big time.'

Spence looked at her sharply. 'Because of Raider?'

Rosie nodded. 'She doesn't want him around her and Jaden anymore. I feel bad. If I hadn't told you, then it wouldn't have happened.'

'It would have got out either way, and Natty wasn't going to hold back. You know how he feels about her. About both of them. Still, I haven't spoken to him since the fallout.'

Rosie sat closer to Spence, resting a hand on top of his.

'Spence, I know you're hurting, but Natty needs you.'

Spence shook his head.

'I'm not sure he does. He seemed pretty mad when I saw him. I still can't believe he would snap on me like that, or that he wouldn't tell me about Cam and Anika.'

'The only way you'll get those answers is to speak with him,' said Rosie. 'Despite everything, he's your best friend.'

Taking a risk, Rosie rested her head on Spence's shoulder, gratified when he didn't pull away.

* * *

SEVERAL DAYS after his fight with Spence, Natty was in a club. He'd had several drinks, trying not to think about his problems. Cameron had been unable to meet him, and Natty hadn't had a proper conversation with his friend about the current state of affairs. He didn't know how to initiate the conversation, and he had no plan in place.

Nothing but getting drunk and distracting himself.

With that in mind, he headed towards a group of women, shocked at how shaky his legs were. Zeroing in on a curly-haired mixed-race woman, he smiled at her.

'What's your name?' He asked, noticing her eyes slightly widen. She gave him a coy smile, obviously surprised he'd approached her in such a way. Natty waited her out. Despite his mounting issues, he knew how to approach and deal with women. *Most women*, he corrected, Lorraine flitting across his mind before he ruthlessly pushed her out.

'Gaby,' she replied, her soft voice barely heard over the music. Natty gave her his name, gave her friends a cursory greeting, then took Gaby to get a drink. It took her a second to warm up to him, but soon she'd given him her life story. She'd broken up with her boyfriend a few weeks ago, and though she claimed it was for good, Natty had dealt with enough of these women to be able to read between the lines. He predicted she would be back with him by the end of the month.

'What about you?' She asked, twirling her hair with her free hand, eyes glistening. 'Are you seeing anyone?'

Natty shook his head.

'It's been a while since I've done the relationship thing,' he said.

'That's too bad. How come?'

'Guess I've been waiting for the right woman,' he replied, keeping eye contact. It was a corny line, but Gaby still giggled.

'I guess you have. What happens when you find her?'

'I'd have to shoot my shot and see what happens.' Natty stepped closer to Gaby, watching as she instinctively moistened her lips. He could see in his mind how this would all play out. They'd go back to her place and undoubtedly have sex; after that, it would be up to him. Maybe this was what he needed. It was easier than the complexities of dealing with feelings, and actually *liking* people.

Try as he might, he couldn't shake the memories of sitting on Lorraine's sofa, with her head on his shoulder, content and happy in a way he'd never felt with another woman. Internally he groaned, feeling his stomach tighten.

'Natty?'

He blinked, now back in the sweaty, dark club. It had lost its splendour. Even the drink didn't taste the same anymore. He didn't want to be here.

'Natty? Are you okay?'

Gaby was trying to talk to him, a look of concern quickly giving way to annoyance when she realised he was ignoring her.

'Yeah. I'm fine.'

'Are you sure?'

He nodded. Gaby placed her hand on his, but he pulled away.

'I can't do this. Gotta go,' he said, disposing of his drink and leaving the club.

By the time he made it home, it was almost midnight. He'd been off the radar for the past few days, trying to avoid thinking about his problems. It was becoming clear that approach wasn't going to work. He knew his feelings for Lorraine were the real deal. He'd been hiding from himself, and his attitude had led to this isolation. Most of his world was alienating him, and he couldn't blame them.

Natty slumped on his sofa and stared into space, thinking of his dad. He knew of his dad's killer reputation, but he wondered if he'd ever gone through issues like this. He wondered if he'd ever had feelings for a woman like Natty did. He wondered if his dad had ever felt such a way for his mum, but he wasn't sure.

His whole life, Natty had fought his way out of any problems. He'd developed a reputation, refusing to back down, doing things his way, always ready to take it to the next level, but that wasn't what he wanted to be, and the high of battling always left him feeling hollow afterwards. Fighting always led to more problems, and in the end, none of it was worth it.

Natty didn't regret his decision with Raider, but knew it could have been handled better. He could have shown more maturity, but the rage had taken over. It had taken over his conversation with Spence too. Spence had always dared to be himself; to show his feelings even at the risk of being mercilessly teased by his friends, and now he was hurting. He had come to Natty for support. Natty had shattered his world further, and he hadn't heard from Spence since.

The longer he sat there, the longer Natty knew he couldn't go on like this. He couldn't hide from the world and pretend things weren't going on. He had to show some of the maturity Lorraine and Rudy had previously lambasted him about. Even if he didn't get the resolutions he wanted, he still needed to try. With that in mind, he left the house.

* * *

SPENCE'S STREET was empty as Natty hesitated outside his place, some of his newfound courage dissipating. He rubbed his hands, feeling the early morning chill. He'd said some horrific things to Spence, and now he was terrified that he might have gone too far to be able to fix the friendship. That desire to show maturity emanated through, though, and he knocked on the door. Spence opened it almost a minute later, his expression hardening when he saw Natty standing there. He rubbed his eyes, adjusting the dressing gown he'd clearly thrown on before answering the door.

'Hey,' said Natty.

'Nat,' Spence's tone was icy, but Natty wouldn't let that bother him.

'I wanted to talk to you.'

'Are you sure you didn't say everything you needed to say last time? You were pretty thorough.'

Natty sighed, lowering his head.

'I shouldn't have thrown Anika and Cam in your face like that,' he said. 'I'm sorry, Spence. You're one of my best friends, and you deserved better.'

Spence blinked, but maintained his stiff demeanour. Natty blew into his hands, rubbing them together. Noticing, Spence stepped aside so Natty could enter. Heading into the living room, Spence switched on the light, both men remaining standing.

Natty glanced around the room, thinking of the last time he'd been to Spence's. Life had gotten so hectic for him lately, that he couldn't recall. The living room remained the same; various books splayed across the dark brown coffee table. Several plants dotted around, along with a bookshelf, a sofa, and several smaller chairs. The walls were a caramel colour that gave the room some nice character.

'Why did you never tell me?' Spence spoke after a long moment.

Natty searched for the words.

'Those two were in the past, and I guess I thought it wasn't such a big deal. Besides, you were happy. You both were. I didn't wanna say something that caused issues.'

'It was obviously a big deal. Cam had a thing about my relationship for the longest time. Anika was distant and awkward about our future, and all of that was probably because the pair of them had a history, one

I was too stupid to see.' Spence sighed, a tear leaving his eye. 'I . . . don't know how I'm supposed to feel.'

Stepping forward, Natty gripped his friend's shoulder.

'Spence, you can feel any way you like, fam. You have the right to be hurt, and I had no right to speak to you like I did. Deep down, I always respected you for owning your feelings and being honest, even when I was teasing you for the same thing. Avoiding my own problems has landed me in my current pile of shit.'

Nodding, Spence bowed his head for a moment.

'How are you doing with not working? Must be tough to get used to.'

Natty blew out a breath.

'I deserved it. My life is in complete shambles right now. Lorraine won't speak with me. Fuck knows what Elijah is gonna do. Tonight, I hit a club by myself, so I could get a woman, but when it came time to close the deal, I flinched. Should have listened to you instead of getting caught up.'

Spence shook his head.

'Your heart was in the right place. Right now, you seem like you're thinking clearly. You should speak with Lorraine and Rudy, and tell them how you really feel about things.'

'Speaking with Rudy won't get me my role back.'

Spence met Natty's eyes.

'Is the role what you really want?'

'What do you mean?'

'The life . . . hustling. Is that what you really want? You have an opportunity to truly reinvent yourself. Not many people get that.'

Natty felt a smile coming to his face, overwhelmed by positive emotions towards Spence.

'You're a little genius, Spence, you know that?'

'Less of the *little*,' chuckled Spence. 'Don't forget, I still couldn't solve my own problems. My girl still left me.' Some of the light left his voice then.

'You had the balls to try. It'll take time, but you will come out of this stronger. Onto bigger and better things. Speaking of which . . .

have you spoken to Rosie lately?' Natty smiled warmly at his friend, who returned it.

'It's just that easy for you, isn't it?' he replied. Both men laughed, feeling truly better for the first time in days.

* * *

LORRAINE SAT AT HOME, watching television. She was still recovering from her injuries. Rosie had kept her company, but left a short while ago. Lorraine had appreciated the distraction, and with Rosie around, hadn't had much time to think about her issues. At first, she'd been annoyed at her friend for going against her wishes and telling Spence about what Raider had done, but Rosie's heart had been in the right place.

Jaden had already gone to bed with little fuss. She still hadn't told him what had happened to Raider, but he'd asked several times about Natty, and whether he would be coming around to play with him. Lorraine did her best to avoid giving a definitive answer.

Truthfully, she didn't know what to say to him. Deep down, Lorraine accepted that Natty had been protecting her, but she still wished the situation had been handled differently. Things with Natty had never been simple, though; it was just another thing she had learned to accept.

Despite all of Natty's flaws, his heart had always been in the right place. Lorraine only wished that was the same where she was concerned. Looks and demeanour aside, she had always wanted more from Natty, and for a while, it seemed things were trending in that direction. Their recent interactions before their fight had evolved, going from arguing at parties and drunken sleepovers, to conversations about careers, Natty letting her confide in him, and most importantly, being there for her son in a way his dad had never been.

He'd even bought her a new laptop so that she could keep studying. The gesture had meant so much to her. It was a sign Natty was no longer just invested in what he could get out of the situation; he was invested in Lorraine; her success.

Lorraine blinked, emotions ablaze, realising she had delved far further into her feelings than anticipated. When her phone beeped, she gratefully seized the distraction. Her heart clenched when she read the message from Natty:

Come outside.

After reading the message twice, Lorraine sat still, weighing up whether to do it. They'd had harsh words last time they'd seen one another, and she didn't see how things would be better this time. Still, Natty had sent a text, rather than knocking at the door, or shouting for her to come out, and she was curious enough to wonder what he would say. Clambering to her feet, she slipped on a pair of sliders and unlocked the door.

Natty stood in the garden, hands in his pockets. The first thing Lorraine noticed was that he didn't seem as cocksure as he usually did. He appeared to be standing straighter, and was meeting her eyes. Lorraine kept her eyes on him, waiting for him to speak.

'How are you?'

Lorraine blinked. She hadn't expected that. Instinctively, her hand went to her ribs.

'I'm getting there. Is that all you came to say?'

'I came to apologise. Seems to be a running theme of mine. I've been saying it a lot lately.' Natty rubbed the back of his neck. 'I've fucked up a fair few things.'

Lorraine stayed quiet, not knowing what to say. Natty cleared his throat.

'I . . . have feelings for you. Proper ones. I hid from them for a long time because I didn't think we could work out, and I *knew* you were too good for me. I knew it then just as I know it now. Doing that, though, it led me here, with everything around me turned to shit.'

Lorraine opened and closed her mouth before she realised she'd done it. Her heart raced, unable to believe it was Natty speaking.

'I grew up wanting to be just like my dad. Then, he died, and I was just there, pushing forward in a life that didn't love me. The only one that I knew.' Again, Natty cleared his throat. 'I wish I'd spoken to you before I went after Raider, but I'll never feel bad about protecting you, Lorraine, because I love you.'

Lorraine gasped, the first noise she'd made since Natty started speaking, unable to believe what she had heard. Natty's eyes blazed as he stared at her.

'Anyway, look after yourself. You have my number if you need anything — anything at all.' He left, swallowed by the darkness before Lorraine could unstick her throat enough to speak actual words. Helplessly, she stared at the spot he'd vacated, a storm of emotions swirling inside her.

'Natty . . .' she whispered to the night.

* * *

As Natty headed to Delores', he expected to feel bashful at baring his soul to Lorraine. He hadn't expected to use the *L word* during his speech, but didn't regret it. Once he said it, he knew it to be true. It had been true for a long time, and he was done hiding from it.

When he reached Delores' place, he knocked at the door, but no one answered. The light was on, though, so Rudy was likely inside. Delores never stayed up late. He tried the door, which was unlocked. Natty entered, going over the words he planned to say to Rudy, intending to keep it short and sweet as he had with Lorraine and Spence.

'Did you handle the pickup?'

Rudy's voice made Natty pause. He hadn't realised he would be interrupting a meeting. He almost turned to leave.

'Course I did,' replied a familiar voice. Natty's eyes widened. He hadn't realised Wonder and Rudy were on speaking terms. 'The Money is low. Second week running.'

'That's the *Natty effect*,' said Elijah. 'Say what you want about him . . . He knew how to keep that team humming.'

Natty stepped closer. Despite the harsh words last time they were face-to-face, Elijah sounded impressed. It was a reminder to Natty of how well he had done to establish a base in Little London.

Before he messed it all up.

'I'll get them in line. Don't worry about that,' said Wonder, snorting. 'Natty's not the only money-maker.'

'Forget that.' Rudy's voice cut through the conversation, and the others fell silent. 'Little London served its purpose, but we have other things to consider. Who should we use for the hit?'

'I'd have used Raider, if your stepson hadn't nearly killed him,' replied Elijah.

'I could do it,' said Wonder.

Natty's heart pounded, wondering if they were talking about killing him. Warren had been the last major casualty, and that was due to his refusal to fall in line. In his time running Little London, Natty hadn't heard of anyone kicking up a fuss, and didn't see what could have changed in a few weeks.

'Clearly, we need to think on this some more,' said Rudy. 'Mitch won't be easy to get.'

Natty's brow furrowed. He couldn't think of any *Mitch* involved with Little London, and certainly not one that warranted such a discussion.

'Anyone can be taken out,' said Elijah. 'We've already gone over this. Our people won't wait forever.'

Natty was half-listening, going over the name *Mitch* in his head. Stomach jolting, he thought of his uncle.

Was it possible they were talking about him?

Rudy grunted. Natty had never heard him sound so tired.

'We won't get a second chance. I've worked with him for decades. I know how he thinks.'

'You mean you've worked *for him*,' retorted Elijah.

Natty froze. Blood pounded in his ears. They *were* talking about killing his uncle.

The men continued talking, but Natty wasn't listening. He needed to let his uncle know what had happened.

Moving back slowly to escape, a floorboard creaked beneath his feet. Heart thumping, Natty stopped, wondering if they'd heard. When the sounds of their voices continued, he breathed a sigh of relief.

He turned to leave, only to find himself face-to-face with another man.

For a second, neither moved, and then the man charged. Natty forced him into the coffee table, then to the floor. Taking in the man's face as he groaned in pain, Natty realised he didn't recognise him. As he coughed and spluttered, the air driven out of him, footsteps ensued. Elijah and Rudy stumbled from the kitchen, Rudy's eyes widening when he saw Natty.

'He heard everything. Kill him.'

Natty didn't hesitate. He turned and ran as a flurry of bullets were fired his way.

CHAPTER TWENTY-SEVEN

NATTY SURGED DOWN THE STREET, ducking low when he heard the crack of another nearby bullet. His heart raced, stunned over what had transpired. *Rudy was working against the crew.* Elijah's men were after him, and he needed to get away before they killed him. Once he'd done that, he could make sense of what was happening. He didn't know who was involved, but he needed to get to people he could trust.

Right now, that meant Spence and Cameron.

Increasing his speed, he hurried down an alleyway, his long legs helping him accelerate from his pursuers. Hearing their shouts, he ducked into a garden, crouching down, stilling his breathing. He knew he was on Markham Avenue. He was close to his mum's house, but he couldn't involve her in this mess. It was his problem to sort out. He pulled out his phone, but the heavy breathing of his pursuers caused him to pause.

'Where's he gone?' One of them asked.

'He must have run ahead,' a voice Natty recognised as Wonder's, replied. 'He's one of those fitness freaks. We should have popped him in the room, the little pussy.'

'Can't believe he outran us, still. I used to win awards for running in school.'

'No, you didn't. You barely went, and you were never a runner. Remember, I knew you back then.'

'Whatever, Wonder. You don't know everything. You just think you do.'

Natty listened. They weren't directly outside the garden he'd hidden in, but were close by, and were taking little care to keep their voices down. Their sloppiness worked to his favour.

Natty was tempted to jump out and attack the men. He knew he could take Wonder, but didn't recognise the voice of the second man, and the fact they were both armed stopped him. He just needed to wait a while longer.

'Fuck it, let's go back to Elijah. He'll know what to do next. We'll get Natty next time. Better still, Rudy can do it. This is his problem.'

After the pair stomped away, Natty waited another five minutes, stunned by his good luck. In their shoes, he'd have searched every garden on the road, but the fact they hadn't suited him. He tried his uncle, but the number wouldn't connect. Chest heaving, Natty dialled a special number he'd left for him years ago. After he told his uncle what was going on, he would meet with Spence and Cameron and devise a plan.

'Yeah,' a voice answered, not one Natty recognised.

'I need to talk to my Uncle Mitch.'

'No *Mitch* here. Think you've got the wrong number.'

'Don't take the piss. I was given this number, and told to call if there was an emergency.' Natty's voice rose. He'd have torn this man's head off in person, but he needed to keep his wits, now more than ever.

'Was the number the only thing you were given?'

'Yeah . . .' Something went off in Natty's head. 'Wait! *Loyalty1212*,' he said, remembering the code phrase he had been given. The person on the other end paused.

'Okay. Leave your message, Natty.'

He blinked, surprised the person knew his name. He assumed it was tied to the word he had been given, and that each person had a different one. It was a clever bit of skill, but he didn't have the time to admire it.

'Listen, Rudy's dirty. He's working with Elijah, and the plan is to take out my uncle and take over. I don't know how many people they have, or who is involved, but they tried to kill me.'

'I'll relay the message. For now, you need to stay out of sight.'

'Did you hear what I said? Rudy's a snake!'

'Like I said, I will relay this, but now is the time for you to listen. Do you have a spot you can lie low in?'

'Yeah, I'll—'

The line went dead. Eyes widening, Natty glanced at the phone, his stomach lurching as he realised the battery had died. Stupidly, he'd forgotten to charge it in the morning, and now it had cost him.

Clambering to his feet, he left the garden, running down the road. He needed to get to Cameron's as quickly as he could. Once there, he could regroup and ring Spence. Natty thought about the man who had answered the phone, annoyed that he didn't know more about the inner workings of his uncle's organisation.

For all he knew, they were in league with Rudy, and he had just tipped him off.

Taking another deep breath, he forced down the negative thoughts. They wouldn't help him in this situation. Cameron didn't live far away, and he would have weapons. Natty didn't want to kill anyone, but if it came to his life or theirs, he wouldn't hesitate.

Through sheer luck, he didn't run into any of Elijah's or Rudy's men on the streets. By the time he reached Cameron's, he was panting, his t-shirt sticking to him. Sucking in air, he knocked twice then tried Cameron's handle, pleased to find it was unlocked.

Cameron sat in the living room, sipping a glass of brandy. When he glanced up and saw Natty, he gave a start, spilling the drink on himself.

'Shit,' he cursed, leaping to his feet and wiping away the mess. Natty looked from the glass, to the bottle on the table, then to his friend.

'Why do you look so shook?'

'I didn't expect you to just burst in my door like the police,' said Cameron. 'I'm a little drunk; plus, I had a few lines earlier.'

'Why?' Natty asked. He knew Cameron liked to dabble, but indulging in drink and drugs when he was alone, with no events or parties on, seemed strange.

'This chick was meant to roll through, but she cancelled.'

'Fine,' replied Natty. 'My phone died. I need to make a call.'

'What's going on?' Cameron asked. Natty was tempted to have a drink, but needed to keep a clear head.

'Rudy's working with Elijah.' Natty gave it to him straight. Cameron's eyes narrowed.

'Course he is. We all are.'

'No, not like that. They're in an alliance,' said Natty. Cameron still looked confused, so Natty broke it down, telling him of the meeting he had interrupted.

Cameron shook his head.

'I can't believe that . . .'

'It's happening, so you'd better believe it,' replied Natty. 'They're gonna take out anyone who doesn't go along with the plan.' He watched Cameron, expecting him to start panicking and overreacting. Instead, Cameron refilled his drink and took a sip, his brow furrowed.

'What are you going to do?'

Cameron's reaction pleased Natty. He hadn't wanted to talk his friend around, and he'd simply reacted how Natty had wanted. No dramatics; keeping things simple, wanting to know the plan.

'They had me trapped, and my phone died as I was calling for backup,' Natty replied.

'Who were you trying to call?'

'Do you have a charger? I need to use it.'

Cameron pointed to a corner of the room. Natty located a frayed charger. It had seen better days, but would do.

'Ring Spence. Get him over here ASAP.'

'I can ring some other people too. Get more bodies.'

'We don't know who we can trust, bro. Rudy is talking about a takeover. It only works if he has pieces on the inside. Until we know who we can trust, it needs to be me, you, and Spence.'

'Spence is probably holed up with his bitch.'

Natty's nostrils flared.

'Anika left him. But that doesn't matter now. Just do it.'

Cameron smirked, but didn't say anything. Natty headed to the kitchen and downed a glass of water. He refilled it and downed the second, then let the water run, washing his face, feeling refreshed afterwards.

'Spence ain't answering.' Cameron stood in the doorway. Natty wiped his face with a paper towel, then disposed of the rubbish.

'Shit. They could have sent people there already. They know he's down with us. Rudy knows everything about us.'

'What are we gonna do? Wanna go to his house?' Suggested Cameron.

'Nah, we need to stay holed up here for now. I need a strap.'

'I've got one hidden upstairs.' Cameron hurried from the room, and Natty took a deep breath. It worried him that Spence was off the radar. He thought about how logical his friend was. Spence not answering his phone was serious. There could be multiple reasons he wasn't responding, and Natty hated that his paranoia had set in. He hated himself for questioning Spence's loyalty, but based on everything that had happened tonight, it was justified.

Panic rising, Natty hurried to his phone. It had only been charging a few minutes, but he turned it on, and saw a text message from Spence:

> Heard there was a shooting near your mums.
> You good?

Natty's heart stilled. Cameron had said he couldn't get through to Spence, yet Spence was active. Before Natty could consider this, he pushed the call button. It rang twice.

'Nat?'

'Spence?'

'Who else would it be? Glad you're alright. What's the deal with the gunshots?'

'Look, there's no time. I'm at Cam's, and—'

'Hang up.'

Natty turned, unsurprised to see Cameron aiming a gun at him. Without a word, he ended the call and dropped the phone.

CHAPTER TWENTY-EIGHT

'WHY, CAM?' Natty asked, trying to maintain control.

'You're not the only one who has plans,' replied Cameron, the gun aimed at his chest. 'Big things are happening. I was smart enough to get in on the ground floor.'

Natty shook his head, his stomach dropping. Cameron was one of his oldest friends, someone he had known since childhood. He couldn't believe he had betrayed him.

'I may have had plans, but you were always with me, fam. I'd have taken you wherever I went, and you know that,' Natty replied.

'Don't give me that crap!' Cameron exploded. 'All you care about is yourself. You didn't bring me into Little London to get money with you. You put Spence in charge over me, and just expected me to take it. When did you ever do anything for me?'

Natty kept his eyes on Cameron, knowing now more than ever, he needed to remain calm. He would deal with Cameron's betrayal if he ever got out of his predicament. Right now, he needed to keep him talking.

'Who turned you? Elijah? Rudy? One of the flunkies?'

'Does it matter? You're finished either way. Your uncle can't survive what's going on. He'd never have gotten as far as he did without Rudy.'

Natty tried putting the pieces together, his chest jolting from all the possible implications.

'Is Spence involved?'

Cameron scoffed.

'Spence is as soft as you. You're both pussy whipped, especially you. You should have died for the beating you gave Raider.' Cameron smirked. 'Truthfully, Elijah pushed for that, but Rudy talked him out of it.'

That fact surprised Natty, and he struggled not to show it. *If Rudy was out for his blood, why wouldn't he let Elijah kill him?* He wanted to ask, but knew he wouldn't get the answers.

'How long have you hated me?' Natty decided to go in another direction. He needed to keep Cameron off balance. By any means necessary. He couldn't rush him. Smartly, he kept himself out of reach, his hands unwavering.

'I don't hate you.' Cameron's mouth fell open a moment, then he smiled. 'You're just weak. The moves you've made have been trash. You're a little bitch for your uncle, and he's a damn coward. Too scared to even show his face in public.'

Natty was intrigued, but didn't know where Cameron was taking it. When Cameron didn't add anything else, he spoke.

'What happens next?'

'I called Rudy. Men are on their way to take care of you.'

Natty smirked. Cameron's grin vanished.

'Why are you smiling? Did you hear what I said?'

'No matter what team you're on, you end up as the bitch, don't you? Whether it's me, or Elijah, or Rudy, no one respects you. We use you for the little things,' said Natty.

Cameron stepped forward, fury lining his face.

'I'm a big part of the plan. For once, you're not the main guy, and you can't deal with it.'

Natty laughed.

'I'll die knowing I'm not a boot licker like you, Cam. People only respect you because of me, and deep down, you know that. I bet that's how they got to you. I'll tell you this, though: first chance they get, you'll be out, because without me, you're nothing.'

Cameron's finger tightened on the trigger. Natty's heart slammed against his chest. He needed to play it carefully here. He didn't want Cameron to shoot him, but he also didn't want him thinking clearly. He needed to keep him distracted.

'Are you even *allowed* to kill me?' He laughed. 'We keep our instructions simple with you, so you don't fuck them up. It's part of your programming.' Natty resisted the urge to tremble, breathing slightly deeper to steady himself.

'You lost, Natty. I could take you if I wanted to. I don't take orders from anyone.'

Natty grinned. His attempts to distract Cameron by preying on his obvious insecurities was working.

'You still need to wait for backup, right? You ran to call as soon as I got here. Didn't have the guts to take me on without a gun, right? And you have the nerve to call me and Spence pussies?'

That was the clincher. Cameron's jaw jutted, putting down the gun and kicking it away. With a yell, he charged Natty, who didn't move, allowing himself to be taken to the floor. They wrestled around, Natty quickly getting the momentum.

Cameron was no slouch, but Natty was bigger and more scientific. Landing several solid punches to his chest and stomach, he wrapped his arm around Cameron's throat and squeezed. Cameron began kicking, trying to break the grip, but he had the move locked in, feeling his movements growing weaker.

Heavy footsteps distracted him, causing him to loosen the hold. Cameron took advantage, elbowing Natty several times and breaking free just as Spence burst in, aiming a gun at Cameron. Before he could act, Wonder and the other man came through the front. Cameron grinned.

'I was wondering when you guys—'

The rest of his words were cut off when Wonder shot him in the shoulder. Cameron toppled to the ground with a yelp, cradling his bleeding arm. Once Spence entered, Natty had grabbed the gun, now aiming it at Wonder. Spence trained his gun on the second man, and no one moved.

'Drop the guns. We've got people on the way,' drawled Wonder. 'If you hurry, we can get some help for your friend there.'

'He stopped being my friend when he held a gun on me and took your boss's money,' replied Natty.

'You can't win. You already ran from us once. Make it easy on yourself and come quietly.'

'I'm not going anywhere with a little pawn like you,' said Natty. Wonder grinned.

'*Pawn*? You're calling me the pawn? That's rich.'

'Let's be honest: if I hadn't beaten Raider within an inch of his life, he'd be the one stood there, not you.'

'You think?' Wonder's brow furrowed.

'I know. We all know. You're a little punk, and you always have been. If you had any brains, you'd have gone for Spence, not that idiot.' Natty jerked his thumb at Cameron, still whimpering on the floor.

Before Wonder could speak again, more people entered, their weapons far larger than any of the others in the room. There were six in total. Natty's stomach plummeted. He hadn't done enough, and now he and Spence were dead.

Before he could put his hands in the air, the group aimed their guns at Wonder and the other man. Natty's mouth fell open.

'One time only: drop them or die.'

Wonder and the other man didn't hesitate. They placed the guns on the floor and were quickly overpowered by four of the men. Their arms were zip-tied behind their backs.

The leader stepped forward, lowering his gun.

'I'm Clarke. We spoke on the phone. You need to come with me.'

Natty nodded, not bothering to argue. Clarke gave more instructions to his men. Spence stood stupidly, gun by his side, watching everything with his mouth wide open. Without a word, Clarke swept from the room and Natty followed, stunned by everything that had transpired.

'You're lucky, Natty. After the phone cut out, we sent men to Spence's. We figured you would be at Cameron's when he wasn't in.'

Natty didn't respond. They climbed into a car, and the driver immediately pulled away.

'What are you going to do with Cameron?' Now that his adrenaline ebbed, Natty couldn't believe what his friend had done, and how quickly it had bounced back on him.

'He will be taken care of.'

It wasn't much of an answer, and Clarke added nothing further. Natty stayed silent as they drove to an area he recognised as Harehills. They walked into a house, and down to a cellar. Natty's stomach lurched when he recognised the two men tied to wooden chairs.

'You lot are going to pay for this. You know who I am and what I can have done to you, so you'd better let me go.' Rudy's eyes were alight, nostrils flaring in fury as he struggled against his binds. By contrast, Elijah sat calmly, not attempting to fight. He was resigned to his fate. Rudy's eyes narrowed when he saw Clarke.

'You work for me. Stand down, and get me out of here. Now.'

Paying him no attention, Clarke handed Natty a gun. Natty glanced at the heavy weapon, then to Clarke, whose expression remained placid.

'As you can see, we were able to get these guys too. Your warning helped . . . but it was always in hand. Your uncle wants you to kill them both.'

Natty didn't respond, nausea bubbling in his stomach. Rudy faced Natty.

'Nat, this is me. You know me. You're better than this. The stuff that is going on is business. You're like a son to me, and you wouldn't have been harmed. You know that. The bullets were just to scare you.'

Natty let him speak, trying to control his fluctuating emotions. He had history with Rudy, and the idea of killing him filled him with dread.

'Think about your mum. She loves me. If you do this, she will never forgive you.'

Natty ignored Rudy, taking a minute to weigh up his options.

Regardless, the men would die. He didn't have to know everything about his uncle's business to realise that.

But, could he do it?

Natty thought about his dad; imagining all the times he'd been in similar situations. It didn't make him feel any better about his current predicament.

'If I don't do it, what happens?' He finally asked Clarke.

'Nothing will happen to you.'

Even in the middle of the situation, Natty understood the double meaning. If he didn't do it, he would never ascend. Taking a deep breath, he stepped in front of Rudy, raising the gun to his head. Rudy's face was ashen, his lips and chin trembling.

'Nathaniel,' he said.

Natty's finger tightened on the trigger, and Rudy sighed, his hope evaporating. Natty squeezed the trigger, blood spraying the wall behind Rudy, his head falling limp.

Without consideration, Natty moved to the side, standing directly in front of Elijah. They shared a look. Elijah smiled.

'So, this is it then?'

Natty raised the gun, pointing it at his head, just as he had with Rudy.

'This is it.'

Elijah's smile faded, giving way to a defiant look of anger. Through gritted teeth, he said, 'get it over with then.'

Obliging, Natty pulled the trigger, spraying the wall with identical splatter.

He held the gun in place for a moment, his eyes exploring the scene. Giving way to the gun's weight in his hand, he felt it slip to the side. As it did, Clarke reached out and took it from his hand.

'Breathe,' he said.

Natty didn't respond, eyes still studying the men. Unlike Rudy, Elijah's head had shot backwards, allowing Natty to see the bullet wound in his head. Worst of all, he could see the look of terror in Elijah's eyes as the light was extinguished from them. In a way, Rudy's head slumping after he shot him was fortunate, because if Natty had seen the same look on Rudy's face, he probably wouldn't have been able to shoot Elijah.

Falling to his knees, Natty emptied his stomach. When he'd finished, he remained on his knees.

'You did well,' said Clarke. 'Your friend has already been taken home. Ant will take you. People will be in touch.'

Natty said nothing as he was led out. In the car, he remained in a daze. He had killed two men. Cameron's betrayal had rocked him, and he wondered how much of their friendship had been a lie.

When the men dropped him home, Natty crawled into bed, the numbness growing, realising he could easily have died tonight.

He probably should have, he thought.

Instead, people were dead because of him.

Clutching the covers tightly and pulling them closer, he considered which option would have been worse.

Squeezing his eyes shut before he could decide, Natty's body gave into his exhaustion, falling asleep, cheeks still wet.

EPILOGUE

FRIDAY NIGHT PLAYED host to yet another gathering in the Hood. Music played, people congregating, dancing, and having fun.

Natty stood in a corner, his face solemn as he sipped his only drink of the night, doing nothing to stand out. There had been so many spots like this one where he'd sought to be the centre of attention, and he felt ill thinking back on that fact.

Everything had changed.

The bodies of Rudy and Elijah were found, with people immediately pointing to an attempted gang war between their respective crews. Wonder had sworn revenge, but did nothing, left in place to sell the lie. Elijah's crew now worked for Mitch, paying large percentages to remain in business.

Cameron had disappeared, with Natty unsure if his former friend was still alive.

Even now, the killings continued to take their toll. He lived in fear of being arrested, or never getting over what he had done. He and Rudy had been close, and to learn he'd attempted to engineer his downfall was hard to swallow. His mum was worse than ever, refusing to admit her heartbreak over Rudy's death. Consequently, he spent less time around her.

Natty nodded at a man he knew, ignoring the hungry eyes of several females. When another man approached him, he was relieved.

'It's time.'

Natty was led to a backroom, where his uncle waited, sat in a leather office chair. He remained as wiry as ever, but looked worn and far older, other than his eyes, which were as intelligent as ever.

'You've grown, Nathaniel.'

Natty didn't reply, trying to remember the last time he'd talked business with his uncle. For so long, word had come down through Rudy, and to be here in his presence was almost surreal.

'How's your mum doing?'

'She won't accept what happened.'

'I doubt she will,' said Mitch. 'We can discuss her another time. I want you to take Rudy's position. Money goes up, of course.'

Natty froze, unable to believe what was happening. He had dreamed of the moment he would get a promotion more times than he could count, and now that it had happened, he was astonished.

'Are you serious?'

'I don't joke about business.'

'Why?'

'Because you finally showed me something. You've been a star from day one. Rudy saw it. It was just that temper of yours getting you in trouble. You've gotten over that. You showed real character keeping your little friend calm until Clarke arrived. You put down our enemies, and you kept your mouth shut afterwards. You've learned what you needed to learn. This is the result.'

Natty weighed over those words, part of him thinking this must be a dream. After a moment, he opened his mouth to reply.

'I can't take it, Unc.'

Mitch didn't react. His eyes remained locked on Natty.

'What if I offered you half a million pounds up front?'

Natty's stomach fluttered at the amount offered, but it didn't change his answer.

'It's still a no.'

'Why?'

Natty blew out a breath.

'For the longest, this was all I wanted. I was so mad at you and Rudy for holding me back, but lately, I've realised how right you were. I jeopardised so much with my attitude, and I held myself back. Even now, I've still got a lot of growing up to do. One thing I've realised is that I'm not a leader.'

Mitch smiled, his eyes twinkling.

'Yes, you are. The fact you don't see it, only enhances that fact. I won't force you, however. I'll promote someone else for now.' His smile vanished, all business once again. 'Rudy and Elijah are not the only ones clamouring for the throne. Leeds has been quiet for too long, and the little crews aren't gonna stay subservient forever.'

Natty nodded his understanding, shocked to see his uncle's face soften.

'I'm proud of you, Nathaniel. Your dad would be too. Gangster stuff aside, you stepped up for the family, when you could have said no to taking care of Rudy and the other one. We will talk soon. Feel free to stick around for the party.'

With those words ringing in his head, Natty walked out, almost in a trance. As he left the building, he wondered if he had done the right thing in turning down the promotion. There was no guarantee it would be offered again.

Putting that to one side. He climbed in his car and drove away.

* * *

NATTY STOOD OUTSIDE LORRAINE'S. He'd been there for nearly five minutes, his heart racing. He had been here more times than he could count, routinely walking in. Things were different now. Everything had changed, and he was trying to find himself amid that.

With a deep breath, Natty finally knocked, his heart leaping into his throat when the door opened.

Lorraine gazed out at him. He looked right back, and for a few seconds, neither moved. Without a word, Lorraine stepped to the side and let him in as Jaden came running to tackle him. Natty felt weightless as he embraced Jaden, his heart racing. He looked up from the hug to Lorraine, and they smiled.

DID YOU ENJOY THE READ?

Thank you for reading Good Deed, Bad Deeds!

This was the first book I planned after finishing the Target series, and it took a while for the pieces to align, but I love the end result, and hope you did too.

Please take a minute or two to help me by leaving a review – even if it's just a few lines. Reviews help massively with getting my books in front of new readers. I personally read every review and take all feedback on board.

To support me, please click the relevant link below:

UK: http://www.amazon.co.uk/review/create-review?&asin=B0B7JZXF2J

US: http://www.amazon.com/review/create-review?&asin=B0B7JZXF2J

DID YOU ENJOY THE READ?

Make sure you're following me on Amazon to keep up to date with my releases, or that you're signed up to my email list, and I'll see you at the next book!

PRE-ORDER HUSTLER'S AMBITION

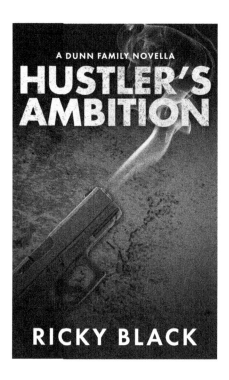

Due for release February 8, 2023, Pre Order the latest novella in the gritty and gripping Dunn Family Series, Hustler's Ambition Now, for a reduced price of £0.99p.

READ BLOOD AND BUSINESS

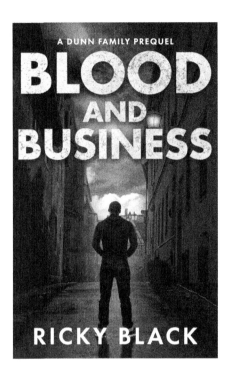

Tyrone Dunn wants to take over Leeds, and he is willing to battle anyone who gets in his way.

Even family.

Will it be settled by blood . . . or business?

Order now, and find out.

ALSO BY RICKY BLACK

ABOUT RICKY BLACK

Ricky Black was born and raised in Chapeltown, Leeds.

In 2016, he published the first of his crime series, Target, and has published ten more books since.

Visit https://rickyblackbooks.com for information regarding new releases and special offers, and promotions.

Printed in Great Britain
by Amazon

18676408R00171